D0429098

timepiece

Also by Myra McEntire

hourglass

timepiece

An Hourglass Novel

Myra McEntire

EGMONT

USA

New York

EGMONT

We bring stories to life

First published by Egmont USA, 2012
443 Park Avenue South, Suite 806
New York, NY 10016

1 3 5 7 9 8 6 4 2

www.egmontusa.com
www.myramcentire.blogspot.com
For more about the Hourglass world:
www.murphyslawcoffee.com

Library of Congress Cataloging-in-Publication Data
McEntire, Myra.
Timepiece / Myra McEntire.
p. cm.
Summary: When vital research about the time gene is stolen, Kaleb must join
Emerson and the Hourglass team to find the criminal, who could be anywhere
in time.
ISBN 978-1-60684-145-7 (hardcover)—ISBN 978-1-60684-332-1 (ebook)
[1. Space and time—Fiction. 2. Psychic ability—Fiction. 3. Science fiction.]
I. Title.
PZ7.M47845424Ti 2012
[Fic]—dc23
2011027159

Printed in the United States of America

To Ethan, Andrew, and Charlie,
the lights of my life. I love you all the time, no matter what,
and I'm so glad you are mine.

To CJ Redwine and Jodi Meadows.
I can't list all the reasons why,
because some of them aren't appropriate,
but we know. We know.

Be not the slave of your own past. Plunge into the sublime seas, dive deep and swim far, so you shall come back with self-respect, with new power, with an advanced experience that shall explain and overlook the old.

—Ralph Waldo Emerson

Chapter 1

*M*aybe getting drunk and dressing up like a pirate for the masquerade was a bad idea.

Okay, definitely a bad idea. At least the pirate part.

I stared openly at the girl standing in line next to me, who did everything she could to avoid looking in my direction. Her mouth was a masterpiece, the lower lip slightly fuller than the top. Or it could've been a pout. Either way, it was the kind of lip that begged to be between my teeth. I had no idea how she got that ridiculously curvy body into a skintight golden cat suit, but I was all for helping her get out of it.

I leaned toward her. "Meow."

Best come-on line ever.

She assessed me through a slim, black mask. "If you ask to rub my belly or make any of the obvious body-part jokes, I'll steal your sword and you'll leave here needing a peg leg. Or worse. Got it, sailor?"

"Aye, aye, Captain." I gave her an enthusiastic salute.

She turned her back to me and stood on her tiptoes, craning her neck to check the progress of the line. The rear view was so spectacular, I considered not saying anything else to her until we were inside so I could enjoy it in peace.

But she caught me looking.

"You are dressed like a cat, right? Or a tiger?" I said quickly, the words slurring a little. Everything in my line of vision shifted to the left. "Are you here for the masquerade?"

"No. I regularly walk the streets of Ivy Springs dressed like a jungle animal."

"Rawr." I pretended to swipe her with imaginary claws and hissed.

No response.

I rested my back against the rough brick wall, pulling the pirate wig off my head to scratch my scalp before putting it back on. It felt cockeyed. Or maybe that was just my brain.

"They aren't going to let you in looking like that without asking questions." Tiger Girl eyed my dreadlocks warily. "How much did you have to drink? Are you going to puke on my shoes?"

I wanted to close my eyes because my head was spinning, but I couldn't stop staring at her. I let my mind loose for a second, trying to get a read, but the alcohol had done its job.

"I won't puke on your shoes," I told her, while promising myself to get my hands on those curves. Giving in to the dizzy, I closed my eyes for a second. "I've just had one hell of a day."

2

"And I guess now you're going to tell me about it?"

There wasn't really any good way to tell a girl I'd never seen before that my dad had recently come back from the dead, my mom was in a coma, and an entire battalion of Civil War soldiers had appeared on my front porch that very afternoon. "I'm more of a doer than a talker."

"Somehow that doesn't surprise me."

I winked suggestively. "By any chance, would you be a doer?"

"Do you kiss your mama with that mouth?"

Hurt blistered into anger, sizzling beneath the surface of my skin. She didn't know. It wasn't intentional. Her eyes told me that she'd seen evidence of my temper, and I pushed it down, hard.

"The line's moving." I inclined my head in the direction of the doors, fighting my own emotions harder than I'd ever fought anyone else's.

To my relief, the girl followed the crowd into the Phone Company.

The inside was transformed. The Phone Company was no longer a classy, upscale restaurant but a garish, fall-themed explosion. Huge webs with hundreds of tiny fake spiders hanging from the spun cotton strands adorned the walls, and a scarecrow graced every corner. Ghosts strung up on invisible wires swooped through the crowd at random, leaving shrieking laughter in their wake.

There were pumpkins everywhere, and an ungodly amount of candy corn, but what would've truly scared the partygoers were the things they couldn't see.

A veil shimmered on the stage. Veils were gateways that served as holding places, lobbies to the future or past, where travelers stood before they entered the bridges that took them to other times. They looked like walls of sunlight shining on water.

Wherever there was a veil, there was usually a "rip."

A rip—or ripple—was like seeing the same scene from a film on a loop, over and over, except it's a person stuck in time and superimposed on the present. Not corporeal, and not visible to anyone who didn't carry the specific time travel gene.

Until lately. Because now, I could see rips, too.

Which probably explained the jazz trio people kept walking through. When Em appeared and walked *around* the trio toward me, my rip theory was confirmed.

From the expression on her face, I was about to get hell handed to me on a platter.

"Kaleb Ballard. I should kick your ass."

No one as tiny as Emerson Cole should have so much power over me. She dropped her parasol on an empty table, pushed her hoop skirt to the side, and did her best to wrestle me into a sleek leather booth. I put my fingertips on the edge of the table to gain equilibrium, but I was too unsteady on my feet. I sat.

"I thought we'd cured you of your drinking problem." She punched my bicep. Twice.

"Ow." She could hurt me physically, too. "I thought we'd cured you of your violence problem."

With her blue silk dress, white gloves, and blond hair curled

4

into perfect ringlets, she looked like a deranged escapee from *Gone with the Wind's* Tara. Or from a Southern-themed wedding party whose bride really hates her bridesmaids.

"Seriously, Kaleb." Her concern sliced the cut a little bit deeper. "Why?"

"You know why." At least part of it. I breathed in, blew out a deep sigh, and lowered my forehead to the table.

"Seeing the rip after school freaked me out, too. Although I guess it was seeing *you* see the rip that freaked me out. But I went for a run. You knocked back a fifth of . . . what? Lighter fluid?"

"Cut me a break, please." I looked up at her with what I hoped was effective pleading. "You know it's different for me than it is for you. I didn't know what else to do."

"Getting trashed wasn't the answer." She plucked a glass of ice water off a passing waiter's tray and pushed it into my hand. "We all need to be alert—all the time—until we figure out what's going on."

"I'm not trashed. Just buzzed." Unfortunately. I took a long drink of water and eyed her outfit. "Why are you dressed like Scarlett O'Hara?"

"It's a private joke," she said.

"With who?"

"Myself."

"Are you going to sit down?"

She frowned and pointed to her huge skirt. "I haven't figured out how yet."

I shook my head and took another drink, letting my laugh escape into the glass, but I couldn't hide from Em.

Instead of allowing her fist to hit my arm again, I caught it in my much bigger hand and held on for a fraction of a second too long. A tall shadow fell across the table.

"Hey, guys."

Michael.

Em pulled away from me, turning and rising up on her tiptoes to greet Michael with a kiss. The light above us dimmed for a millisecond, and my stomach dropped. I focused on the tabletop as the rush of angry heat in my chest made its way to the tips of my fingers. Since they'd become a couple, the "setting off sparks when they saw each other" side effect had started to become a problem. I made sure all my major electrical appliances were plugged into a surge protector. I hadn't yet found a way to protect myself.

Once the lights stopped flickering, I sensed silent communication. I caught Emerson imitating a guzzling motion, her hand curved around an imaginary bottle.

"So . . . Yeah," she said. Michael, presumably dressed as Rhett Butler, gestured for her to sit. She looked down at her skirt and shook her head. "Kaleb might be taking the pirate thing a little too far. You know. With the rum obsession. "

"It wasn't rum," I argued. "It was bourbon. I found it in my glove compartment."

Michael slid into the booth across from me and leaned close, speaking in a low voice. "Drinking and driving *and* an open container?"

"Listen, Clark Gable, I didn't drink and drive because I didn't drink until I got here. There isn't an open container anymore, because I drank it all. And also, I recycled the bottle."

A telltale vein pulsed in Michael's forehead. I could feel his anger, too, ripe and unyielding, which meant the three shots I'd taken in the Jeep were wearing off.

Emerson sounded a warning in her throat. "Don't make a scene, please. My brother is watching, and I don't want to upset Dru."

Thomas, dressed as Gomez Addams, stood with his wife, dressed as Morticia, next to the bar. Probably double-checking IDs. Em had told me that Dru was pregnant. She didn't have a baby bump yet, but her hand always rested on her belly. Her emotions exuded a fierce protectiveness I recognized. Mama Warrior. You don't mess with that. My mom had been just like her.

My fingers flexed, itching for a bottle.

"Kaleb, hand over your keys right now, and we'll give you one free pass. But if it happens again, I'm talking to your dad myself," Em said.

At least Em cared. Just not in the way I wanted.

"You're vicious." I met her eyes and slid my keys across the table. Michael pulled them from my hand before Emerson could touch me, giving them to her.

"I'm also short. Which means it's that much easier for me to take you out at the knees." She tossed the keys up in the air with one hand and caught them with the other. Making light. "I'll hide these puppies. Try not to kill each other while I'm gone, and if you're going to argue, get under the table to do it." I watched

7

her walk away, her hoop skirt swinging from side to side, hitting ankles, knees, and chair legs. I didn't look at Michael.

"I'm sorry," he said.

I snapped my head toward him. Neither one of us had seen his apology coming. "What?"

"About this afternoon." He frowned before he ran his hand through his hair and slouched back against the booth. "Em told me."

"Oh. That."

I didn't want to think about the uniformed soldiers posing for a picture on my hundred-and-fifty-year-old porch. A porch that had suddenly appeared to be so new I could smell sawdust.

"If Thomas hadn't caved and let Em come to the Hourglass school…," I trailed off. "I don't know how I'd have handled the ripple on my own. She only had to touch one soldier, and then everything dissolved."

"I'm glad she was there for you," Michael said. I could hear the underlying "don't get used to it."

Leaning back, I crossed my arms over my chest. "She said it was the same kind of rip she saw the night she went back to save you from the explosion in the lab. A whole scene."

"Like you stepped into a painting."

I nodded.

"I can't explain it, Kaleb. I can't explain the ones I've seen myself."

"Why should you explain anything to me?" A quick glimpse of skintight gold fabric caught my attention from across the room.

I didn't have anything else to drink, but the next best distraction was making her way to the dance floor. "You aren't responsible."

"We don't know who's responsible."

I gave him a scathing look. "Yes, we do."

He disregarded the statement. "Did you tell your dad what you saw?"

"No." Dad had enough to worry about. "Maybe you should tell him. He'd take it better from you, anyway."

"That's not—"

"You and Em have fun. I'll find you later for a breath check so I can get my keys."

"Kaleb, wait," Michael said, but I was already up. Shaking off the conversation and any responsibility, I took a deep breath, adjusted my sword, and went with my gut.

And took a wide step around the jazz trio to get to the dance floor.

I banished any thoughts of Em and Michael, or Michael and my dad.

Tired of being on the outside looking in. In both cases.

I followed Tiger Girl onto the dance floor. I had way more than dancing on my mind, but I had to start somewhere. She'd almost reached a group of girls in a circle when I caught her by the hand. She turned to face me.

"Oh. You."

"Try to contain your excitement." I gestured to the crowd around us. "I wouldn't want you to cause a scene. Riots can be very dangerous in this kind of situation."

"Right," she replied in a monotone, pulling her hand away. "I'll bring it down a notch."

"I thank you, and the Ivy Springs Public Safety Department thanks you." I bowed slightly. When I stood, wearing my most winning smile, I saw only her retreating backside. "Wait!"

Stopping, she dropped her head. After a couple of seconds, she looked at me over her left shoulder. "What am I waiting for? You to stop being so conceited? Because I don't have that kind of time."

My earlier anger licked at the edge of my vision and I blinked. I usually didn't have to try so hard. "I wanted to ask you to dance."

She pivoted on her heel and faced me.

"May I?" I extended my hand, pushing the anger away and pulling out the smile again, this time with increased wattage.

"Will you take no for an answer or will you bug the piss out of me until I say yes?"

"I like to think of it as persistence." I made the mental stretch, looking for amusement behind her words.

None.

"One dance," she said, relenting. "Then we go back to our separate corners."

"You might enjoy it so much you change your mind about that." I was either going to have to work extra hard for this one or move on to an easier conquest.

"And monkeys might fly out my butt, but I wouldn't bet on that, either."

An easier conquest it was.

To speed up the rejection process, I pulled her toward me and slid my hands down to cop a quick feel of what was truly the finest ass I'd seen in my entire lifetime, and I'd been paying attention.

She reared back and smacked me. So hard my ears rang.

"What do you think you're doing?" *Wide-open rage.* It poured out of her, with no mental stretch required from me to read it. "I don't care how much you've had to drink, you douche bag, no one touches me like that without my permission."

Part of me felt like turning that rage around on her, letting all of it go, and something black and vicious clawed its way up my throat. At that exact moment, a loud whine came from the sound system. Everything went dark.

Screams and laughter filled the space as the crowd anticipated a prank. The emergency lights flashed on and illuminated a man holding a handgun. Raising it, he shot at the ceiling and hit the chandelier. The room erupted in chaos as tiny crystals rained to the floor.

One silent emotion carried over every scream. Paralyzing *fear.*

Emerson.

I took a better look at the man standing on the stage, holding a gun in one hand and a pocket watch in the other.

Jack Landers.

The bastard who killed my dad.

I grabbed Tiger Girl and dragged her behind me, fighting against the tide of the crowd.

After pushing her to safety under the staircase, I stood in front of her, scanning the room for Emerson and Michael. I caught a glimpse of blue silk and black tux as they escaped through the front entrance.

Jack had been on the run for more than a month, and now he was in my sight line. The rush of adrenaline through my veins sobered me up *real* quick.

My hand was still wrapped around Tiger Girl's wrist. "Stay here and stay down. Don't take any chances. He can't see you from the stage."

"He has a gun," she said from behind me, her voice choked with terror. I could feel it coursing through my fingertips to my brain. "Have you lost your mind?"

"A long time ago."

Riding the adrenaline, I let go of her and stepped into Jack's view. Faint shapes hurried toward the doors in the glow of the security lights. I squared my shoulders with the stage.

Jack was here to do damage—his expression confirmed it.

I wanted to do a little damage myself.

Our eyes locked as I fought my way through the last few people in the crowd toward the temporary stage located at the end of the restaurant. I stopped halfway to try and get a read on his emotions. Nothing.

"Typical. Making a grand entrance." I didn't break the stare.

"I'm surprised you didn't hire an orchestra to play a theme song for you."

"Shouldn't you be somewhere brooding and angsting? You're even wearing eyeliner." He tucked the watch away, and then lowered the gun to his side. But he kept his finger on the trigger. "Or have you passed the brooding and angsting over to—"

"*Don't* say her name. After what you did to her, you don't have the right." He'd messed with the time line and truth of Emerson's life so badly that she couldn't sleep without having nightmares.

"I'd like to see Emerson. We do have some unfinished business. She might disagree with you about what I 'did to her.'"

"You deserve to die for all the things you've done—all the people you've hurt." My dad, my mom, Em. I'd wished Jack Landers dead for months, and now I had my chance. The muscles in my gut tightened as I prepared to make a move. "How about we make that happen right now?"

He smiled. "Killing me would be the worst mistake you could ever make."

"I see it as a service to humanity."

"Then you're seeing it all wrong." So egomaniacal. "Don't force my hand, Kaleb. You'll wish you hadn't."

"I don't have a choice." I took two steps toward him before he lifted his weapon and took aim. I ducked and rolled behind a table, expecting a blast of gunfire.

Nothing.

I carefully lifted my head to peer over the edge of the table and saw him shaking the gun, checking the barrel.

I didn't think of what my choice would do to my father, or my mother if she ever woke up. I pulled the dull metal sword free from my costume, extended it, and rushed the stage.

Somehow, through all the mental noise from outside, I heard the bullet slide into the chamber. Time slowed down, and I wondered if this was what everything looked like right before you died. I kept running as he leveled the gun and sighted the barrel.

Everyone else's emotions ceased to matter. All I could focus on were my own.

Rage.

Retaliation.

Revenge.

Taking what I believed could be my final steps, I leapt with the sword outstretched. As I flew through the air toward him, Jack flickered like a CGI ghost in a bad horror movie, anger twisting his features, a loud curse ripping its way from his throat. I watched his finger squeeze the trigger as my ribs caught the edge of the stage.

Before the bullet escaped, he disappeared.

The gun went with him.

Chapter 2

The Phone Company was a disaster of glass and overturned tables. The lights that were still in working order reflected off puddles of spilled drinks and shattered chandelier crystals.

After Thomas and Dru cleared the general public from the premises, including a protesting Tiger Girl, they went outside to deal with the authorities. Michael still wore his masquerade costume, but Em had changed into street clothes and piled the mess of Southern belle ringlets into a hyperactive ponytail on top of her head.

I lay flat on my back on the stage, my Captain Jack wig and pirate shirt on the ground. A garbage bag full of ice from the bar covered my ribs. Jack's words kept rebounding off the sides of my brain. He'd been so sure of himself. How would killing him be the worst mistake I could ever make?

Propping myself up on my elbows, I looked at Michael and

Em. "I can't believe you called Dad. What good is it going to do for him to come down here? Jack's gone."

"You're hurt. He said he'd have Nate and Dune stay with your mom," Michael said.

"I'm fine," I said through clenched teeth.

"Then why do you have ice on your ribs?"

"Stop fighting." Em scrubbed her hands over her face and leaned back into Michael. No uncontrollable electrical currents now. Those disappeared if the two of them touched a lot, and Michael hadn't taken his hands off her since she'd changed out of the poofy dress. For all I knew, he hadn't taken his hands off her while she'd been changing.

The twinge I felt came from my ribs.

Had to.

"I wanted your dad to see the setup, get his opinion on how Jack got here." Michael put his hands on Em's shoulders. "How he got out so fast. If he could have been traveling."

"He wasn't traveling." I sat up and threw the bag of ice to the ground. The crunching sound it made when it hit satisfied me. "He's *not traveling*. Jack doesn't have the travel gene."

Emerson blew out a deep breath. "That didn't stop him before."

"Doesn't matter." I slid to the edge of the stage and grunted as I leaned over to scoop up my pirate shirt. Em kept her eyes averted as I pulled it over my head. I used the edge of the stage as leverage to stand up, and turned my grimace of pain into a frown. "He doesn't have any way to travel. No one does."

16

Em flinched. The formula she'd managed to steal from Cat and Jack hadn't been complete. No exotic matter meant no one had traveled since Cat had disappeared.

"He has Cat," Michael said. "There could have been a lead on a traveler in the Hourglass files he stole."

"Maybe." I shrugged and quickly regretted it. I hadn't expected a simple shrug to hurt. "But even if Jack found another traveler, that doesn't mean he can travel too."

Em frowned and an unexpected wave of anxiety flowed in my direction.

"What?" I asked. "What's wrong?"

"There are so many unanswered questions," she said. I sensed from their expressions and the sudden tension that she and Michael had talked about this a lot, more than he'd wanted to. Probably because he didn't have the answers. "We don't know why Jack didn't just change his past himself. Why did he need me or your mom to do it? Is he the kind of guy who'd worry about the consequences of messing with his own time line, or would he think twice about it?"

Michael's jaw flexed as he clenched his teeth. "I still think there were limitations because of the exotic matter formula. Remember how much he'd aged when he came out of the veil in Liam's office? I was shocked he was healthy tonight."

"I can't stop thinking about something Cat said." Em stared at the floor. "That Jack piggybacked my travel gene to get out of the bridge when he was stuck. I know only travelers can move through time, but the continuum is so screwed up now. He could still be manipulating it."

"That could mean . . ." I stopped cold and waited for Em to finish.

"If Jack could piggyback a gene to get *out* of a bridge, could he piggyback to get *into* one? And if he can get into a bridge, can he use it to time travel?"

The massive oak doors to the Phone Company swung inward to admit my dad, putting a quick end to our theorizing.

He picked his way through glass and overturned furniture to the stage. He kissed Em's cheek and gave Michael a long look. My ribs gave another twinge before he turned his attention to me. "Show me."

Keeping my eyes on the far wall, I lifted my shirt just enough for him to see the beginnings of a nasty blue bruise starting where my ribs had caught the stage.

"Do you think they're broken?" He tapped the pocket of his brown tweed jacket and pulled out a pair of glasses.

I still didn't look at him. "I don't even think they're cracked."

He slid the glasses on and leaned in closer, furrowing his brows in concern. "You wouldn't tell me if they were."

I shrugged and dropped the shirt. There were lots of things I didn't tell him. From the way he'd looked at Michael, he had secrets of his own.

Dad straightened and removed the glasses, dropping them back into his pocket. His eyes fixed on the exact spot where Jack had appeared and disappeared.

"A veil," he murmured. "Is that where Jack showed up?"

"And where he disappeared." Em shuddered. "Wonder when he'll be back. And what he wants this time."

Dad and Michael exchanged a look over Em's head. I knew what they were thinking.

Jack wanted her.

"You can't worry about that," Dad said to her, with a gentleness he used to reserve for my mom, or me when I was a lot younger. "We can't anticipate Jack's every move."

"We can anticipate that he doesn't care about the continuum," Em said, "or all the ways he can screw it up."

I knew what was coming next, and not just from Em's pointed stare at me. Bossypants.

She crossed her arms over her chest. "Are you going to tell him?"

"Tell me what?" Dad asked.

Coerced *and* trapped. "I saw a rip today. I know it was a rip, because Em was with me."

He didn't say anything, just rubbed his beard the way he always did when approaching a problem.

"Why aren't you surprised?" I asked, the uneasiness growing in my gut.

"Because it's not a surprise." He dropped his hand and sighed deeply. "I didn't have to call Nate and Dune to come and stay with your mom. They were already at the house, along with Ava. They've all seen rips, too."

Chapter 3

I stared at Dad, thrown by the implications.

"From what I can gather, anyone with the time gene can see rips now. Dune, Nate, and Ava were all alone in different public places, and yes, it's happened more than once to each of them."

"Do you think that means they can travel, too?" Michael asked, uncertainty drawing his voice taut.

"I don't know." Dad shrugged. "But without exotic matter, there's no way to test it. I'm not interested in taking any risks."

The sound of Thomas's black boots hitting the floor made us all jump when he entered from the kitchen. His footsteps echoed as he stalked toward us, his anxiety preceding him.

"Thomas. I'm sorry for the mess and the trouble," Dad said with regret. "I'll be glad to cover anything your insurance won't."

"Absolutely not. You aren't responsible. But I have a few questions about the ass—man who is." His slicked-back Gomez

Addams hairdo and drawn-on, pencil-thin mustache were at odds with the fierceness in his eyes.

"I'll do my best to answer," Dad said.

Thomas directed his words toward Dad but pegged Michael with an accusing stare. "I'd like to speak with you two outside."

"Why can't you just ask your questions here?" Em argued, her anger at being left out obvious.

"I can get any information I need from you later." He gave Em a parental look when she made a sound of protest. "This is an adult conversation."

Em's spark of fury told me Thomas would pay for that comment later. I knew she was fighting hard to hold her tongue.

"Lead the way." Dad gestured toward the doors with his head, and he and Michael followed Thomas outside.

Em watched them walk away. The second they were out of earshot, she let out a truly impressive stream of curse words and took out a couple of fall decorations with her fists, finally punching a plastic pumpkin to the ground and kicking it across the room.

Even though I was tempted, I knew laughing would prove deadly. "Are you picturing Thomas's face on that pumpkin?"

"In my mind's eye, his nose is bleeding."

"At least he acknowledged you. My dad thinks I'm completely useless."

"Don't say that." She pulled herself up to sit on the edge of the stage. "You aren't useless."

We were quiet for a few seconds, long enough for me to realize she was trying to figure out the best way to say something.

"Spill it, Em." I grinned at her. "No need to sugarcoat."

She uttered a sound of frustration. "Stop reading me."

"You know I can't help it."

"Since it's just you and me,"—she patted the stage beside her—"sit."

I leaned back, putting all my weight on my arms before sliding carefully into a sitting position. It was rare we were alone together, and her nerves were skipping around like live electrical wires. "What is it?"

"I wish . . . you and Michael could . . . make up."

"I didn't know we were in a fight," I lied, as smoothly as I could. "What's it about? You?"

Her immediate blush confirmed it. "I've already capped my awkward quota for the year, and it's only October."

"I don't hold back, Em. You and Mike both know where I stand when it comes to you."

She stared down at her hands. "And you know where I stand."

"Maybe we should arm wrestle for you," I said, trying to make a joke. Failing.

"Stop." Her voice was sharp and loud, the usual smooth edges disappearing in her anger. "I'm not a thing, and I'm not joking around. I care about you both."

"One of us more than the other." There was no reason to bother trying to keep the disappointment out of my voice.

"You aren't being fair. I don't want to be the thing that ends your friendship. You two used to be like brothers."

A fat plastic spider hanging from a fake web in the corner fell to the ground with a thud. We both jumped.

It was time to put the truth out on the table. She could do whatever she wanted with it. "Michael and I were like brothers, because Dad wishes Michael were his son."

Em started to respond, but I caught sight of movement by the dining patio and held up one finger. I looked up, expecting another spider to fall, or for one of the scarecrows in the corner to be wobbling on its bamboo stake. Then I sensed emotion.

I signaled to Em to keep quiet again and peered through the dim light. *Fearlessness and determination.*

A guy I'd never seen before stepped inside the building.

A quick flash of light reflected off the knife in his hand.

I stood up on the stage in front of Emerson when he started toward us. Shorter than me by four or five inches, his shoulders were as wide as mine. His nose curved slightly to the left, as if he'd broken it in a fight and set it himself afterward.

"No one's supposed to be in here. The police made everyone leave," I said, pulling myself up to my full height. I inclined my head toward the front of the Phone Company. "They're right outside if you're looking for them."

"I'm not." He had an accent—either British or Australian— I could never tell them apart. He kept his tone low, regulated. Controlled.

"How can I help you?" I hoped Em would keep quiet and not draw attention to herself. I heard her climb to her feet, and stopped hoping.

"You're Kaleb Ballard." He climbed the stairs to the stage, stopping just in front of the veil.

Squinting at him in the dark, I tried to remember if I'd seen him somewhere before. He didn't look much older than me, but there was a weird air of maturity about him. "Who're you?"

"Call me Poe." He scanned my costume, and I pulled at the strings of the pirate shirt. "You need to pass on a message."

I raised my eyebrows. "Do I look like an envelope?"

He didn't laugh, and from the way his body stiffened, the efforts to keep his temper restrained were considerable. "The space time continuum is compromised."

"Thanks." My muscles tensed, too. "I'll alert Doctor Who."

Em's fingers closed over my wrist. She was staring at Poe's right hand. The knife. Her fear made me bite down on my tongue to stop any more smart aleck responses.

"The continuum is compromised because of the choices those associated with the Hourglass have made." He sounded muffled through the veil.

I didn't respond. The first rule of Hourglass is that you don't talk about Hourglass. Like Fight Club, but without the merciless beatings.

Em let go of my wrist and took a step closer to Poe. "What if those associated with it didn't understand their choices?"

I gritted my teeth. She'd given us away.

"Ignorance of the law is not an excuse." He spoke in a creepy monotone, as if he were some kind of puppet. The anger inside him didn't match his voice at all.

"The *law*?" Em snorted. "I guess you're the sheriff?"

Her response snapped a tenuous thread. Instead of acknowledging her, Poe stared directly into my eyes and smiled. The hair on the back of my neck stood up.

It didn't happen in slow motion, more like stop motion. I felt no fear or anxiety coming from Poe at all, just a dark resolve as he lunged, knife pointed directly at me.

Emerson jumped forward to block him. Before I could react, he grabbed her upper arm and jerked her into the veil.

The same one Jack Landers had used.

Em kicked to find leverage so she could do damage, but Poe was holding her off the ground. She growled with the effort, her fury hot. I kept my eyes on the knife. "Let her go."

When he shook his head, I launched myself at the veil.

And slammed against what felt like a rock wall.

I hit the ground, landing on my back, disoriented, my ribs screaming in protest. Something that looked like water shouldn't be so solid. I tried again, putting my shoulder into the attempt this time. Still no give.

There was only one way for Poe to get into the veil. He was a traveler.

I pushed at the veil with my palms, hoping against hope that it would somehow give way. "You can't travel with her. You don't have what you need."

"Who says I'm a traveler?" His voice sounded slightly muffled.

I pulled my head back. What the hell? "How did you get through the veil?"

He shrugged and smiled.

"Let her go," I repeated through clenched teeth, punching the veil with each word. "And I'll deliver whatever you want."

Keeping his eyes on me, he lowered Em enough that her tiptoes touched the ground. He kept one arm around her neck, the knife pointed toward her chin. Her fury cooled as fear started to set in. "The Hourglass has made some very poor choices."

"People make poor choices every day," I said, throwing his words back.

"People like Emerson. Michael. Your father. Jack."

"We aren't responsible for what Jack did."

"Your father is." Still the monotone voice.

"My dad wasn't alive when Jack betrayed us," I argued, his lack of reaction sparking a bigger one from me. "Because *Jack* killed him."

"But he was alive when Emerson went back to save Michael. Jack didn't throw the continuum off by himself."

"She was *tricked.*" I dug at the veil with my fingers, but it remained as unyielding as stone. "Cat purposely misled her. Em didn't know what she was doing when she went back to rescue Michael. Dad didn't know she was . . ."

The words died on my lips. All of Em's anger was gone, and she was pulling frantically at Poe's forearm.

He was cutting off her air supply.

"Time," Poe said, "the natural order of things, is not something you can alter. I believe Emerson knew that there would be consequences." The tip of the knife touched Em's throat, just under her ear. An ominous prickle slid down my spine. "The pattern woven into the fabric of time is changing, and we know exactly where to place the blame."

"It's not her fault. We can fix it." I kept talking, not fully aware of what I was saying, unsure of whose fear was the strongest, mine or Em's. Hyperfocusing on the point of the knife and the fact that Em couldn't breathe. "The Hourglass will fix it."

"The Hourglass can't fix it."

My hands formed fists as I spoke through clenched teeth. "We can try."

Em gasped for air, digging her fingernails into Poe's flesh. Now there was no emotion coming from her. There was nothing coming from her at all.

"No," Poe said, entirely too self-satisfied. "You can't fix anything."

He moved so slowly, so deliberately, that if he'd been outside the veil, I'd have had him pinned to the ground with my elbow in his throat in less than a second. But he was inside, with Em, and he knew he could take his time.

He met my eyes, smiling, and executed one swift slice with his blade.

Across Em's throat.

Everything went quiet.

Chapter 4

*B*lood seeped into the neckline of Em's white sweater before spreading like the ocean across the sand, darkening everything it touched. Even though Poe held her up, she listed to the left, her feet dangling like a small child's. Red liquid pooled in the hollow above her collarbone.

"No!" The scream came from my very center, tensing all my muscles, making me shake. I attacked the veil with a vengeance, pounding my fists against it so hard I could feel the blood vessels bursting. "Emerson! *Emerson!*"

Poe didn't watch me, he observed me, as if I were an animal in a cage. His expressionless calm was as unnatural as a walking corpse. Then he dropped her to the ground and carelessly dusted off his hands.

Grief and rage scrambled for purchase in my chest. Neither won. I tried to scream Emerson's name again, but it caught in my throat, choking me. I kicked the veil repeatedly, over and over, until I hit the ground on my knees.

She lay unmoving at Poe's feet, blood pouring from her throat. Her eyes were open, but empty.

Tiny. Helpless.

Gone.

"You need to deliver a message to your father." Poe's expression was blank. He reminded me of a robot, programmed for a specific task and nothing else. "Find Jack Landers."

"Come out here. Come out here and bring her with you." I held my fists down by my sides, speaking through my teeth but still trying to sound calm. I thought about his knife, and how I would get it away from him. Then gut him. I wanted to see his blood spilled, along with everything inside him. I wanted to grind his heart into the floor with my heel.

"If Jack is found, there's a chance that everything that's happened can be repaired. Then the Hourglass can choose the time line on which it would like to continue. If the request is refused, or not met, time will be rewound."

In. Out. In. Out. I had to breathe. I had to make Poe think I wasn't a threat so he'd come out of that veil. He had to come out of the veil so I could destroy him. "I don't understand."

"Time will be rewound, and your time line will be chosen for you." Poe looked at me as if I were dense before he continued, speaking slowly. "There's only one way to clean up the mess the Hourglass has made without consequences."

"There are already consequences." The flow of blood from Em's neck was starting to slow. It just touched the edge of Poe's shoe. He'd track her blood out of this restaurant and down the streets of Ivy Springs if he walked away.

But he wouldn't be walking away.

"There's a great possibility the continuum can be repaired without consequences to your personal time lines, and there are several time lines from which you can choose. The one where your father is a pile of ash or the one where he's restored. Same goes for Michael. And Emerson could be in a mental hospital, or she could be part of the Hourglass." It was as if he were ticking off something as unimportant as a grocery list. "You choose, or we will."

"Why bother mentioning Em's time line as a threat? She's dead." And you're next.

"Is she?"

Poe extended his arms, still holding the blade.

The blood went from dark and dry to shiny and wet.

Em rose from the ground in backward motion, returning to Poe's arms. The stain on her sweater faded from the bottom up, the pool of blood in her collarbone disappeared, but the life was still absent from her eyes.

Poe stopped then, staring at me. "You'll pass on my message?"

"Yes." My voice was a pleading whisper. "Please, yes."

Slowly, so slowly, the knife made a return path across Emerson's neck. The blood disappeared completely, and her hands once again pulled at Poe's arm.

I froze, afraid to move. Afraid Poe would kill her again.

"You have till October thirty-first. Midnight."

Poe lowered Em to her feet and smiled.

I shook with the desire to jump him and peel his face off. When they stepped out of the veil, I snatched her away and pulled her to my side. Her skin felt cold.

"Oh, and one more thing. Anything taken can be returned. Anything given can be destroyed," Poe said, still smiling, walking backward to the exit. "Teague said your dad would understand."

With that, he turned on his heel and left the Phone Company.

Em shook her head, looking confused. "What just . . ."

I grabbed her and squeezed her so tightly that now I was the one cutting off her air supply. She smacked at my arms, and I loosened my hold.

"Kaleb?" Her voice was muffled, her breath warm through the thin cotton of my pirate costume.

The shirt had seen entirely too much action, and not the good kind. When I got home, I was going to burn it.

"You're okay?" A flood of relief replaced the anger in my blood as I released her, looking her over from head to toe. "You feel okay?"

"I don't remember what happened, exactly. I thought . . . I thought Poe was going to stab you, so I jumped in front of you—"

I wanted to hand in my man card and cry. "Which was insanely stupid."

"Protective instinct?"

"You, protecting me." I cupped her face in my hands, knowing she wasn't mine to touch, but unable to stop. "Insanely stupid."

She shivered, and when she spoke, her voice shook a little. "I'd call you a sexist pig, but I'm feeling off my game."

"I thought I'd lost you."

"But you didn't." Reaching up to entwine our fingers, she pulled our hands away from her face. "Anyway, he pulled me into the veil, and then things got . . ."

"Em? Are you okay?"

She grabbed the hem of her sweater and pulled it out in front of her, her eyes searching for something that was no longer there. Then her hands flew to her neck. "He cut me . . . he slit my throat."

"To make a point."

She sank into a chair. "Which was?"

"We have to find Jack."

Her mouth dropped open and the waves of her confusion and outrage swept over me. Before she could say anything else, the front doors slammed open.

Concern, then a split second later, fear so fierce it made my teeth ache. Michael.

"Are you two all right? Someone said a guy with a knife just walked out the back . . . what's wrong?" Michael crossed the room in two heartbeats before landing on his knees in front of Em, gathering her hands into his. "What happened?"

Em looked up at me, and then at my dad, who'd followed Michael in. "I think . . . you'll have to get the details from Kaleb. I was kind of busy. Being dead."

Chapter 5

"*D*amn." The morning sun flooding my father's office temporarily blinded me. I pulled my baseball cap down over my eyes.

For my own safety, I waited for my vision to return before I walked any farther. The office had definitely become messier since Dad returned from the dead. Without my mother to clear them away, coffee mugs littered the top of his huge desk, and a stack of newspapers in the corner grew taller by the day.

"You're late." Em's voice sounded hoarse, either with tears or with sleep. She and Michael sat hip to hip on the love seat.

"Didn't realize it was a party." I rubbed my eyes to pull the room into focus. Dune occupied the wingback chair in the corner, while Nate sat on the floor. I noticed the fresh neon green streak in his black hair when I dropped down beside him.

"We used our time wisely." Dad leaned his head from side to side, stretching the muscles in his neck. Tense already. "Everyone knows about Jack's appearance last night. And Poe's, as well as his ultimatum."

That explained the fear and uncertainty I could feel pulsing around the room. There was no anger from Michael or Em for having to wait until this morning to get details. That was all me. But something was off with Em.

"Poe mentioned someone named Teague last night. Who is that?" I asked. Might as well get things started.

"Teague," Dad said, and was quiet for a minute, as if he were shuffling through mental files for information. "She used to be the head of the parapsychology department at Bennett University before it was dismantled," Dad explained. "Her unconventional ideas stripped the credibility of some very sound research and led to a major loss of funding for the department. Once the money was gone, so was she, along with several staff members who chose to leave."

Everything from melancholy to fear jumbled up inside him. The past mixed with the present, too tangled for me to sort out.

"Wait a second." Nate switched positions on the floor beside me so fast it made my head hurt, and his mind moved as quickly as his body did. "You said that the staff *chose* to leave. If staying at the school was one choice, what was the other?"

"Joining Teague." Dad's lips pressed together in a grim line.

"Where? What makes her powerful enough to send an assassin and demand—" I stopped. I already knew the answer.

So did Em.

"She's part of the consequence Cat warned me about before I went back to save Michael." Em slumped back hard on the sofa. Dust flew two feet in the air. "Teague must be part of the Powers That Be."

"The Powers That Be." Dad nodded. "Chronos."

Dune placed his elbows on his knees, and one of his dark brown dreads escaped the leather tie, swinging into his eyes. He ignored it. "I thought Chronos was a myth."

"That's what they want you to think." Dad's voice was grim and layered in what felt like years of frustration.

Dune's focus drifted toward Dad's bookcase and his hourglass collection. They were the only things on the shelves that weren't dusty.

"I didn't follow Teague," Dad explained, his expression resigned. "I'd begun researching the time gene, and I was ready to start the Hourglass. Cameron College offered me a position, and Cat and Jack followed me to Ivy Springs. It was past time to get out. She wasn't completely certain how it worked, but Teague knew about my ability and Cat's, as well as Grace's."

My stomach took a dive at the sound of my mother's name.

"Why does Teague want Jack now? How can he repair the damage he . . . *we* did to the continuum?" Em focused on a spot on the floor. *Pain. Sadness.* But not one hint of regret. Michael took her hand.

"Poe didn't say that Jack could repair the continuum." I nudged Em's knee with my elbow. "He said if we found Jack, there was a possibility the continuum could be repaired. You were kind of . . . out of pocket for that part."

"Oh yeah. I was on the ground bleeding to death." Em laughed halfheartedly.

No one else did.

"*Can* Jack fix the continuum?" I asked.

Dad put his hands in his pockets and leaned against the bookcase. He was hiding so much. I could feel it, but I couldn't explain any of it. "I don't think that's why Teague wants him."

"Why, then?" Em asked.

"That's not for you kids to worry about." He was protecting us. He was also terrified. After pausing for a moment, he seemed to make a decision. "I've already said too much. The message from Teague was for me, not all of you."

"What? That can't be it. We still have questions." I pulled myself to my feet, angry. "You have to let us help you."

"No, I don't." Dad shrugged with an air of finality, and then stepped forward to shuffle papers on his desk.

"Yes, you do." I spoke firmly, enunciating, letting Dad know that I didn't plan on backing down. "Everyone in this room was part of the plan to bring you back. If that doesn't give us full rights as Hourglass members, then something is way wrong."

"I have the help I need." Dad's words didn't give the answer away, but Michael's emotions did. I spun around to face him.

I shook my head in disgust. "Why doesn't somebody just make you a freaking superhero cape?"

Michael's expression didn't change.

"Son. Michael's an adult, and he's capable of making his own decisions."

"He's nineteen."

"I refuse to put anyone else in jeopardy, especially if they're underage. What happened last year almost ruined us."

"Oh, what, you mean how enrollment at school dropped after you blew up in your lab?" I laughed bitterly. "Or when it dropped after you came back from the dead? I can see why you'd jump to Michael for help, considering what an 'adult' handle he had on that situation."

"All of this falls squarely on me," Em spoke up. "Jack compromised the continuum because he wanted my ability to travel to the past. It's not right for me to sit safely and act like I'm not responsible."

"Jack didn't kill me because of you, Emerson," Dad assured her. "He wanted the Hourglass, and after that was his, he got greedy. He tried to use you as a tool for some grander scheme to change something in his past."

"Please, Liam." Em scooted to the edge of the couch and leaned forward, staring until Dad met her eyes. "I want to be a tool for the right reasons. Let me help."

"Michael and I can handle it," Dad insisted, his eyes shuttering any emotion. "I only wanted to catch you all up to speed. Oh, but I do need one thing. Someone to tell Ava that Jack is back."

Everyone looked at me.

Chapter 6

I didn't believe in delaying unpleasant tasks.

I went straight from Dad's office to the stone gatehouse on our property and knocked.

"We have to talk," I said, when Ava answered.

She tried to slam the door in my face.

I stuck out my foot to block it, glad I was wearing boots. It bounced off and swung open. "I'm serious."

"I'm serious, too. I don't want to deal with you today." Ignoring me, she went to the couch and picked up the television remote. When she pressed a button, a scene from nineteenth-century England disappeared from the TV screen. "Besides, there's nothing we need to discuss."

She wore a tank top, and I could see every detail of her shoulders and collarbones beneath the tiny straps. Too skinny to begin with, she was starting to resemble those runway models who ate cotton instead of real food because it was chewy and calorie free.

"Actually, there's a lot to discuss."

"Go home, Kaleb," she said, with barely concealed disgust.

A couple of weeks ago, Ava and I had run into each other after school. Physically ran into each other. I'd tapped into her emotions against my will. She'd been wound so tight I went against my better judgment and asked her if she was okay. One word of kindness, and she'd spilled her guts. We'd ended up huddled together on the floor while she cried until all her tears were gone.

Jack Landers did terrible things to her that no one deserved. Things she couldn't remember, but could still feel.

Until that day, I'd had no idea. We weren't exactly friends now, but we weren't enemies, either. I didn't call her The Shining anymore, but things were at least twelve shades of awkward between us.

I pulled at the roots of my hair, glad I'd started growing it out so I had some to grab in frustration. I tried again. "I know you don't like me—"

"And I'm your favorite person?"

I stood my ground.

"Fine," she said. "Why are you here? Have you added sadomasochism to your list of extracurriculars?"

"No. It's about Jack—"

She raised a long, skinny arm and pointed at the door. "Get out."

39

"Stop cutting me off," I yelled, instantly sorry when she flinched. I tried again in a lower voice. "You have to hear this. We called a truce, remember? All I'm asking for is a few minutes."

Her face remained blank. "I'll give you three."

"He's back."

She stared at me, her face going paler with every passing second. "Are you sure?"

"Yes."

"Did you see him? With your own eyes?"

I nodded.

She seemed to lose the strength to stand, and slid down the arm of the couch onto the cushion with a soft thump. "Where?"

"Last night. He showed up at the masquerade party, but he was gone before I could get to him. Popped in and out. Not before he tried to take a shot at me. With a gun."

Across the room, a mug on a sideboard rattled and then jumped before slamming into the wall. Black coffee dripped down the patterned wallpaper.

I stared openmouthed. I'd never seen any evidence of Ava's ability in person.

"What do you mean 'popped in and out'?" she asked, ignoring the splattered coffee. "Why didn't you stop him?"

"I tried." I explained Chronos and the ultimatum, but left out the part about Em and the throat slashing. "We have until Halloween to find Jack. Or we're at the mercy of Chronos."

When she shivered, I handed her a sweater from the back of

the couch. She pushed her arms into the sleeves and wrapped herself in it.

"Hey," I said in what I hoped was a comforting voice, "it's going to be okay. He won't get to you again. We won't let him."

"How? Is someone going to be with me twenty-four/seven?" The remote rattled on the glass end table but stayed put. Ava closed her eyes and took a couple of deep breaths. "Not just me, what about Emerson? What about about your mom? He worked here, for years. He knows this place inside and out."

Dread.

"You're alone out here," I said in sudden realization.

"Thank you, Captain Obvious."

One of Ava's roommates had graduated; the other two didn't return to the Hourglass school for the year. Probably because of the whole "the school's founder blew up in his lab and then came back from the dead and, by the way, your classmate killed him" thing. I made a snap decision. "I think you should move into our guest room."

"What?" Ava snorted in disbelief. *Shock. A little bit of hope.* "Are you drunk?"

"Not right now." I stared at the coffee stain on the wall. "What Jack did to you is wrong. The things he did to all of us are wrong. We're going to have to get past it all if we're going to find him, and you're going to have to trust me."

"Trust you?" She shook her head. "Me, trust you?"

"Please stop fighting with me all the time."

Abruptly, she stood and disappeared into the tiny kitchen, staying away long enough that I wondered if I should go after her. Then she returned with a handful of paper towels and dropped to her knees to wipe furiously at the coffee-stained wall.

"Kaleb, I don't want to fight with you. I don't want to fight with anyone. But you just asked me to trust you. What about you trusting me? How can any of you stand to look at me?" An ocean of desolation and loneliness waved across the room. "After everything that happened, how could you ask me to move into *your house*? I killed your father."

"The past is the past." A world of hurt revolved inside her, so twisted I wasn't sure how to respond. I stood, reached her in three steps, and kneeled down beside her. She stilled but didn't meet my eyes. "What happened wasn't your fault. It was Jack and Cat's. They used you, forced you."

"That's not true. How could I have done those things—pursued Michael that way, been jealous of Emerson to the point of hating her, tried to *kill* your dad—and succeeded—unless I wanted to?" There were tears in her eyes, and her skin was blotchy. "I had to want to, right?"

"I don't think we understand everything about Jack. We didn't even know about his ability to steal people's memories. Think about it. No one ever asked why he was here. Or maybe we did, and he took the memory away from us."

Ava picked up the now empty coffee cup and placed the remaining paper towels on the sideboard. "Taking too many memories without replacing them leaves a void."

42

A void like the one inside her. It was terrifying, the nasty, black, hate-filled pockets of self-loathing, the empty spaces where fear and doubt took up residence. Nothing changed her emotional landscape. Joy never managed to creep into the mix, overtake the darkness, offer hope.

If my mom ever woke up, I wondered if she'd feel the same way.

"Well, then, let's make sure it doesn't happen again." I took the coffee cup out of her hand and nodded toward her room. "Just start packing."

I'd carried the last bag to Ava's new room in my house when my cell rang.

"It's Em," she said when I picked up. She hadn't waited for a hello, and she didn't take a breath before continuing. "After the meeting today, Michael and I had an argument—I mean, a discussion—and now we need you to come downtown."

"I don't do couples counseling."

She made a raspberry sound into the phone. "Just come meet us. Have you ever heard of Murphy's Law Coffee?"

Chapter 7

I stepped into the coffee shop, and a bell rang over my head.

I'd walked past Murphy's Law a million times, but I'd never been inside. I wasn't one for sitting, and sipping a hot beverage while chatting someone up wasn't on my list of favorite things to do. Even so, I inhaled deeply, appreciating the mingling smells of baked goods and freshly ground coffee.

Stunning framed nature photographs hung on every patch of the sunny yellow walls. Shelves were packed tight with new and used books, and a children's section boasted low tables full of puzzles and toys.

I found Em and Michael in the front corner of the room at a table surrounded by a grouping of overstuffed orange chairs. They reminded me of the giant toadstools from *Alice in Wonderland*.

"What's so mysterious you couldn't share it over the phone?"

I asked Emerson when I reached them. I dropped into one of the chairs and tried to relax against the fat cushions.

"Nothing, now," Em said, gazing out the huge plate-glass window, holding a tiny cup containing something very dark.

Her voice didn't hold a tenth of the energy I'd heard when she called.

"What's going on?" I asked.

"I thought I had an answer. To the finding Jack thing." She tipped the cup and drained it of its contents before placing it on the empty saucer in front of her. "But I was wrong. And stupid. And a terrible friend."

"No, you aren't," Michael reassured her, touching her lightly on the knee. "It's not like you asked for a frivolous reason."

"She'd never ask me to do something like that." The trust she had in him—the trust they had in each other—was so intense that I felt alien and intrusive.

I rapped my knuckles against the table, wishing I had something productive to do with my hands. "I can go . . . if you need me to . . ."

"No, don't leave," Michael said. He inclined his head slightly away from the table. "Just give us a second."

I followed the smell of baked goods. Even though the building had obviously been around for a while, everything in the place was neat and organized, from the highly polished floor, which was stained a dark chocolate brown, to the selection of books in the bookcases. I reached the bakery display case and leaned down to peer through the impeccably clean glass.

I spied a sight that enticed me way more than any éclair or doughnut ever could.

I'd know that back end anywhere. Just last night, my hands had been on it.

Tiger Girl was behind the counter.

Knowing she most likely hadn't forgotten or forgiven, I stayed down and tried to figure out how to escape without belly crawling to the exit. Then she moved out of sight, and I heard the swinging door to the back of the shop open and close.

I stood and shot back to the table. Emerson and Michael looked up at me in surprise. "You know what? I need to go. Can we meet up later? I'll find you. Okay."

Their focus shifted to something behind me, and I cursed under my breath.

"Em, can we talk in the back for a sec? I feel like I need to explain," Tiger Girl said, her husky voice insanely close to my right ear. "I'm so sorry—"

Em interrupted. "No, I am."

Tiger Girl knew Emerson. Emerson knew Tiger Girl.

When she noticed I hadn't moved, Em started to make introductions. I shook my head furiously and eyed the front door. So close, yet so far.

Em ignored me. "Lily, I want you to meet my friend Kaleb. Kaleb Ballard, this is my best friend, Lily Garcia."

Best friend. Awesome.

I turned to face her and all brain function ceased. Long dark hair knotted on top of her head, skin like butter, and curves that begged me to reach out and touch, all combining to completely obliterate the memory of her solid smack across my face.

For the first time in my life, the morning reality was exponentially better than the fantasy of the night before.

When I found my voice again, I said, "I'm Kaleb. And I'm also sorry."

Lily leaned her hip against the side of Em's chair, crossed her arms, and stared at me with hazel eyes. "*Not* so nice to meet you, sorry."

"How do you two know each other?" Em asked.

Lily's nuclear gaze remained steady. "Remember how I told you about the guy grabbing my junk right before that lunatic took the stage with his gun?"

"No," Em breathed. "Kaleb, you didn't."

"Oh, but I did."

"Are you hungover?" Lily asked me. Not in concern. Her hair slipped out of the loose knot to fall around her shoulders.

I shook my head and tried not to pay attention.

"Too bad. So." She looked at me with the perfect combination of disinterest and disdain. "How is it that you happen to know my best friend?"

The hissing and whirling of the coffee machine behind her stopped, and the shop held its breath.

"His dad is Liam Ballard." Em, eager to diffuse the situation, hurried to answer for me. "The man Michael and I went back in time to save."

"The director of the Hourglass? Oh crap."

Lily dropped into an empty chair, and the shop exhaled.

"She knows?" I asked Em.

Lily's frown started in her eyes, spreading to her forehead and mouth like an afterthought.

Em worded her answer carefully. "She knows about the time travel thing, and what happened with your dad, and about the purpose of the Hourglass. I got permission from your dad to tell her that much."

So she hadn't given Lily specifics about other people's abilities. Hopefully.

"What does *he* know about me?" Lily asked.

"Nothing," Em answered.

"Nothing," I repeated. "At all."

Lily looked up at me balefully. "Except how my ass feels in your hand."

A group of older women spilled into the shop, chattering in delight. Tourists, definitely, here to antique shop and soak up small-town atmosphere.

"I need to get back to work," Lily said, scooting to the edge of her chair. "Pumpkin Daze is starting, and I have to stock the pastry case so I can go hand out candy."

"Do you need me to stay and work?"

"No, I'll be fine."

"Call me?" Em asked.

"After my shift." She lifted her arms to adjust the apron strings around her neck, and then shook out her hair before catching it up in another knot. She caught me looking.

"What?" I asked, with a failed attempt at innocence.

"Did you need me to stand up? Twirl around?" Lily stuck her index finger in the air and made a spinning motion.

I had the good sense to respond by mumbling, shaking my head, and staring at the floor.

Chapter 8

E merson's expression was priceless as we filed out of the shop onto the sidewalk. "I can't believe you grabbed Lily's . . . You know, Kaleb, maybe you should start drinking organic milk. It has less hormones."

The town square teemed with people and energy. The fall festival ran for the whole month of October, kicked off by the masquerade. Today was the Town Trick or Treat, and little kids rushed around everywhere, holding out bags and taking candy from shop owners and employees. A cauldron with individually wrapped chocolates sat unattended in front of Murphy's Law.

"Exactly how much does she know about the Hourglass?" I asked Emerson.

A tiny ballerina in a purple tutu danced up and held out her bucket. I scooped some chocolates from the cauldron and gave her two. She smiled up at me with sparkly pink lips, exposing the space where her two front teeth should have been.

I gave her the whole handful.

"Lily knows everyone at the Hourglass has a time-related ability," Em answered. "But I kept the details to myself."

"We gave her specifics about travelers, but we didn't go into anything else," Michael said. His cell phone rang, and he read the caller ID. "Be right back. Hello?"

"Why were you and Lily apologizing to each other?" I picked up the cauldron and passed out more candy to a couple of boys with king-sized pillowcases bursting at the seams.

Em stared at Michael's back and sat down on a bench flanked by flowerpots filled with yellow mums and purple pansies. "I can't really talk about that."

Even though I could sense emotions, I didn't always know the cause of them. When someone was angry, it could be directed at me, something I did, or it could be because the Yankees won. If someone was afraid, it could be because of a social situation or because they were awaiting the result of a medical test. I hated never being sure.

Like with Em right now. I didn't understand why I felt fear from her, especially fear wrapped up in guilt.

"Why can't you talk about it?" I asked.

She dug at the concrete with the toe of her sneaker. "It would mean betraying a confidence. Not that I don't trust you . . . it's just . . . I can't."

I picked a piece of candy out for myself. "But Michael knows?"

Em hesitated for a brief second before answering. "Well, I had to tell him."

"Sure you did." Putting the cauldron back in its chair, I smiled thinly at her, turned on my heel, and walked away.

"Kaleb, wait!"

I'd just crossed the square, weaving through craft booths bursting with canned vegetables and jars of jam, as well as home-made candles and really creepy-looking dolls, when Emerson caught up to me in front of the Ivy Springs Cinema.

She grabbed my arm. "Please."

Her face was so vulnerable, just like it had been the second before Poe had cut her throat open. The memory of her bleeding and broken on the ground made me soften. "What?"

"Michael's known about this particular situation for a while. . . . I'm not trying to hide anything from you on purpose. But I promised to keep a confidence and I can't break it."

Her raw honesty almost leveled me. This girl wouldn't know betrayal if it punched her in the face. "You're excellent at keeping your word. Aren't you?"

Her hand was still on my arm. "I've never told him how you took the pain from me when we thought he was . . . dead."

"You mean how I *tried* to take it." I'd been completely willing to carry her grief for her, but she'd stopped me.

"What happened was between us," she said. "And it's not like it was a betrayal."

I knew part of her felt it was. Taking emotion from someone was intensely personal. It created a strong bond. And with Emerson, it was a bond I didn't want to break, even though I knew I had to.

"You can tell him. I want you to. It was your pain, your business," I argued, when she started to disagree. "It's your place to share that, not mine."

"Only if you promise to talk to him about it after I do."

I nodded. She'd tell him how it connected us. I'd have to promise to disconnect it.

"Soon. And you need to talk to your dad, too. After the way you argued with him today—he just wants what's best for everyone."

"I'm not ready to talk to my dad." I stared at the line of movie posters on the brick wall in front of the theater. They must have been running a revival of some sort, because all of the posters advertised black-and-white films, with the exception of *Gone with the Wind*.

"He loves you. He's proud to have you as his son. His *only* son."

"Yeah." He loved me. But he trusted Michael. Everyone did. The last thing I wanted to do was to get into that with Emerson.

A faint breeze brought the smell of caramel corn and cider. It sent Em's hair flying, and she tucked it behind her ears. "Also, about Lily—"

"Oh no." I shook my head. "You don't get to yell at me now. Lily already took care of the shaming portion of the day. I won't bother her again, swear."

Em laughed. "I'm not worried about you bothering her. If you do, you're the one who'll be in trouble."

I got a really strange feeling, and I looked around. We were in a crowd of people, but none of them were little kids in costume. The smells of the festival had disappeared and been replaced by the smell of popcorn.

"The line for the theater is really long," I said, mostly under my breath. "What's so exciting . . ."

"Everyone has on hats. Those are 1940s-style coats," Em said slowly. "Hells bells."

We looked up at the giant marquis at the exact same time.

GONE WITH THE WIND
MIDDLE TENNESSEE
PREMIERE TONIGHT AT 7:45
ADMISSION $1.10

"What do we do?" I asked, overwhelmed by the sheer number of bodies lined up on the sidewalk. Em and I were the only modern people in sight. "Where did *our* Ivy Springs go? What happened?"

"Time slipped. Maybe you can help me pick it up?" Em extended her arm to touch a woman wearing red lipstick with hair in big, fat loops on top of her head. "And who decided to call a hairstyle a victory roll, anyway? Dumbest name ev—"

She froze.

Dread, the kind that makes your stomach bottom out.

"What is it?" I asked.

"They don't see me." Em waved her hands in front of the

woman's face, careful not to touch her. When the woman didn't react, Em ran down the length of the movie line, stopping every few feet to try to catch the attention of one of the patrons.

I followed, almost knocking her over when she stopped short.

Em was shaking her head. "Why don't they see me?"

"I'm not sure I understand what you're asking."

"Rips. I've had conversations with them. They notice me, and I notice them. These rips don't see me." She closed her eyes. "The rip at your house yesterday—the soldier I touched didn't see me coming. The rip the night I went back to save Michael was the same way. I was in a house with a mom and her kids, a small house, but they didn't *see* me."

"Hey," I said, concerned with her whirl of fear and anxiety. "It's okay."

"I actually think it's a huge sign that it's not okay at all." Em reached out to touch the closest rip. As the scene dissolved, she sighed in relief. "We need to get out of here. And then Michael and I need to talk to your dad."

Chapter 9

*F*ingertips tapped a staccato rhythm on my bedroom door. I took the ice pack off my ribs and shoved it under my pillow before marking my book with a wayward candy wrapper. I opened the door to my dad.

"Ava is getting settled." He reached out to ruffle my hair on his way in. A year ago, I would have ducked. Now I fought the urge to lean into his touch. "I'm glad you asked her to move in. Wish I'd thought of it."

"It's not like she'll ever come out of her room." I noticed a beer bottle cap sticking out from under the edge of my dresser. I walked over, kicked the cap underneath it, and leaned against the edge.

"Maybe not, but we'll know she's safe," Dad said, frowning in the direction of the bottle cap.

"As safe as anyone can be from Jack." I twisted the drawstrings hanging from the hood of my sweatshirt. "Did you and Em and Mike come to any conclusions about the way the rips are changing?"

"Just combined our observations."

That was all I was going to get. Something else I couldn't be trusted with.

"Switching topics." He sat down on the end of my bed, smoothing out the wedding ring quilt. It had been passed down through my mother's family and was mine since I was little. I loved the comfort and the weight, knowing generations of Walkers had slept under it. "Have you been taking your emotion control meds regularly?"

"Depends on what you mean by regularly." I was. But alcohol definitely dulled the effects.

"Daily is preferable. I wondered if something was going on. I've noticed a . . . change between us." It hurt him to say it. I wasn't interested in making it easier for him.

"You were dead for six months. A lot of things changed."

He flinched, as if I'd swung at him and barely missed. "Fair enough."

"What are you getting at?" People not saying what they meant made me weary. Especially people I cared about. I could do with some complete honesty, but I'd never find it here. Not from Dad.

"You seem more emotional than you used to be. We don't talk about your mom, you don't visit her—"

"I don't want to visit her." I never went near her room. I was too afraid that if I did, I'd curl up beside her and never leave. I reached for one of the Atomic Fireballs on my bed and popped it in, welcoming the rush of heat.

"Your prerogative." He didn't try to hide his disappointment.

"You've changed, too." I shoved my hands into the kangaroo pocket on the front of my shirt, stretching it toward my knees. "You and Michael have secrets. You didn't . . . before."

"I had other adults to depend on before."

But I'm your *son*.

I wanted to say that out loud. Instead, I pushed the candy into my cheek, feeling the roundness of it stretching my skin. "You aren't going to change your mind about the rest of us helping?"

"Not right now. It hasn't even been twenty-four hours. Why don't you have some faith in your dear old dad?"

"Maybe you should have some in us." I said around the candy, exhaling to cool off my mouth and to distract myself from my own emotions. It didn't work. Biting down hard, I broke the Fireball in half and traced the circles inside it with my tongue.

"It's not a matter of faith in you. My interests lie strictly in keeping you safe." He stood. "Consider this the end of the discussion. Understand?"

I didn't answer him.

"I promised Thomas and Dru we'd help them finish up the move. We'll leave for the Coles' at five. I'll meet you at the car."

Em was moving in next door. A mile down the road to be exact, but she and her family would still be our closest neighbors.

Since Thomas was so slammed during Pumpkin Daze, Dad had offered the use of our combined muscle mass to help situate the furniture. Michael's convertible already occupied one side of the driveway by the time we arrived. I hung back once Dad got out.

"All right," I lectured my reflection in the rearview. "You will behave. You will not argue with anyone. Dru is pregnant, so you'll think of helping her and not yourself, put her needs ahead of your own. You are sweetness and light. Human cotton candy."

My laugh started as a snicker but ended up a snort.

I opened the Jeep door and stepped out onto the driveway. Into Lily Garcia.

"You really take vanity to a new level." Her hands were on her hips. "Talking to yourself in the mirror, laughing at your own jokes . . ."

What had she heard? "Were you spying on me?"

"Your window's rolled down there, genius." Her messy bun, combined with the tiny wire-rimmed glasses she wore, gave her a librarian vibe. A slightly sexy, seriously judgmental librarian vibe. "I assume you're here to help unpack boxes."

"No, genius, I'm here to help move the furniture." I made an exaggerated show of flexing my pecs.

"Putting all that beef to use. Too bad your intelligence just atrophies away in that tiny little brain."

"Aww, you think I'm intelligent?"

She just sighed and turned her back. I followed her up to the house.

Arranging the furniture didn't take too long. Thomas came in halfway through and stole a kiss from Dru, rubbing her belly before he got to work. Dad watched them out of the corner of his eye.

He couldn't stop watching them. His intense ache for my mother never eased. When I couldn't take any more, I stepped outside on the back deck to cool off, to put some distance between myself and my father's heartache. Leaning back against the outside wall, I closed my eyes and listened to the brisk breeze rustling the tree branches. I smelled burning leaves, the best part of living out in the country in the fall, in my opinion. Unless you counted bonfires. And hayrides.

Hayrides were the perfect place to make out with a girl and get away with grabby hands. Could always blame it on bumpy farm roads.

I was almost ready to go back to the house, when I heard two people arguing in the side yard. I couldn't get back up the stairs to the porch without my heavy boots echoing on the wooden plank stairs, so I listened.

"You have to let me do it." Urgency saturated Lily's voice. "Why won't you?"

"Your grandmother will freak," Em answered. "She'll freak, cause me bodily harm, and she'll never make me another Cubano. She's made it very clear that you aren't allowed to look for people."

"You are my *best friend*. That makes it different." For the first time, I noticed Lily's slight Spanish accent. It probably became more pronounced when she was angry or upset, like she was now.

I peered around the house to find that the ferocity of Lily's emotions matched her expression.

"I said no." Em's denial almost outmatched Lily's insistence. "You're loyal, and your loyalties to Abi should outweigh any you have for me. She's your family."

Lily grabbed Em's hands. "So are you. This time, what Abi doesn't know won't hurt her. I'm not going to break her rule. Not exactly."

"How are you going to get around it?" Em's green eyes were full of pleading. "Finding a megalomaniac who can time travel isn't like knowing a bank bag is back in a building. You can occasionally find things, but never people, right?"

"That's the rule." Lily let go of Em. "Abi's never explained why I can't use it—just that I can't."

"She wouldn't have been so adamant about it for so many years if she didn't have a good reason."

"Ugh, this is so frustrating." Lily dropped her hands. "What's the point in being a human radar detector if I can't detect?"

A human radar detector?

I thought back to the conversation I'd overheard between Em and Michael at the coffeehouse.

Disbelief exploded like a bomb in my chest. I took off down the back steps and across the short stretch of lawn.

I crashed through a pile of crunchy leaves, causing them both to jump.

I moved into Em's personal space, so close she had to tilt her chin all the way up to meet my eyes. "Lily can find people. That's why you wanted us to meet at Murphy's Law. You thought *Lily* was our answer to finding Jack."

"I *am* the answer," Lily growled, and stepped between Em and me. "Maybe you need to learn to mind your own business."

"But"—I looked at Em and then at Lily in confusion—"you said you couldn't look for a person. Just things."

"I'm working it out. It'll be *fine*," Lily said. "I'm helping. But I have to do it on my terms."

"Your terms? There's no room for *terms*, sweetheart."

"Listen, jack hole, I wasn't aware until recently that Ivy Springs is some kind of . . ." Lily waved her hands around, searching for the right word. "I don't know . . . freak magnet."

"*Freak* is my word, not hers," Em contributed, her gaze bouncing back and forth between us.

"Whose word is *jack hole*?" I asked.

Lily kept going. "You might be comfortable with whatever your abnormality is, but mine's not something I usually talk about, and it's definitely not something I'd choose to discuss with *you*."

"Did Em tell you the consequences if we don't find Jack?"

"No." *Bewilderment.*

"The people who want Jack claim to have a way to rewind time," I informed her. "If we don't find him and turn him over, they'll rewind it. My dad will be dead, and Em will be a vegetable in a mental hospital."

Frustration and anger, moving quickly into fear.

Lily shook her head as if she didn't believe she'd heard me properly. "A vegetable in a mental hospital?"

"Okay, *enough.*" Emerson pushed her way between Lily and me. "I don't want guilt to be Lily's motivation for breaking a promise to her grandmother."

"Breaking a promise or jeopardizing lives," I said. "Which is more important?"

"Why didn't you tell me about the consequences?" Lily asked Em.

I took Em's hand, concentrating, reading her. She tried to pull away, but I wouldn't let her. "Why are you trying to hide the truth?"

Em finally broke away, reminding me how much strength there was in her petite body, and took off toward the back porch at a jog.

"Give us just a second?" I pleaded with Lily. She nodded, and I caught up with Em.

"We'll stop Jack," I said. "But we have to find him to do it."

"No, that's not it." She fought tears. "Jack never mentioned Lily specifically in the list of all the things he 'did' for me. But I'd be an idiot to think otherwise. A best friend with a supernatural ability? A coincidence?"

"I'm sorry, Em."

Her fear was for Lily. "And I don't know where she'll end up. Her life . . . it hasn't been easy as it is. What if it was as easy as Jack could make it?"

"Why don't you just tell her?"

Em lowered her voice as Lily walked toward us. "How would you feel, hearing that? Knowing your whole life was manipulated because someone wanted something from your best friend?"

"But you don't know if—"

"If he did put her here, he knows what her ability is. Jack has a reason for everything he does." The tears she'd been fighting filled her eyes. "Why would he put someone in our direct path who could find him, especially when he doesn't want to be found?"

"That's it. Private time is over." Lily interrupted and pulled Em into her arms, hugging her long and hard. "Em. Go inside."

"What?" Em wiped her eyes and frowned.

"I want to talk to him. Alone."

She was looking at me.

Chapter 10

*O*nce Em was gone, I faced Lily. "I usually find bossy to be a sexy trait in a girl. You've broken the streak."

"I don't give a damn what you think about me." Lily didn't mess around; her words always matched her emotions. "You haven't broken any streaks at all. I've met a hundred boys like you in a hundred different scenarios, even dated one or two, and you're all exactly the same."

"It's not nice to stereotype."

"Don't talk to me about stereotypes." She stared up at the pale pink sky and frowned. Her eyes matched the tiger's-eye pendant that hung from her neck. "I'm not here for friendly conversation. Michael's solidly on Em's side, so I'm not going to get any information from him. But you're selfish enough to tell me the truth."

"Perceptive."

"Very."

"Maybe Em's already told you the truth," I countered. "Catch me up on what you know."

"Smooth."

"Very."

Lily sighed. "I know that Jack Landers messed with her time line. I know what the Hourglass does, sort of, and that you all have to find Jack." *Worry. Helplessness.* "I knew there was an ultimatum, but I didn't know what it was, or the consequences of it. Until you."

"Now that you do know, why did you ask me to stay out here with you, alone?"

She crossed her arms over her chest and tilted her chin up at me. "Do you have any other way to find Jack, or am I the only option?"

"I don't know," I answered honestly. "Dad says he'll handle it. Well, that he and Michael will handle it."

"So Em's being her usual self by trying to circumvent the problem and take care of it herself?"

"Yes."

Lily's face was screwed up in concentration, her features smoothing out as she put puzzle pieces in the right places. I didn't want her to fit in the piece about how she ended up in this exact time and place.

"Ivy Springs isn't a magnet for freaks," I said abruptly, trying to derail her train of thought. I fished a stick out of a pile of leaves and peeled off the bark, throwing it on the ground.

"This many 'special abilities' in one tiny town makes it a magnet," she said, disagreeing.

"How do you know there aren't fifty freaks living in Nashville? Or five hundred in Atlanta?" I peeled off another piece of bark. "Maybe they're keeping it a secret, too."

"There are *at least* five hundred freaks in Atlanta, but that doesn't mean any of them have a special ability." She jerked the stick out of my hands and snapped it in half.

"Okay." I raised my eyebrows.

"You're trying to change the subject." She chucked a piece of the stick toward the woods. "I don't know why, but if you want to succeed, you'll have to try harder."

"One point to Lily."

"If you don't find Jack, and time is rewound, how do you know things wouldn't play out the exact way they did the first time?" she asked. Too perceptive. "How do you know people wouldn't make the same choices, live the same lives?"

"I think the people who want Jack will take him out of the picture. From what point do they take him? After he killed my dad but before he changed Emerson's time line?"

She threw the other half, harder this time. "That sucks."

"That sucks," I agreed.

"If I do help . . ." She stopped, catching her breath, and stared over my shoulder. I turned around.

A man sat on a horse twenty feet in front of us.

"That's . . . not . . . right," Lily choked out from behind me.

One end of a long rope circled the man's neck in a makeshift noose, and the other end draped over the highest branch of a black walnut tree. None of it had been there two minutes ago. His hands were tied behind his back, his feet tucked into stirrups. A shotgun came into view behind the horse he sat on, aimed at the sky.

The man attached to the gun came into view next.

"We don't take to thieves here." He leaned the gun against the trunk of the tree as he took the rope and tied it tightly, working it into the grooves of the bark. "Not of our livestock or our women."

"I didn't touch your wife."

The sound of the shotgun pump echoed across the empty landscape. Lily's shoulders jerked at the sound.

"I didn't, and I'm not a thief. I thought it was my horse, I thought . . ." Desperation tainted the excuse. Sweat beaded on the thief's forehead.

"I caught you red-handed with both. I took care of the woman, but you're welcome to another turn on the horse." The man holding the gun curled his index finger around the trigger.

"You'll be sorry," the thief said. "My men will make you sorry."

"They'll have to find me first. Enjoy the ride."

I jumped forward, grabbing Lily's arm. She made a sound of protest as I spun her around and pulled her into my chest.

A shot echoed through the twilight air.

The horse reared and took off at full speed, and the man jerked backward with a loud snap. His feet twitched as his face turned red, and then blue.

Lily struggled to free herself from my arms. I held her tighter. "Don't look. Please don't look."

The man who shot the gun had disappeared.

"Kaleb? Lily?" A voice broke in, faint, sounding far away. I looked toward where the house was supposed to be. Em.

The three of us stood in the middle of a field, empty, except for a dead man hanging from a tree.

Em watched the man swing from side to side, not looking at his face. Her voice remained calm, but she kept swallowing as if she was trying not to throw up. "Lily?"

Lily pushed her way out of my arms before I could stop her. Her focus shifted from Em to the man hanging to the tree and back again. "What the hell . . ."

"You can see him?" Em whispered.

"Where are we?" Lily asked, spinning around in a complete circle. "What happened to the house?"

Em and I exchanged a look that asked a singular question. If Lily could see the full-blown rip, did that mean the rips were changing? Or did it mean Lily had the time gene?

Em turned toward the hanging man and walked the twenty feet to the trunk of the walnut tree. She tried touching it first, but nothing happened. Squeezing her eyes shut, she gingerly reached out in the direction of the man's foot.

When she made contact, the scene in front of us melted from top to bottom.

To reveal Thomas and Dru standing on the back porch, staring at us.

Em gazed back in horror. "What are you doing?"

"Checking to see what was keeping the three of you," Thomas said. "What are *you* doing?"

"Did you . . . did you just see that?" Em waved her hand in the direction of the place the rip had disappeared seconds before.

Thomas and Dru replied in unison.

"See what?"

Chapter 11

I was pretty sure I was awake, but if so, why was Lily Garcia sitting at my kitchen table on a Sunday morning? I rubbed my eyes with my fists.

"Did you forget your shirt?" she asked.

I blinked. Still there. I was glad I'd pulled on basketball shorts instead of coming downstairs in my boxer briefs. "No. I wasn't expecting to see . . . anyone."

"Surprise." She waggled her fingers. Jazz hands.

I grabbed some pineapple-orange juice from the fridge. Screwing the plastic lid off, I started to drink out of the carton before I caught myself. I extended it to Lily. "Thirsty?"

"No," she said, wrinkling her nose.

"Not to be rude, but why are you in my kitchen?"

"I'm here to see your dad. He ran over to the college to get supplies from the science department. I guess he didn't expect me to come for testing so soon."

Anxiety.

"For the gene," I said.

"Yay you for keeping up. Are you going to tell me Ivy Springs isn't a freak magnet now?"

Avoiding the question, I chugged what was left of the juice and tossed the empty container in the trash. "Did you sleep?"

"My grandmother said I called out a couple of times." There was a hint of dark circles under her eyes.

I hadn't slept at all. In my mind, the man swung from the tree all night. "You live with your grandmother instead of your parents?"

"We escaped from Cuba when I was little. My parents are still there." *Pain.* It so often led to avoidance. "Have you always lived in Ivy Springs?"

"No. We moved here when Dad took a job at Cameron College." I shut the refrigerator door. "But this house has been in my dad's family for generations."

"Nice."

There were a couple of awkward seconds of staring—neither one of us knew where to look—but I could sense Lily trying really hard *not* to look at my bare chest or tattoos.

Instead of going upstairs for a shirt like a normal person, I reached for the hook magnet on the side of the fridge, grabbed my KISS THE COOK apron, and slid it over my head.

"Are you kidding me?" Lily's eyebrows almost met her hairline.

"No. I'm . . . hungry." Suddenly desperate to make the apron look somewhat normal, I took a coated cast-iron pan down from the rack over the kitchen island. "As for the apron, I like cooking. I like kissing. I like giving orders. About both."

I stared at her until she blushed.

"You okay with garlic?" I snagged a bulb from the counter and held it up. A piece of papery-thin skin fluttered to the floor.

"On your breath or in my food?"

Solid comeback.

I grinned. "In case I have enough leftovers for a doggie bag."

"If 'doggie bag' is meant to be an insult, up yours."

I clicked on the burner under the pan, squeezed a clove of garlic through a press, and then added chopped onions and red peppers from my stash in the fridge. After dropping in a couple of tablespoons of butter, I set the flame to medium.

"Why are you being . . . well, not nice, but not completely hateful?" Her cheeks were still flushed.

"I'm not good with mornings. I need a full belly to crank up to bad-boy mode." I looked at her from the corner of my eye. "I wouldn't stick around for lunch."

"Not in a million years." She leaned forward in her seat, tapping her fingers on the table. Working up to something. "Em said that your parents are travelers, just like Michael and her."

"That's true."

"That made me wonder . . ."

"Wonder what?" I asked.

"I want to know what your ability is."

"Wow." I grabbed a spatula and shifted the vegetables in the pan. "Such subtlety. Never would've expected it from you."

"You found out about me by eavesdropping." She shrugged. "I thought I'd keep it classy and ask."

I rested my elbows against the kitchen island, ducking my head to avoid the pot rack. "Empathy. Sensing people's emotions. Mostly of people I know, but even those I don't—if I touch them."

"Is that why you grabbed me at the masquerade? To feel my 'emotions'?"

"No." I grinned. "Not at all."

Lily rolled her eyes. "How did you find out that's what your ability is?"

"My mom is an actress." I turned back to the stove to pour in beaten eggs. To give the pain a chance to leave my eyes before I faced her again. "She quit the business to stay home with me, but she still does the occasional gig."

"No way! Your mom is Grace Walker," Lily said. "You look exactly like her."

That's what everyone always said.

"Lucky for me."

That's what I always said back.

"I'm not following. What does your mom being an actress have to do with empathy?"

"Mom started work on a remake of *Cleopatra*, lots of emotional scenes. I was about three." I wiggled the pan to make sure the eggs weren't sticking. "A couple of days after she left home to go on location, I started having irrational reactions to things. Dad called her to talk about it. They tracked it. I was reacting to her scenes as she filmed them."

"That's not so strange, right? I mean, she's your mom."

"She was filming in Egypt."

"Oh." Lily chewed on her thumbnail. "How does empathy relate to time?"

"Everyone has an emotional time line." I sprinkled a handful of cheese over the omelet, eyed it, and then added more. "I can travel yours, in the right situation."

"Backward or forward?"

"I don't mess with the future." Anymore.

"How do you use it?"

"Something smells good." Dad popped his head into the kitchen and I jumped. "Thanks for waiting, Lily."

Saved.

"No worries." She smiled at him before looking back at me, straight-faced. "Thanks for fighting off your inner bad boy for so long. Looks like breakfast is all yours."

Dad extended his hand to show her out of the kitchen. Before he followed, he took in my chest and apron. "Son?"

"Yeah?"

"Maybe you should locate a shirt."

Chapter 12

After Lily and her questions, I couldn't stop thinking about my mom.

I drove to the gym for some peace in the indoor pool.

I discovered the difference water makes when I was little. My mom had taken me swimming every day, rain or shine, hot or cold. When we'd moved to the house in Ivy Springs, she'd insisted we put a pool on the property.

Since Jack had put her in a coma, I couldn't bear to swim there anymore.

Because of my ribs, I walked into the water instead of diving. Sinking to the bottom of the pool, bubbles rising as I slowly released my breath, I allowed myself to think about her. Nobody else's emotions nudged in to confuse me, convolute the sorrow.

She gave up everything for me. A lucrative career, a place in the spotlight, any chance at normalcy. She didn't even know she was a traveler until she was pregnant with me. When she started seeing ripples, my dad was there to guide her through it.

Then I was born, and she became the mother of a little boy who was constantly bombarded by every emotion around him.

Once she and dad figured me out, what my needs were, she walked away from her life to keep me safe. Protected. She did her job so well that, until it was time for me to start school, the only emotion I ever felt was love.

She surrounded me with it.

I let myself float to the surface. The cool air was a sharp contrast to the warmth of the water. I took another deep breath.

This time, I pushed off the side of the pool and swam freestyle. My arms and legs pumped, churning up water but smoothing out my emotions.

We still didn't know exactly what Jack Landers had done to my mother. He told Emerson that he'd taken enough of her memories to render her suicidal. I didn't know if he'd taken her memories of me.

My mom wouldn't have lived her life for me the way she had only to throw it all away. I never once felt her desire to be anywhere but with us.

The fact that she was still breathing confirmed it, even though she'd been unconscious for almost eight months.

I'd been serious about taking Jack out with that sword when I'd rushed him.

How could killing him be a mistake?

Now my emotions and purpose were as linear as the blue line on the bottom of the pool. I pushed off to swim the length of it one last time, and then came up to the surface for air.

Sunday night football.

The converted pool house was all latte-colored paint, dark brown leather, and huge windows. Tonight, it smelled like nachos and chili. I didn't want to think about what it would smell like later.

"Boom!" Nate cackled and threw the television remote down so hard it bounced off the couch pillows. "I told you he'd score three touchdowns. You've got to take my garbage duty for a week."

"Oh yeah?" Dune looked down at least half a foot at Nate's triumphant face and flexed. "Make me."

Nate groaned.

Neither one of them noticed me.

I went straight back to Michael's room, but stopped with my hand on the doorknob when the TV went dead and the lights flickered off and on in the hall.

My parents had the same abilities as Michael and Em, and the same electrical connection. For as long as I could remember, the electricity was settled, and the love between them was so constant that it became emotional background noise. I barely noticed it until they were both gone.

Michael and Em's love created the kind of electricity people noticed.

I'd let go of the knob and was backing away when Em abruptly opened Michael's door. "Kaleb! Hey. Were you looking for us?"

Michael was stretched out on his bed in jeans and a T-shirt, and he was smiling. The covers were wrinkled, and a small hooded sweat jacket lay on the ground, along with Em's black Converse. My stomach twisted into a tiny ball of regret.

At least I hadn't interrupted anything too serious. Michael still had on his socks.

"I can come back."

"Stay." Em's feet were bare, her cheeks pink, her hair a rumpled mess. "I was going to grab some water, anyway." She nudged past me, and I heard the television in the living room switch back on.

"I'm sorry," I mumbled to Michael when I stepped into his room. "Maybe next time hang a sock over the doorknob?"

"I'll remember that." The smile disappeared, and he sat up. "Just taking advantage of our time together."

His words were casual, but the ache coming from Michael echoed the one my dad lived with every day. I took it in, let it roll around in my chest, spread out, and settle.

"We'll find Jack. He won't hurt her, or anyone else, again," I promised. I meant it.

"Em told me what happened, how you tried to take her pain."

My heart skipped a sudden, painful beat. "I thought she might."

Michael stared at the floor, feeling as unsure about how to proceed with the conversation as I did, but determined to have it. "I didn't know you could do that."

"It's not something I talk about."

"Do your parents know?"

"Mom does. Dad? He has an idea. I don't do it for just anyone." But Em had been so small in my arms. Tried so hard not to cry. I'd rocked her back and forth when she broke, wishing she'd let me take it all away.

She'd handled it on her own.

"I guess what I don't understand is"—Michael paused, searching for the right words—"after all those years of keeping it to yourself, why did you do it for her?"

Michael's guitar leaned against his dresser. He'd tried to teach me chords for years, but I only ever managed to remember three. I picked it up and played each one twice before slapping my hand down on the strings to silence the sound.

"The morning I met her, I was hungover. Remember?"

He nodded, curious, but willing to wait for my answer.

"My emotions were wide open, and . . . she climbed right in." I touched my hand to my heart, expecting an ache that didn't come. "She listened."

Before Em, no one had listened to me in a long time.

"She was completely devastated when she lost you," I said, remembering just how broken she'd been. "Like a repeat of Mom, after Dad and the lab. You know how terrible it was."

"I remember."

Mom was larger than life, but so much of her life had revolved around Dad. I'd watched her close in on herself after the accident, convinced that her love for me was the only thing keeping her breathing.

I discovered that I'd failed her the morning I found her unconscious on her bathroom floor. She'd been that way ever since.

"I knew I could change it for Em. Make it better." I stopped and stared up at the ceiling for a second. "I didn't with Mom. I let her carry around all that grief instead of stepping in to take it. I didn't try until she was already in the coma. There was nothing there. Too late. I didn't do one thing that made a difference."

"Em said it hurt you, physically."

"That didn't matter." Emotional pain was layered. Taking it to ease one situation opened the doors to the past, where every emotion leaned against the one beside it. Pull out one, all the others fell. It was hard to know where to cut it off, if you got it all or if pain still remained to destroy, like cancer.

"Did your mom know? Would she have let you take her grief?"

"I would've insisted." And she'd be here now.

"No one knew what Jack was doing. I should have paid attention, done more to help you both," Michael said.

"You did enough. You took action. That's why my dad is at my mom's bedside right now. If anyone can bring her back, he can."

"Thank you," he said, meeting my eyes. There was absolutely no pride in him. Everything he felt was for Em, about Em, about her best interest. "For taking care of her. If . . . anything ever happened, I hope you'd do it again."

Sorrow. Way too much for an offhand comment. I started to ask what he meant, when Em walked in, glass in hand.

"Are y'all done?" Em hopped up onto the edge of Michael's desk. She smoothed down her hair and then smiled, as if she was remembering how it got that way.

"Yes." I put the guitar back in the corner. "I'll get out of your way."

"No, sit. I wanted to talk to both of you. About Jack."

I warily lowered myself into a chair shaped like a giant baseball mitt. Cheerful Em made me nervous.

Putting down her glass, she cleared her throat. "I've been thinking about Liam, and how he doesn't want our help to find Jack."

"He has reasons." Michael's fingers curled around the edge of the bed.

"Oh, I know he does," she said. "But I don't like them."

I snorted.

Em grinned at me. "There's one easy way to find Jack, and that's to travel through time to somewhere he could be intercepted. Dune tracked Jack and Cat making a cash withdrawal in New York and then buying plane tickets to Heathrow, so we have times and places to look."

"But traveling is impossible without exotic matter," Michael said.

"Which gives Liam a good reason to be in the lab, searching for what's missing from the exotic matter formula. Michael and I need to be there to help him." She turned wide, innocent eyes on me. "That's where you and Lily come in."

"I thought you didn't want her to help," I said, more than nervous. Almost twitchy.

"I didn't. Then she yelled at me." Em winced at the memory. "A lot."

"What does that have to do with me?" I asked.

"She's never really used her ability outside Murphy's Law. She also told me that she can't track things unless she's seen them, so to find Jack, she'll need to see something he keeps with him. All the time."

"That's impossible, unless we track him down." Michael looked at Em as if she'd lost it.

"No, it isn't," Em answered smugly.

"How?" Michael asked.

"You forget Lily was at the masquerade. Kaleb pushed her under the stairs, but she got a good look at Jack first." She waited for the answer to register, and we spoke at the exact same time.

"The pocket watch."

Chapter 13

I took a picture of Jack and the pocket watch to Murphy's Law on Monday afternoon. He'd always carried the watch with him. I thought it was pompous, but I also thought he was a tool, so I hadn't paid much attention.

I waited for Lily at a table in the back. She took care of her customers with efficiency and a smile. Confidence. The Hourglass school was too small to provide complications like popularity and gossip, but I knew other girls who were caught up in all that. I'd bet Lily wasn't.

She knew what she wanted, and she was all about achieving it.

"Where are Em and Michael?" Lily asked when she finally made it over to me. She stretched, rubbing the small of her back. She was wearing the Murphy's Law apron again, and the strings were wrapped around her waist and tied in the front.

I focused on the bookcase just behind her and tried not to

notice how curvy she was. "Dad needed them after school for some research."

"So they sent you?" She sounded disappointed.

"Calm yourself, you're going to scare the customers," I deadpanned. "This seems to be a persistent problem with our interactions."

"This is where I remind myself how much I love my best friend. Abi's at the farmers' market in Nashville, so I have a couple of hours." She sighed and took off the apron. "Let me get rid of this so no one asks me for help."

I watched her walk away. Such a hot little package.

Such a pain in the ass.

She disappeared behind the swinging door and returned with a plate of cookies and hot tea that smelled like mint. Setting the cookies between us and pushing a bottle of cold water at me, she asked, "What's the plan?"

"Who's Abby?"

"Abi is my grandmother. Short for *abuelita*."

I opened the bottle but didn't drink. Just twisted the cap on and off. "How are you going to keep what we're doing a secret?"

"I'm going to be very careful." She stared into her cup of tea for a second before inclining her head toward the picture on the table. *More determination.* "That's Jack, isn't it?"

I slid it over to her. "That's Jack."

Leaning back in her chair, she called over her shoulder, "Sophie, will you throw me my glasses?"

Lily caught them one-handed and slid them on without ever putting down her tea.

I picked up a cookie. Peanut butter. "That was a really impressive catch for a girl."

She leaned over so far her nose almost touched the photo. "Your mouth is talking. You might want to look to that."

I bit into the cookie and ignored her. "Need a magnifying glass?"

"Yes." She abruptly put down her tea, went to the children's section, dug around in a bin, and pulled out a book. It was roughly the same size as our tabletop and had photos of magnets, microscopes, and graph paper on the front. "There's supposed to be a plastic magnifier in here, unless some little rug rat stole it. Aha."

She gently removed it, careful not to damage the book, and held it above the picture. I scooted my chair closer to her and caught the scent of vanilla and peppermint.

"You're sure he keeps the watch with him all the time?" She looked at me from the corner of her eye. "The engraving is detailed. It looks really valuable."

I put down the cookie, dusted off my hands, and reached for the magnifier. "May I?"

When she handed it over, I held the picture up to the light and studied the engraving.

Infinity symbols.

"It looks like duronium," I said.

The duronium disc my parents had made for me when I turned

sixteen was in my pocket, just like always. I felt for it from habit, reassured by the shape, if not the sentiment engraved on it. *Hope*.

"Aren't the rings Michael and Em wear made of duronium?" Lily asked. "Em said it's so rare I'd never see it on a periodic table."

I handed the magnifier back to her. "It is rare, and really hard to come by. The general public doesn't know about it. Neither does most of the scientific community."

She closed the book and put it on an empty chair. "Why?"

"No one can explain its properties. Not even my dad."

Fragments of information started sewing themselves together in my mind. Jack had a duronium pocket watch, and he was able to hide in veils. He'd used them to disguise himself when he first approached Emerson last summer. Poe had a duronium knife. He was able to pull Emerson into a veil, kill her, and then bring her out again without any repercussions.

"How did Jack end up with duronium if it's so rare?" Lily asked.

"No idea. I've never looked at his pocket watch up close. Jack and I avoided each other, kind of like never and always." I took my duronium disc out of my pocket and held it tightly in the palm of my hand. "I don't know if the pocket watch has always been duronium. He could have replaced another piece that was silver."

The shop was crowded when I came in, but now things were starting to thin out. Out of nowhere, I got the weird feeling that someone was watching me. I looked around the shop, and then outside. All I could see was a man reading a newspaper. He'd been there when I came in, a full cup of steaming coffee in front of him. I kept staring, and he lowered the paper.

Blond hair. Cold blue eyes. Gratified smile. Pocket watch in hand.

Jack.

I pushed back in my chair, shaking the table. Lily grabbed her mug of tea to keep it from toppling to the floor. "Hey! What's going on?"

One second he was there, the next he was gone. I rushed to the front door, slinging it open so hard the hinges squeaked in protest. There was a veil beside the table where he'd been sitting. He'd left a message on a white napkin, written in black ink.

Now you see him, now you don't.

Chapter 14

*L*ily burst through the front door of Murphy's Law. "Was that . . . ?"

"Yes." I shoved the napkin with the cryptic message into my pocket. I didn't want her to see what Jack had written, or the threat it implied. That he was everywhere.

"I looked right at him. Served him coffee. I *touched* him." She shuddered and rubbed her upper arms. "But I didn't recognize him."

"He's playing a game. It's what he does. Exposes weaknesses and dangles possibilities." I leaned against the window. The coolness of the plate glass on my back was a welcome relief. But the second I started to relax, Lily's tension jumped up and punched me in the gut. "Something else is bothering you. What is it?"

She leaned against the window beside me. "Did you just read me?"

"Like I could help it." I gave her the side-eye. "You're shooting off anxiety like fireworks shoot off sparks."

"Your dad called earlier." She sighed. "I wasn't going to tell you."

"Uh-oh." I turned my head to look at her. "Which one of us is in trouble?"

"I tested positive for the time gene." Her laugh was short and bitter, and she dropped her face into her hands. Her fingernails were short, perfect ovals. "This day. What's next? Blood-filled water? A plague of locusts?"

"Apocalyptical references?" I crossed my arms and stared back out into the afternoon traffic. A red sports car kept driving around the town square, either on a joy ride or lost. "That bad, huh?"

"I think I'll classify you in the boils category."

"Ow."

"Okay," she said, relenting. "Maybe frogs."

"You know what happens when you kiss a frog, don't you?" I asked, appreciating the moment of levity in the middle of disaster.

"I think they pee." She stepped forward into my line of vision, her hands on her hips. "Your dad's phone call didn't surprise you."

I shook my head. "Nothing does anymore."

"Why?"

"Something's . . . off. In our world." I didn't want to say "wrong," because that would be like saying "Welcome to hell, now with hotter fire."

"Off? That's all you have to say?" She threw her hands into the air in defeat. "That's sad. I thought you and I'd come to an agreement."

"What kind of agreement?" I couldn't understand why she felt so let down.

"That you'll tell me the truth." She pursed her lips.

Even though we didn't like each other, that bottom lip was still tantalizing. "I'm not exactly known for honesty."

"This is different. We're working together for a common goal. I'm not a conquest," she said, "or even a possibility, so please be real with me."

Uncommon request. "Okay."

"I think my Ivy Springs as Freak Magnet theory is correct," she said. Her hair was twisted up into a sloppy bun. "Three people from the same hometown with a time gene?"

"Technically, my hometown is Memphis."

"Really, Kaleb?"

"Just keeping it specific." I made a motion of surrender.

"It doesn't matter if we were physically born here, we were attracted here. *Magnet*." Lily drew the word out, speaking with precise enunciation as she touched her pointer fingers together.

I tried not to laugh. "What's the other possibility?"

"I'm here because of him. Here in this situation and here in this town. Because of Jack." When I didn't answer, her hands dropped limply to her sides. "Why would any of you keep that a secret?"

"Because we don't know anything for certain." I couldn't

answer her truthfully. I didn't want to give her any information that wasn't absolute.

"If he isn't found, and time goes into rewind, it could affect me."

"If you're here because of him, yes, you'd be impacted by a rewind."

"Which means my grandmother would be, too." I heard the realization dawn in her voice. "Possibly my extended family."

"Possibly."

"This throws a whole different perspective on things." She took a deep breath, and I could feel her mind shifting to accept the truth. "I really am the only option for finding Jack."

"No. If my dad can re-create the formula needed to time travel, it would provide a really easy fix. Intercepting Jack at a known place in his past would be the fastest way to find him."

"How's that working out?" she asked, her eyes steady on mine.

I frowned. "It's not, exactly."

"His past," she mused. "What about his past?"

"If they make the formula work, I'm not sure where they'll go to find him—"

"I'm not talking about the formula. Jack's stirred up all this trouble because he wants something changed. He wants a ticket back to his past." She almost bounced as she asked her next question. "Has anyone ever asked why?"

I sat at our table with my back to the kitchen door. Sophie had been assigned as the lookout for Abi. Even so, Lily stood with an order pad in her hand, leaning against the table instead of sitting down with me. Her apprehension at being caught by her grandmother made me a little afraid. Abi appeared to be the kind of woman you didn't want to mess with, and I was helping her granddaughter break a huge rule.

I wished I could see enough to keep an eye out for Abi, too.

"We've never tried to figure out why he wants the past changed," I said, continuing our conversation from outside. "Just why Jack didn't change his past himself, and why he needed Em to do it for him."

"No one knows the reason?"

"There are a couple of theories. Em thinks maybe there's some reason he didn't want to mess with his own time line, but I don't think Jack cares about breaking rules. Michael thinks it's because the exotic matter formula was unstable, and Jack couldn't travel far enough to do what he wanted."

"I have no theories. Time travel makes my head hurt." She bit her bottom lip. "How old is Jack?"

"Midthirties."

"Your dad is in his midforties." She made a note on the order pad. "And Jack's known your dad how long?"

"About fifteen or sixteen years. That's when Jack became Dad's lab assistant."

"Fifteen years is a long time," Lily observed, still writing. "And a lot of memories. Not to mention how hard it would be to keep track of who knew what. Lots of people are involved at the university level. Staff, students, colleagues at other schools."

"Keep going."

"I agree with you. I don't think Jack cares about rules, which makes me think what he wants changed didn't happen recently. I think it happened way before he came to Ivy Springs. Maybe even before he started college at Bennett."

"We don't know where he came from." I rubbed my temples. "Our friend Dune's been researching, but we don't know anything about his background."

"But someone has to, somewhere." She leaned one hand on the table and tapped the end of the pen against her lips. "He could erase memories, maybe even find someone to help him erase complete computer databases, but not paper trails. Not every single one. Think about all the things that were on paper twenty-five years ago that are on computers now. Report cards, school records, annuals."

I gave her a sarcastic smile. "I'm sure Dune's taken all that into consideration."

"Don't condescend to me, Kaleb Ballard." Lily snapped to attention, standing straight up. "I'm thinking out loud, and you're supposed to be helping me brainstorm, not making judgments."

I sat back in my chair and laced my hands around one knee. "Sorry."

"We've established that you're sorry." I caught a hint of amusement under the harshness of her words. "I'm only saying, there's no harm in asking Dune if he's thought of that angle, and if he has, to ask if he has a plan for how you guys are going to approach it."

"Lily," Sophie whispered urgently over the counter. "She's back."

"So," Lily said brightly, pen poised over the order pad with efficiency. "That's two cheese and tomato paninis, a side order of sweet potato fries, another side order of pasta salad, and two vanilla cream cupcakes? What can I get you to drink with that?"

I stared at her. "A water tower?"

"Coming right up." She smiled, ripped the paper off the pad, slammed it down on my table, and walked toward the kitchen. She called out something in Spanish as she walked through the swinging door.

I looked down to see what the order ticket said. She'd written down the entire list she'd rattled off to me, with the addition of *water tower*.

And below that, *Twenty-five percent tip included. XOXO, Lily.*

Chapter 15

I stared across the quad at the science building, waiting. A pile of red and brown leaves whipped into a tiny little tornado and bounced against the brick foundation.

"Well?" I asked Dune.

"Nothing online," Dune said. He'd left his laptop at home. Bad sign. "No evidence of his existence."

In addition to his excellence at research, Dune had the supernatural ability to control the tide and the phases of the moon. I was glad the power to cause multiple natural disasters was contained in one of the most kind and logical people alive.

"I couldn't find anything in Dad's office." I stuck my thumbs in my back pockets. "Paychecks from the Hourglass don't exactly run through any of the normal government processes."

Nate kicked at a rock on the ground. "And there's no one to ask around here, because Jack pulled his Jedi mind tricks on anyone who'd have any decent information."

Dune turned his entire huge frame to the side and stared at Nate. "Please do not disparage the Force by including it in the same sentence as Jack Landers's name."

"You just did," Nate pointed out, making an "oof" sound when Dune elbowed him.

I knew it had to hurt. Dune had told us he was the smallest of his Samoan brothers, coming in at *only* 220 pounds and 5 feet 11. Just one of the reasons I tried to stay on Dune's good side.

I cleared my throat. "So Lily was right. A paper trail is the best chance we have to find out what Jack wants. And since he used to work here . . ." Dad had just started a three-hour staff enrichment, along with the rest of the physics department, so we were free and clear to get in and dig around. We'd stood behind a couple of trees and watched them trek from the science building to the administration office.

"Let's go," Dune said, and we followed him across the lawn.

Getting in the building was easy enough, and so was getting into the records room, thanks to the key I'd lifted from my dad. Rather than a dusty storage space, it was a former classroom, a little on the small side. There were at least twenty boxes that held files, along with a model of the planetary system, Pluto included, a couple of defunct microscopes, and a teaching skeleton missing its left leg bone. The skeleton hung from a rolling stand by a silver hook in its head.

The room also had a window, which meant we didn't have to turn on lights and draw unnecessary attention.

"Nate, keep a lookout, would you?" I took a box off the top of a stack and handed it to Dune, and then I picked up the one below it.

"Why would you make me be the lookout when I can go through those boxes at ten times the speed you two can?" Nate asked.

"Excellent point." I shoved the box in my hands at him and let go. It landed on the ground with a solid thud and a cloud of dust as it slipped right through his fingers.

"Nate, what are you—"

"Holy hell." Nate's voice hit a really high pitch. He was pointing out the window.

A hundred or so young men in caps and gowns sat in the middle of the quad on white folding chairs set up in rows, all staring intently at the stage and podium in front of them. The fallen leaves that had littered the ground two minutes ago were gone, replaced by a lush green summer carpet of bluegrass.

At the podium, a distinguished-looking gentleman reigned over the festivities, wearing a cap and gown.

The banner behind him said CONGRATULATIONS, CLASS OF 1948.

"Please tell me you see that," Nate said. "Do you see that?"

"I do," Dune said, setting down the box in his hands. "There are no women. Where are the women?"

I paid a little more attention to the scenery. The stone on the side of the buildings lacked a significant amount of moss from what I was used to seeing, and the art building was completely missing. "This was a men's college until the 1950s."

"So this is a ripple," Nate said. "From before then."

I heard a crash and a yelp behind us.

Nate and I turned to find Dune on the ground, tangled up with the teaching skeleton.

"I realize this is probably plastic and used for teaching purposes," Dune said, handing Nate a tibia with the foot attached, "but I want it *off me*."

Nate proceeded to use the metatarsals to scratch his back, and then he started to giggle.

I interrupted. "Guys. Look around."

Either my tone or the situation put an end to the giggling.

The storage space was now a classroom. Neat desks lined up in rows, and a blackboard full of equations. The only similarity between this room and the one we'd walked into five minutes ago was the skeleton. Dune was still tangled up in it.

"Where are we?" Nate touched a couple of the desks with his free hand. "Is this a rip? Because I'm still holding this leg bone in my hand. That's not normal. Right?"

"Shut up," I hissed. "Someone's coming."

The door to the classroom opened slowly. A tiny woman holding a mop stuck her head in and looked around, her gaze landing on the leg bone.

"I'm sorry," Nate said, gesturing with the bone. "It was an accident. We . . . we're visitors from . . . out of . . . state?"

I groaned. This wasn't going to end well.

The woman didn't seem to hear or see him, but from the

way her eyes moved, she did see the leg bone. From the way she dropped the mop and covered her mouth to stifle a scream, it must have appeared to be floating in midair. I rushed across the room and tapped her on the shoulder before she could run.

The dusty file boxes reappeared, and I heard a combined gasp from Dune and Nate.

The skeleton was upright and hanging from its hook, slightly more yellowed than it had been a few seconds ago in the rip from the past. It was missing a left leg bone.

The exact bone Nate still held in his hand. It looked brand new.

Chapter 16

"*Can* we just . . . regroup?" Em sat on the corner of my bed, staring at Dune, Nate, and me. "Number one, Lily pointed out to you that we needed to know what Jack's ultimate goal is, so that we can better understand where to look for him."

I nodded.

"Number two," she continued, moving her attention to Dune, "you did a computer search, and there's no information on Jack in any database anywhere."

Dune nodded.

"And number three." Em took a couple of deep breaths and looked at Nate, and then at each of us in turn. "Y'all looked through paper records at the college, and that led to you pulling a *leg bone* out of a ripple?"

Nate nodded and then patted the leg bone awkwardly. "I'd put it back, but . . . I don't know how."

"Why did you take it out of the rip with you in the first place?" Em asked in disbelief.

"We didn't do it on purpose," Nate assured her. "Don't worry. It didn't belong to anyone . . . who needed it."

"It doesn't matter why or how it happened, but it did," I said. "I couldn't tell Dad, because I didn't want him to know I stole his key or what we were looking for, but I couldn't leave the rest of the skeleton there, either. It's evidence."

"It's creepy." Em looked up at me. "And it's a skeleton. In your closet. Your *bedroom* closet. I mean, the irony . . ."

I shut the closet door. "Back to regrouping."

Em closed her eyes and dropped her head into her hands.

"You okay?" I asked her. "Want me to round you up some water or something?"

She peered up at me through her fingers. "How about your flask?"

"Trust me, that's not the answer."

"That's the wisest thing I've heard you say in a while," Michael said from the doorway. Em's eyes opened wide, and I could see and feel her relief. It went all the way to her soul.

Dune tapped Nate on the arm. "We should head out. Liam's going to know something's up if he finds us all in Kaleb's bedroom."

"Wait." After Nate dropped the bone on top of my dresser, I tossed him the key to the science storage area. "Can you get that back on Dad's key ring?"

"Lickety-split." He was gone before I could blink. Dune rolled his eyes and followed, but a little more slowly.

Michael threw his coat on my bed and sat down beside Em.

"Is that it?" He pointed at the bone.

"Yes." I opened my closet door, turned on the light, and let him compare the color of the bones.

"Just so I have all this straight, when you went into the storage room, the skeleton was there. It was missing a leg bone," Michael confirmed.

I nodded.

Michael continued, "When you landed in the rip, the whole skeleton was there, and when you came out of the rip, you brought the leg bone with you."

"Yes." I dropped the leg bone on top of my shoes and shut my closet door. "This makes my head hurt."

Em had been quiet. Michael leaned over, bumping her shoulder with his. "What are you thinking about? Because I know your brain's going a thousand miles an hour."

She pulled her legs up and wrapped her arms around her knees. "The rips. They just keep getting stronger, changing. Suddenly, the people in them don't see us, and now we can physically remove things. I'm just waiting for the past to overtake the present."

"What about the future?" I frowned. "Everything we've seen so far has been from the past. No rips from the future."

Michael didn't answer.

"When's the last time you saw a rip from the future, Michael?" Em hugged her knees more tightly to her chest.

"A while. Since the end of the summer. They started disappearing around the time the full scene rips showed up."

"Around the time Jack started messing with the time lines," I said.

"I don't understand what's happening," Em said. "And it's not very comforting to know that you don't, either."

"Jack is still doing damage to the continuum," Michael said. "If I'm honest, I don't think we have until Halloween to find him. I'm afraid the world won't last that long."

Chapter 17

*I*f the world was in danger, it stood to reason that Lily and I had a lot of work to do.

Murphy's Law was so full I'd had to wait for a seat at the bar. Everyone else had a laptop open in front of them, plugged into a power strip in the wall. I tried to look busy and important as I sent a few texts, but I only got dirty looks from people waiting for a seat.

"Not. Now." Lily swung past me with a steaming coffeepot, and I pulled back just in time to avoid being smacked in the face with it. "My grandmother is in the kitchen."

"Sorry, I didn't know," I said. "Where do you want me to go?"

Smiling, she topped off the cups of the people at the table closest to me, pouring with grace and precision. Obviously, she'd almost hit me because she wanted to.

"Clock tower steps. Twenty minutes. Get out."

The stone clock tower served as the perfect testament to how far Ivy Springs had come. Connected to the old train station, it was now home to the chamber of commerce. It even had ivy climbing up the side. The clock hands moved via electricity rather than clockwork, leaving enough space that the top two floors could be rented for meetings or parties.

I sat down at the far left side of the steps and leaned back on my elbows.

Michael had made it very clear that we were running out of time. While he and Em continued to help my dad solve the riddle of the exotic matter formula, Dune and Nate would continue the computer and physical searches for any kind of records about Jack.

That left me to pair up with Lily.

"Kaleb?"

Nervous excitement. I opened my eyes to see the source. A blond girl I almost recognized. "Yeah?"

"I'm Macy?" She said it as if she weren't sure herself. "We met downtown last summer? You let me drive your Jeep down Broadway."

I'd let her park it, too.

"Macy." If I leaned back another half an inch, I'd be able to see up her incredibly short skirt. Patting the space beside me, I grinned. "I remember."

Her laugh reminded me of wind chimes. She lowered herself gracefully onto the step above me, grinning back and extending smooth, bare legs. "I'm shocked you remember anything about that night."

"I remember watermelon lip gloss." I winked and got the laugh again. "But I do *not* remember getting your number."

"Maybe you should get it now."

"Maybe I should." I lightly touched her knee and was pleased to see the chill bumps form on her skin. I seemed to recall giving her chill bumps before. But that could have been someone else.

"Ahem."

Macy and I looked up.

"*Seriously?*" Lily asked. "You've been here what, five minutes? Don't you have enough going on in your life? Do you really need to play to the stereotype?"

"At least I know how to play," I shot back.

"I'm sorry. I didn't know you were seeing anyone." Macy stood quickly.

I caught a glimpse of hot-pink underwear.

Lily caught me looking. She shook her head with just enough disdain to spark my anger.

"Oh, I'm not seeing her." I inclined my head toward Lily. "I'm helping her out with something, for a friend. Kind of a charity case thing."

I froze when Lily's emotions hit. Not pissy mad but hurt mad. She said a couple of choice words and then stalked away, her long legs quickly closing the distance between me and Murphy's Law.

I couldn't afford to have Lily mad at me.

Plus, I kind of didn't want her mad at me.

"Macy, it was great seeing you." I pushed myself up to my feet, standing on my toes to keep my eyes on Lily. "But I gotta jet."

I heard her say something about her number, but I didn't turn back.

I replayed the conversation in my head to figure out what I'd said wrong. When I finally caught up to Lily, I reached for her hand, but I stopped just in time. She wasn't in the mood to be touched by anyone. Especially by me.

"Lily, I was messing with you," I said in a soothing voice, trying to calm her down. "There's no need to take it personally."

My attempt to calm her didn't work. It made her madder.

"There isn't?" She stopped and poked me in the chest, narrowing her eyes dangerously. "You don't know me. You don't know anything about me. You can't make judgment calls on what I can take personally and what I can't."

I took a step backward to avoid her finger. "You made a judgment call on me and Macy, and you weren't even there for two seconds."

"That was an observation." Now her hands were fisted on her hips. "I know what a hookup looks like."

"There was no hooking up. We were talking. I hung out with Macy this past summer. We're friends."

"What's her last name?"

I blinked. "What?"

"What's her last name?"

"I . . . uh . . ." Suddenly, my mouth felt really dry. "It's right on the tip of my tongue."

"Mmmhmmm." Lily spun back around and started for Murphy's Law.

"Wait—"

"No!" The word exploded as she threw it over her shoulder without looking at me. "Go back to your fancy house and scroll through the contacts on your phone. I'm sure if she was good, you've got her number in there somewhere. I'll be somebody else's charity case."

The hurt came through again, tinged with jealousy this time. It couldn't be because of the girl, so it must be because of . . . my house. I'd called her a charity case, but I hadn't meant it at all, much less that way.

"Hey." This time I did grab her arm, turning her around. "I don't have money."

Lily's laugh reminded me of smoke and honey. "Right. Your *family* has it. You have to wait a few years before your trust fund rolls in."

"That's not true."

"Oh, so you get it when you turn eighteen," she said coldly. "Good for you."

"Listen." Irritation began to slide toward anger. "I told you our house has been in my dad's family for generations. We didn't buy it, and, yes, he inherited it, but only the house, not the money for the upkeep. And we need a lot of money for that."

"So your mom makes a movie and pockets five million bucks. The *name* Grace Walker commands at least that much."

"Yeah." I had no idea why, but I was overcome with the need to tell Lily the truth. To let go and stop hiding. "But that doesn't help us much right now. My mom is in a coma."

She drew a sharp breath.

"No one in the media knows. Not that I think you'd say anything, but . . . we've kept it under wraps. People probably just think she's somewhere tropical, drinking piña coladas and having a full body lift." I closed my eyes and waited for the anger to go away—the anger at the situation and the anger at myself for telling Lily anything.

"How long?" she asked.

I opened my eyes to search her face. I didn't feel pity from her, or hear it in her voice. There was only empathy. I was usually the one providing that.

"Almost eight months."

She took my arm and pulled me toward one of the benches that lined Main Street. "Sit. You don't have to tell me anything. But . . . sit."

We both sat. Now that I'd opened up to her, it was like I couldn't stop. I just kept talking, no matter how much I wanted to shut up. "It happened right after Dad died. It wasn't an accident or anything like that. We don't know what's wrong with her. Exactly."

"What do you mean, 'exactly'?"

"She didn't come downstairs one morning, so I went to her room to find her. She was in her bathroom. On the floor. There were . . . pills. They were all around her." I blew out a sigh, trying not to see her now. Trying not to relive the fear and the pain. "My mom doesn't even drink."

Lily didn't say anything. It was the perfect reaction.

We sat in silence for a few moments as I tried to figure out how to explain things, and how much I wanted her to know. "Jack told Emerson he took Mom's memories of everything that was keeping her alive. Her memories of Dad."

"And you."

I wanted to believe that. The doubt had only grown in the past months, that somehow Mom hadn't loved me enough to stick around. I knew deep down it wasn't true, but the lie showed up at the most inopportune times. Like when a bottle, or a girl, was handy.

"When Jack took Emerson's memories, he replaced them," I explained. "But Mom is just . . . empty, I guess. Jack claimed that made her suicidal."

Traffic passed by on Main Street, and I listened to the comforting, familiar sounds of a small town closing out the day. Keys jangling in store locks, car doors opening and shutting, faint snatches of conversations about dinner plans.

"Em told me about Michael," she said, "when he was dead. Your dad was, too. That's so strange."

I didn't mention that Em had been dead pretty recently as well.

"But Michael and your dad are both alive and well now." Her hand moved toward my arm, but then she changed her mind and quickly pulled it back into her lap. "You have to hold out hope that one day your mom will be okay."

Not only did she believe what she was saying, she wanted me to believe it. The honesty in her voice was wrapped with a warmth I wanted to lean on. "Thank you."

"You're really only fifty percent jerk, you know. Maybe forty-nine. But that other fifty or fifty-one? That's solid. And I bet it's because of your mom."

I couldn't respond. I gave in to instinct, taking her hand and squeezing it gently before letting go.

After a full minute of silence, Lily cleared her throat. "I'm glad we had a touching moment and all, but you should be aware of the fact that I still don't like you."

"Not even the fifty percent that's solid?" I fought the desire to laugh.

She kept her focus on the street, but I could see her lips twitching from the corner of my eye. "Don't push it."

"Fine, then." I kept my focus on the street as well. "I don't like you, either."

"Good," she said, sounding authoritative. "You think we can work on this 'finding crap' thing for a few minutes before dark? My calculus homework isn't going to do itself."

I gave in to my smile. "Let's go."

Chapter 18

*T*hree days.

That's how long it took Lily to find an object that didn't belong to her.

"I did it, uh-huh, I did it." She danced around in my laundry room, swinging her hips from side to side, holding up the shirt I'd worn the night at Em's house when I'd discovered Lily's ability.

It took great effort, but I kept my focus off her hips and on the situation at hand. While I was happy about the latest development, I had to fight to ignore the twinge in my gut telling me that we weren't moving fast enough. "Okay, think. What did it feel like? How did you know where it was?"

"Kind of a hook in my belly button." She rubbed her hand across her stomach. "But I could see the shirt, too, like a photograph. Right there under your Batman boxer briefs."

"Those were a gag gift. And my last pair of clean underwear."

"I don't know which of those statements I find more disturbing."

"Try again," I said. "Find my sword."

She tilted her head to the side. "*Lame.*"

"Get your mind out of the gutter, Tiger." I didn't sound half as frustrated as I meant to. "I meant the one from the masquerade."

"There's no room in the gutter. You're taking up all the space." We stepped out of the laundry room into the hall. "I simply meant that finding the sword should be a piece of cake."

"Sure you did."

We'd reached some sort of working truce after the conversation about my mom. I didn't want to blow it by pushing Lily harder, but I needed more from her. We all did.

She'd just closed her eyes to concentrate, when my back door flew open.

Dune had a folder full of papers, and a big smile.

"What did you find?" I asked.

"The jackpot. I searched the public school systems around Memphis." Dune dropped the folder on the kitchen table. "Oh. Hey, Lily."

"Hi, Dune."

They spent more time smiling at each other than was really necessary.

"I didn't realize you two had met," I said, a spark of jealousy popping up out of nowhere. Why did I care who Lily smiled at?

"Yeah," Dune said. "Em introduced us after you told me about Lily's search ideas."

When Dune noticed I was staring at him, he stopped smiling. "Okay, then. I did some editing on a photo of Jack and ran a face recognition program. It only took twelve hours to get a hit."

"Who are you? Bill Gates's younger brother?" I picked up the folder.

"Don't insult me." Dune flipped a chair around and straddled it. It creaked under his weight. "My gene pool is way more impressive than his."

Lily laughed. It was sort of husky and really sexy. I'd never heard that laugh from her before.

Dune started smiling again and slid a picture out of the folder. "Here's the one I created."

"Nice editing work," Lily commented, putting her hand on his shoulder to lean over and look at the photograph. "Is that version 9.5 or 9.7?"

He looked up at her sideways, and his expression rivaled that of a kid getting ready to blow out his birthday candles. "It was 9.5, but I had an add-on and I was able to manipulate—"

I cleared my throat and tapped my fingers on the tabletop.

Dune's smile disappeared, and he pulled out a piece of paper. It was a black-and-white picture, and it was grainy. "Here's what the search uncovered."

A copy of a photograph. I peered down at the face. It wasn't super clear, just a tiny scan from a yearbook, but there was no mistaking it. "That's him. Jack. With a really bad haircut."

"Someone put it up on a social networking site pretty recently. They're trying to organize a high school reunion, and Jack was on the 'cannot find' list. He grew up in Germantown. The rough part." Dune shuffled through the papers some more and removed a set of school records. "No brothers or sisters, no dad. Not even on his birth certificate."

"You found his birth certificate?" Lily asked, sounding impressed.

"It's easier than most people think," Dune answered, sounding modest.

"Well," I said, sounding pissy, "we obviously need to focus our search on West Tennessee."

I handed the school records to Lily. At least Dune finding a location narrowed things down for her.

"The bad news is, this was all I could find," Dune said, tapping on the folder. "So if we're going to focus the search, we're going to have to go to West Tennessee to do it."

✴

"So someone needs to go to Memphis," Michael said when Dune finished explaining his results.

I'd been standing in the corner, watching Lily not look at Dune.

"Yes. Maybe more than one of us," Dune said. "Someone there might still have a memory of him. I think it would be worth asking around, since at this point, any information would help."

"I don't think a lot of us popping up somewhere and asking a bunch of questions is a good idea," Em said. I'd been pretending she hadn't been looking at me while I watched Lily. "The last thing we need to do is draw attention to ourselves."

116

"Then we'd better not waste any time." Dune leaned back in his chair. "We could map out the city, take it by section. Do you have your laptop, Kaleb?"

"Battery's fried," I said. "Michael still owes me money for the last one he and Em shorted out."

"If no one has a map handy, I can pull one up on my phone." Dune started to reach into his pocket. "But a big one would be easier for everyone to see than all of you trying to scoot in close and lean over my shoulder."

"No scooting in close necessary," I said, pushing myself away from the wall. "There's an atlas in Dad's office. I'll get it."

When I got back, I handed the map to Dune, who had just said something to make Lily laugh. She took the atlas out of my hands without looking at me.

Dune crossed his arms over his chest as he watched Lily flip through the maps of the states. He'd always been solid, but not exactly shredded. His biceps were more defined than I remembered. So were his pecs. Probably from working out with Nate, who was on a perpetual quest to build bulk.

I needed to get back to the gym.

"Liam is never going to let us go to Memphis without a fight." Em looked at Michael. "You're going to have to do a lot of convincing."

"We don't all have to go." Michael was doing the superior thing. Em called it protective, but I didn't need protection. Neither did she.

Em punched him in the shoulder. "Don't you even, Michael Weaver. You aren't cutting me out of this."

"Or me," I said.

Everyone started talking at once, arguing about who would go where and when.

Just as we were on the brink of a full-scale blowup, Lily dropped the atlas and gasped.

Shock. Disbelief.

"What's wrong?" Em abandoned her argument and went to Lily's side.

Lily covered her mouth with her hands. They were shaking. "The map . . ." She slowly lowered them. "I touched Ivy Springs. I was going to trace the route from here to Memphis."

"Okay." Em waited for the rest. The amount of concern she was putting out made me tense. Lily didn't seem like the kind of girl to needlessly overreact.

"I was going to look for Kaleb's sword from the masquerade earlier, by using my ability." Lily took a deep breath. "We didn't get around to it. But just now, when I touched the map, I saw the sword. Immediately, and exactly. In my mind—through my fingers. Like I was reading Braille or something."

"Where?" I asked Lily, my palms on the table. "Where was it?"

"In your backyard." She met my eyes. "In your fire pit, surrounded by ashes."

"I tried to set the sword on fire," I said.

"The costume, too?" Lily asked.

"Yes. The costume was the only thing that burned. I needed

to do it." I didn't know how to explain further without talking about Poe slitting Em's throat, and I didn't know how much Lily knew. "It was . . . cathartic. But how did you find it?"

"I felt an instinct, and I knew I needed to put my hand on the map." Lily's voice was stronger now, and the color started to return to her cheeks. "There was a pull, the same kind of pull I felt earlier when Kaleb and I were practicing."

"Has anything like that ever happened to you before?" Michael asked, concerned.

"No." She held her hands over the map, a half inch away. Then she pulled them back and folded them in her lap. "But I've never actively searched for things before, either."

"I have an idea," Dune said. "A way to test this out. Emerson, think of something of yours Lily has seen before but hasn't seen lately. Preferably not somewhere Lily could guess easily, but you need to know exactly where it is."

Em thought for a few seconds. "Okay. I know what and where it is."

Dune leaned down, and he and Em had a hurried, whispered conversation. After they came to some sort of agreement, he straightened.

"Map?" Dune asked.

Lily gave it to him, this time with no teasing.

Dune opened it to the side-by-side pages that featured a full map of the United States. "Okay, Em. Tell her what object you're thinking of."

"It's a movie, *My Fair Lady*. We used to watch it over and over again in middle school," she explained. "We both wanted to be Audrey Hepburn."

Lily laughed softly. "We were so sad that neither one of us looked a thing like her. A curvy Cubanita and a tiny, little white girl."

"We tried, though." Em laughed, too, and the bond between them felt warm and solid. "Remember the hats?"

"And the cigarettes, with the long holders? I thought your mom was going to kill us."

"She never forgave me for the hole we burned in the couch." Em faltered, and tears formed in her eyes. Michael took her hand in his, and she leaned into his shoulder, quiet for a moment. "Anyway, the movie disc. I know exactly where it is."

Dune put the atlas down on the table and flattened the crease. "Ready?"

Lily nodded and lifted her hands. They hovered a half inch over the shape of the United States before landing somewhere in the vicinity of Kansas. She closed her eyes and took a few deep breaths. When she moved her hands, I thought of the motion people make when they play with a Ouija board. Back and forth, in repetitive figure eights.

"Anything?" Dune asked, dividing his focus between Lily's face and the map.

She stopped and her eyes flew open.

"Thompson's Hill?" Lily asked, referring to the next town over. "Behind the courthouse?"

Em bit her bottom lip and then nodded. "Yes. In storage, with the rest of my parents' stuff."

The memory cost Em. Her energy level dropped, and lines formed on either side of her mouth. Michael kissed her on the temple, and her low leveled out as he helped her carry the weight.

"That's a good memory," Lily said, wiping tears from her eyes. "And I'm glad you still have all their stuff."

"Me, too. I had the breakdown before we could go through it. Since I came back here, I haven't been ready. Neither has my brother. I don't think Thomas or I will ever be ready." Em stood up and took a glass down from the kitchen cupboard, filling it with water at the sink.

"Are you ready to try the watch?" I asked Lily, sensing the need to draw attention away from Em.

She bit her lip. "I think so."

"Maybe everyone should clear out," I suggested. "Lily and I are supposed to be working on this together, anyway."

Michael met my eyes, and I saw the unspoken "thank you." Dune . . . not as much.

When Lily and I were alone, I placed the map in front of her on the table. "Ready?"

"Wait." She put her hand on my arm. "It was really decent of you to get Em out of here before we did this. We shouldn't have brought up those memories."

"I disagree." I sat down beside her. "Sometimes, it's good to remember, and you were the perfect person for her to do it with. If

121

she didn't totally trust you, she wouldn't have felt safe enough to open up. She's lucky to have you."

She looked at me for a long minute.

"Okay. Let's try this." There was a moment of complete silence, and then she pulled back as if the map were smoldering firewood. "I see it. The pocket watch, but on the night of the masquerade. I could see the details of the stitching on Jack's vest."

"Okay." That gave me an idea. "Try again, but concentrate on today, right now this very second. But this time, I want you to close your eyes." I fanned through the pages of the atlas, all the way to Alaska. I placed it flat on the table in front of Lily.

Her concentration hung heavy in the air, like wet sheets dripping on a clothesline. "No."

"Try to relax." I turned to Hawaii, but marked Tennessee with my finger. "And try again."

"Nothing."

With as much stealth as possible, I turned the pages. "One more time."

Lily touched the map of Tennessee, and then her fingers slid quickly from right to left. Kingsport, through Knoxville, all the way over to Memphis. "Here. Right here, right now. He's wearing a different suit, but the same vest. The pocket watch is tucked inside it."

Her eyes flew open. Her finger was on Memphis, right over the marking for Bennett University.

Chapter 19

*I*n the end, Michael went to bat for all of us. He hit a home run. Of course.

I packed while Dad argued.

"I might not be able to stop Emerson and Michael, but you're my son. I could stop Lily, since she's about to skip school—"

"But you won't. Lily's calling this a college visit, which is not a lie, and Em can't go unless she has a chaperone." I threw my shaving kit in my bag with my already folded clothes, figuring I'd go with the scruffy look in the morning. Maybe it would make me look older.

Nate and Dune agreed that Em, Michael, Lily, and I should be the ones to go to Memphis. They'd stay behind and keep an eye on things. Including Ava.

I dropped my travel toothbrush into my open suitcase and faced him. "I'm going to be eighteen soon. What are you going to do then?"

"Drink."

Family trait.

I raised my hands. "I'm only packing in case we don't find what we need in time to drive back. I'll probably be home tomorrow night."

"You'll be home all day because you aren't going."

I turned around to get a hold on myself and to make sure my flask was covered. I zipped up my suitcase for good measure. "Dune found Jack's information from high school. And since the university is still in the process of computerizing old student records, we have to physically go there to see what we can find." I kept the part about tracking Jack's pocket watch to myself. "This is the next logical step. You know you can't go without drawing attention."

"Then let Michael handle it."

I ignored the drop my stomach did, but only because I really wanted to get my way instead of getting in a fight. "Michael might be Superman, but even Superman had Jimmy Olsen and Lois Lane."

Dad tapped his chin with two fingers, a sure sign he was about to cave.

He shoots, he scores.

"I still don't like it," he said, but he relented. "You're checking in. Every hour."

"Dad."

"You can take turns."

"I'm positive Michael will make sure you're in the know." I pulled my candy stash out of my bedside drawer. An open box of Hot Tamales spilled and skittered across my hardwood floor, and I bent over to pick them up. "Dammit."

"It's not that I don't trust you," Dad said, backpedaling.

I stared at his scratched-up black boots, with mud crusted and flaking around the heels. Mom would've freaked that he had them on in the house. "But you trust him more."

"You are my son—"

"Glad you noticed," I said, standing up straight. Even in his boots, I had an inch of height on him.

"My job is to protect you."

Super heartwarming.

"It's . . . Your mother was the one who handled the nurturing part. I'm not . . ." He stopped, his wide shoulders dropping, and attempted to explain himself. "I'm trying. I may not show it the way she did, but I do love you."

"Why do you refer to her in past tense?" The candy went sticky in my tightly closed fist. "'Was.' 'Did.'"

His whisper hurt me worse than a scream. "There's been no improvement; in fact, she's declining. You'd know that if you'd go see her."

"Are you saying it's my fault she's getting worse?"

"No, but hearing her son's voice, feeling his touch, that couldn't hurt her. You know how much she loved—"

"Loves. *Loves.* She loves me. I sat with her when you were

125

dead. I did everything I could. I even tried—" I broke off just in time. "I know what my mistakes are; I don't need a list from you. I'll make sure Michael checks in with you while we're all in Memphis. There's nothing else to say."

I stared at him until he shut the door behind him, and bitterness curled around my rib cage until I couldn't breathe.

I dropped the candy into the trash and dug my flask out of my suitcase.

Chapter 20

"My ass is gonna be so flat by the time we get out of this car, I'm going to have to blow it up with a bicycle pump." Lily leaned forward to rub her lower back.

I bit my tongue to keep from telling her that nothing would make her ass less than perfect. It was too early to get coldcocked, especially by a hot girl.

Instead, I fished for my hat on Em's floorboard, retrieved it, and pulled it down over my eyes. My sunglasses weren't doing enough to fight the remnants of last night's poor choices.

Dru had a college friend who worked at the Peabody Hotel, and she'd comped a suite for us. Em made us leave at the crack of dawn so we could go straight to the school. It was still early when we parked outside the administration building. Bennett University sat on the eastern outskirts of Memphis, and the boundary surrounded almost a hundred acres of forest and academia.

"It's like I'm in the English countryside," Lily said as we drove through the open iron gates that led onto the property. The campus was more fairy-tale village than college. Gothic arches, dark patches of forest, cobblestone sidewalks. Everything was green, gold, and shades of red.

I slid out of my seat and walked around to open Lily's door. She managed to tear her eyes away from the scenery. "What is this? Chivalry?"

"No. You have the Hot Tamales." I held out my hand. "I need a hit."

She shoved the box into my stomach and the connection made a loud crushing noise. "Hot Tamales. Atomic Fireballs. Sizzling Cinnamon Jelly Bellys. Red Hots. I'm surprised you have any taste buds left. Or teeth."

"Do I make the obvious hot-stuff joke here, or refrain?"

"Refrain."

She grabbed a square, padded canvas bag from the glove box and slid out of the car. After unzipping the bag, she took out her camera, unscrewed the lens cap, and started snapping.

"Shouldn't we be thinking about what we need to do next?" I asked Em, watching Lily walk away.

"No. Let her go," Em said from beside me. Michael was still in the car. Checking in with Dad, I was sure. "She'll get the buzz out of her system in a minute or two."

"Is she always like this?"

"Yep. She gets kind of possessed. Or obsessed."

Even though she was in earshot of the conversation, Lily never wavered, focusing her attention on a single yellow leaf hanging on to the end of a tree branch. She lay flat on her back in the grass to take a shot from below, and then climbed halfway up the trunk to take one from above.

"She'll catch a glimpse of something she wants to shoot and she's gone. If not physically, like hanging off the edge of a building or scaling the side of a mountain for a perfect shot, then mentally. She frames shots and fiddles with depth of field and apertures and generally does her thing until she realizes a world exists outside her pictures."

"Is she good?"

"Unbelievable." Em smiled like a proud parent. "You've seen the photographs in Murphy's Law."

"Those are hers?" I asked, remembering how amazing they were. "Those photos are masterpieces."

"Yes, they are."

Finally, Lily walked toward us, shaking bits of leaves and grass from her hair, grinning from ear to ear. Her joy was contagious. I was smiling, too.

"I could spend days here. All those curves and lines and shadows. How did I not know about this place before now?" She shoved her camera into her bag, pulled out a tangerine, and made an apologetic face at Em. "I'm sorry. You know how I get excited."

"And that's why we love you," Em said.

"You okay?" Michael stepped out of the car, shut the door,

and approached Em. He massaged her shoulders and neck. "I wish you'd let me drive part of the way."

"Driving helped me focus on something besides what we're about to do." She relaxed under his touch.

"Can we go over the plan?" Lily tossed the tangerine peel, which she'd pulled off in a perfect, complete spiral, into the woods. The calm she'd managed to maintain in the car was fading. "I assume we're still looking for *information* about Jack first, rather than Jack."

"Do you still know where he is?" Em asked, tension entering her voice again. "Or where the pocket watch is?"

Lily popped a section of tangerine into her mouth and nodded. She'd held the atlas open the whole way in the car, her hands constantly returning to the page. "By the river. I think I'll know exactly where, once we get closer."

"Lily and I will go check in with the admissions office, and then try to find Jack's paperwork." Michael held up the key card Dune had made for him. It was supposed to guarantee entrance to the file storage room. "Kaleb, I think you and Em should go to the physics department to see if you can get any information about Jack and his time here and, if the opportunity presents itself, maybe get some information on Teague and Chronos."

"Why are Kaleb and I going together instead of you and me?" Em leaned back on his chest and looked up at him.

That didn't burn.

"Because if I go with you, we can both ask questions, and that's it. Kaleb's perception is invaluable in a situation like this."

"Aww, thanks for noticing," I said.

"As long as Lily's cool with it." Em shrugged.

Lily nodded. "Fine."

"Okay." Michael sounded relieved. "The head of the physics department is named Gerald Turner. He's on campus today, and he has office hours right now."

All the curves and lines and shadows Lily was so excited about became even more evident as we crossed the campus to the science building.

Gothic architecture, pointed archways, and cool gray stone made me feel like I was in another place and time instead of five minutes away from downtown Memphis. "Hey," I said, pointing up. "There's a bell tower. Where's Quasimodo?"

"Look," Em said, also pointing up. "It's a flying buttress!"

"A what?" I cocked my head to the side.

"Never mind."

We entered the building and approached the science department. I took Em's arm. "Walk behind me."

"Kaleb Ballard. That hurts me in my feminism."

"It has nothing to do with feminism, and everything to do

with the fact that a girl is sitting behind the counter," I whispered, reaching for the doorknob.

"How do you know you're her type?" Em asked doubtfully.

"I'm every girl's type." I ignored Em's snicker, since I'd totally set myself up for it, and opened the door.

We made it past the gatekeeper in record time. Em's snicker turned into an eye roll.

The bluesy sound of Muddy Waters poured into the hallway as we approached, along with the faint scent of pipe tobacco. We paused outside the cracked door, jumping when we heard a gruff voice.

"I can hear you lurking. Don't just stand out there. Come on in. Office hours are posted; you're well within the time frame." The voice was deep, that of a lifelong smoker, or possibly James Earl Jones's younger brother. "Twenty years in this department, and students still think my office hours are some kind of cosmic joke."

Twenty years in this department meant he'd been here when my dad and Teague were here, and when they left. It also meant he'd been one of those who'd chosen to stay behind.

"Well?" he barked out.

I looked back at Em for visual confirmation and then pushed the door open. I was immediately assaulted by shiny black leather, Art Deco prints, and a giant moose head on the far left wall. A tiny placard hung underneath it, with one word, FREDDY. A fedora hung on the topmost point of each antler. One of the hats had a cheetah print hatband.

A man with a head full of white hair, and a black goatee

sprinkled with silver, sat behind a desk. His skin, the same color as cocoa powder, sported deep wrinkles in his smile lines. His gaze lingered on Em when she stepped into the doorway beside me. "Can I help you?"

I felt out his emotions. *Curiosity. Mild impatience tempered with tolerance.*

"Are you Dr. Turner?" Em asked, not crossing the threshold. Waiting to be invited in, like a vampire.

"That depends. Are you two ghost chasers?" He considered us over his bifocals as he pulled a bag of pipe tobacco out of his top desk drawer.

"No, sir," I answered, frowning at Em. "We aren't ghost chasers."

"Good. Reality television has created way too many amateurs, if you ask me. None of them ever finds a damn thing. It's because they're looking in all the wrong places."

"I'm Emerson, by the way." She pointed to herself and then to me, as if the professor might have a hard time coming to the conclusion himself. "This is Kaleb."

This time, he looked at me a little bit too long.

"I'm Dr. Turner. Head of the physics department. Nice to meet you both."

In an un-vampire-like fashion, I stepped into the room without being asked. "We were wondering if we could talk to you."

"Certainly. As long as you were telling me the truth about the ghost chasing." He spun his chair around to turn down an ancient-looking record player. The scratchy sound of the blues faded away and he faced us again, waving his hand at Em. "Come in."

He wore a bow tie, and a pink carnation hung haphazardly from a buttonhole in his vest. When he pulled his pipe from an inside pocket, the flower fell on his desk. He picked it up and twirled it between his fingers.

"Had a visit from the grands this morning. Youngest girl brought me a gift." He smiled, tucked it into a leather pencil holder on the corner of his desk, and gestured with his pipe. "May I?"

"Sure." Em nodded. "I like the smell of pipe tobacco. My granddad smoked one."

"Good, then." He scooped tobacco into the bowl of his pipe, the movement habitual. He was going through the motions, but it felt like a thinly veiled distraction. "Have a seat."

Em chose a leather wingback, studded around the edges with brass tacks. The only other chair in the office looked like it might crumble into a heap if I touched it, so I leaned my shoulder against the bookshelves built into the wall, taking note of the many family pictures as well as the titles on the shelves. *Quantum Physics for Dummies, Holographic Man, The Tao of Physics*, and a decent collection of what looked like first-edition Twain.

"How can I help you, children?" *Direct but kind.*

"We had some questions." Em bounced slightly in her seat. It was either exceptionally springy or her nerves were getting the best of her.

"About the physics program?"

"No," Em said, drawing the word out, looking at me for backup.

"No," I said, wishing we'd discussed a plan. "We were talking about the . . . um . . ."

"About the parapsychology department," he said, like he'd said it a million times before. "You discovered it on the Internet."

"Um, yeah," Em said, smiling in a slightly unbalanced way. "That's it."

I could feel his hesitation. Still, somehow, he miraculously asked, "What do you want to know?"

"We were just interested in . . . the basics about the department." Em looked up at me for confirmation.

"The basics." I nodded. We sucked at subterfuge.

"We're doing . . . a school project?" Em said. It came out sounding like a question.

Dr. Turner pressed down on the contents of the pipe bowl with his thumb and looked at Em from the corner of his eye. "First of all, it was never truly a department, not an acknowledged one, anyway. It fell under engineering and physics. Started as a graduate project on random event generators and machines. Spun off into all kinds of fantastical research."

"What kind of fantastical research?" I asked.

"Life beyond our airspace, remote viewing." He took out another pinch of tobacco, placed it in the pipe with practiced ease, and then closed the bag. "Archeocoustics, dowsing."

"I've never even heard the word *archeocoustics*." Em perched eagerly on the edge of her chair, her toes barely touching the floor.

"Tricky theory, that. Idea is that objects record sound. Memories of conversation." He shrugged. "And a perfect example of one of the things that drove the traditionalists here crazy."

"And the university made the grad students stop?"

"They did." His fingers tightened on the pipe bowl. "The department was shut down."

"But the research continued." Em wasn't reading his body language, or she didn't care. "Right?"

"There were certain things everyone was curious about." He spoke carefully, as if everything he'd said up until this point had been canned, and now we were approaching unknown territory.

"Like what?" Em pushed.

His spike of irritation made me wonder if we'd gone too far.

Keeping my eyes on Dr. Turner, I moved to stand beside Em, my arm on the back of her chair. He stared at me for a moment, as if he were weighing something. Then he seemed to make a decision.

"Most specifically, they were curious about the manipulation of the space time continuum."

Em gasped, then tried to cover it with a cough.

Dr. Turner didn't take his eyes away from me. "Not solely in the realm of physics, but in the realm of something . . . beyond."

"I thought universities were supposed to encourage free thinking." I didn't break the stare. He was either testing us or playing us. Either way, I didn't intend to lose.

"Testing a hypothesis and getting a concrete result is challenging even when the research can be proven." He removed a small metal object from his inside jacket pocket. It was flat on the bottom, and a sharp curve of metal arched over a tiny gargoyle—like a handle. He held it carefully as he used it to push the tobacco down. "The abstract idea of a person with preternatural abilities doesn't fit into pure science. But too many believed the abstract was a possibility."

"You did," Em said.

"I believe in the abstract and the concrete."

I decided to stop wasting time and show my hand. "Then why didn't you follow Teague when she left for Chronos?"

The smell of sulfur filled the air when he lit a wooden match, touched it to the tobacco, and took a few puffs. "I wondered when that was coming."

"We're interested in the truth," I said.

"Are you?" He dropped the match into an ashtray shaped like a turtle. Obviously crafted by little hands, it seemed out of place on his monstrous desk.

"That's all we want. We thought . . . we hoped we could get it from you. Will you tell us?" I asked. "The truth about Chronos?"

"That's a little tricky," he said, puffing once more, "because the truth is mixed in with the legend."

I frowned. Waited.

"Chronos's biggest desire is to be part of something that's as ancient as time itself." He stared at the pipe until the fire went out. "And I find it hard to believe that Liam Ballard's son is questioning me about that something, when his father knows far more about it than I do."

My jaw dropped. "How did you know who—"

"You have your father's build. You even have his way of listening, taking things in without giving anything away." He struck another match and relit the tobacco. "And then, of course, your mother's famous blue eyes."

The last observation sideswiped me. Em must have sensed it, because she took control of the conversation again.

"You said Chronos wanted to be part of something as 'ancient as time itself.' What does that mean?"

Dr. Turner took a long draw on his pipe.

"Please tell us?" Em leaned forward, placing her hands on the edge of his desk.

"Again, these are answers you should be getting from Liam." Dr. Turner exhaled, filling the air with the aromatic scent of vanilla.

"You say that like it's simple." I laughed derisively. "He doesn't tell me anything. I don't even know what questions to ask."

"Then I most certainly have to respect Liam's choices, as he's your father." He almost sounded regretful. "But I can say that when Teague left Bennett University, the . . . scope . . . of her interests narrowed."

"What did she focus on?" I asked.

"I can't tell you any more about Teague." He turned a very direct gaze on me. "Except . . . no man—or woman—is an island."

"Okay." Em looked from Dr. Turner to me and back again. Frowning, she took her hands off Dr. Turner's desk and leaned back into her chair. "If you won't tell us about Teague, can you tell us about Jack Landers?"

"Doesn't he work with Liam at Cameron? Or did that change last year after the . . . accident?" He was feigning innocence. I'd have known by his wide-eyed expression even if I hadn't been able to feel it.

"It changed." Our cover to explain Dad's "death" was that he'd survived the explosion, but with a head injury that caused amnesia. We didn't have a solid cover for Jack. "So have you seen him? Jack?"

"Is he no longer employed at Cameron?" Dr. Turner ignored my question as well and took another deep puff on his pipe.

Stalemate. "Maybe you should ask my father."

"Touché." He raised one eyebrow. "Of course, if I did ask your father, I'd have to let him know you'd been to visit. Asked lots of questions."

"Fine." The old man played a serious game of hardball. He knew my questions had crossed a line. "No. Jack is no longer employed at Cameron. Or by my father."

"I see." He lowered his pipe to the turtle ashtray. "No. I haven't seen him lately."

All we'd managed to establish is that neither of us knew where Jack was, but Dr. Turner was feeling satisfied. I was left feeling I'd given something away and not gotten anything in return.

"I'm sorry I couldn't offer you more information." Dr. Turner stood and picked up a briefcase from beside his desk.

"Wait!" Emerson jumped to her feet. "That's it? That's all?"

"I don't have anything else to tell you, and I have a lecture to give. But . . ." He stared at me for a long moment. "Are you doing any sightseeing while you're here?"

"Sightseeing?" I asked.

"I suggest it. You go to London, you visit Buckingham Palace. You go to Egypt, you visit the pyramids." He looked at us pointedly.

"We'll take that under consideration," Em said.

"I hope you do."

We left, and I followed Emerson around the corner out of earshot of the office.

"Do you think he really has a lecture?" she whispered.

"I think we got a little too specific with our questions." We walked down the stairs and toward the parking lot.

"Why was he saying those things about sightseeing and staring at us like that?"

"I don't know, but it was weird."

"He knew about Teague. I wish we'd asked him about Poe," she said. The wind blew her hair in her face, and she reached up to twist it around her hand. "I wonder if his name would've gotten a reaction."

"I'm kind of glad we didn't. We gave a lot more than we got."

"I keep expecting to see Jack." She let go of her hair and wrapped her arms around herself. "I wonder if there's safety in numbers, or if he can steal memories from two people at the same time."

"I'll keep you safe, Shorty." I put my arm over Em's shoulders and pulled her to my side for a quick squeeze. "We'll find him."

"Damn, I hope so." She growled under her breath. "I just realized I haven't had coffee in two hours."

"Oh no. We'd better do something about that real quick. I'd hate for you to get irritable."

Her response was an elbow to the stomach.

Michael and Lily came into view. They were both sitting on the bumper of the SUV, and they looked miserable.

"Oh no," Em said.

Fear. Dread. Defeat.

"Hurry." I walked faster. Since my legs were so much longer, Em ran to keep up.

"What's going on?" Em asked. Lily stood up, and I could tell she'd been crying.

"We got into the records. No details about Jack," Michael said, sounding defeated. "Everything was gone."

"That's not so bad," Em said, giving Lily a quick hug. "It's what we expected, right? We have the high school stuff to work from, and Lily can look for the pocket watch."

"Lack of details isn't the only problem." When Lily's voice

hitched, I realized just how close she was to crying again. She brushed away the forming tears.

Michael explained. "When we got back, we tried to find the pocket watch on the map. We've been trying for twenty minutes."

Lily dropped her hands. "It's gone."

Chapter 21

I held open the elevator of the Peabody Hotel for Lily. We were on a mission that originated from offering to brew Emerson coffee with the maker in the hotel room. She'd thrown a shoe at us.

"I'm sorry." Lily's guilt filled the space around us.

"Stop."

She leaned back against the elevator wall and met my eyes in the mirrored doors as they closed.

"Lily, we're looking for a desperate man who doesn't want to be found. You've chosen to be involved because of your friendship with Em." I pushed the button for the lobby. "Finding him doesn't rest solely on your shoulders."

"But it's like he fell off the map. He *did* fall off the map. How did he disappear so fast?"

"I don't know, but we aren't at a dead end. We have the high school information, and we can still look for people who might have known Jack way back when. And there are other options."

The doors slid open, taking Lily's direct gaze with them. I stopped at the concierge desk on our way through the lobby to get directions to the closest coffee shop. Both Lily and Em had insisted on a non-chain. Supporting local business enterprise, etc., etc.

"Down the street, intersection of Union and South Second," I told Lily, and then followed her through the lobby. She had on jeans and some kind of flowy white shirt with brown embroidery on it. It didn't show any skin or fit tightly, but I could see the outline of her curves through it.

"Are you going to be warm enough?" I gestured toward the shirt, but I didn't really look at it. Or her.

"Worried I might catch a cold?" There was a hint of a tease in her voice.

"I was raised to be a gentleman." I still didn't look at her. "And I follow through. In most circumstances."

"I'll be fine. It's not that far. What's the name of the place we're looking for?"

"Cockadoos."

"Cockadoos," she repeated.

"That's what I said."

The Peabody lobby was grandiose almost to the point of excess. Lots of marble and shiny wood. Intimate groupings of chairs, and jazz playing in the background, softened it just enough to keep it welcoming.

"What's with Memphis and the bird fetish?" Lily pointed to the splashing fountain full of ducks as we walked past. "They get escorted down here every day on a red carpet, and then go back up to their penthouse. Ducks. Have a penthouse. On a roof. I don't get it."

Cold air rushed through the doors as we stepped outside.

Lily rubbed her arms briskly.

I started unbuttoning my shirt.

"Wow, really? Right here on the street?"

"Shut up. You're cold. My shirt is flannel, and warm, and I have a long-sleeved T-shirt on, too." I pulled my arms out of the sleeves and held it out for Lily as if I were helping her into a coat. When she didn't react, I shook it a little.

"I'm not leaving you in a T-shirt and nothing else in this wind. I'll be fine." She waved it away and started walking again. "Let's just hurry."

"Lily." I didn't move.

She turned around. "I'm not going to win, am I?"

"No."

Giving me a half smile, she walked back and slid her arms into the sleeves. "Thank you. That was very . . . nice."

"Sometimes I do nice." I shoved my hands into my pockets. "Let's move. I'm cold."

She swung out a too-long sleeve and hit me on the arm. I broke into a half jog.

"Okay, I take it back," Lily said, stopping short once we arrived at our destination. "The bird thing totally works."

The outside of the café had quaint tables, a bright blue awning, and a neon sign with a picture of a rooster. Inside, we found yellow walls, exposed brick, and comfortable-looking places to sit.

We stood in the to-go line instead of taking a table. I ordered a double espresso for Em and Mexican hot chocolate for myself. Lily ordered a mint tea, and then watched every move the barista made, seeming satisfied with the results.

I paid, Lily grumbled at me for paying, and then we stepped back outside.

"What other options did you and Em come up with for finding Jack?" Lily asked. "Did Dr. Turner tell you something?"

"Not exactly." I sipped my hot chocolate, grateful for the kick and the heat of cayenne.

"Don't waste time being cryptic." The wind blew her dark hair over her shoulders. It was out of the messy bun, sort of half up and half down. It softened her. "We're all on the same team, with the same goal."

"He didn't really give anything away, but some of the conversation seemed odd. I asked him about Teague and Chronos, and then Jack, and he suggested we go sightseeing."

"That's weird."

"And he mentioned an island. Maybe he meant Mud Island. The Pyramid, too."

"What if that was a hint? Do you think we should try to look for Jack there?" she asked.

"Maybe. Or . . ." Em's coffee delivery sloshed around inside the cup as I came to a stop. "Maybe we should focus on looking for Chronos and Teague there."

Lily removed the bag from her tea and dropped it into a metal trash can on the street. "Would he have given you their location that easily?"

"I wouldn't think so, but he didn't claim any affiliation with anyone. Maybe he dislikes Teague and Chronos as much as we do. He didn't leave the college with Teague." I shrugged. "There might be some animosity there."

"It's worth a try. We'll hurry back and look at the map." She replaced the plastic lid and blew into the tiny hole to cool off the liquid.

I was avoiding looking at her lips when I saw him.

Poe, head down against the wind, on Union Avenue. He jay-walked across the street.

I handed Emerson's espresso to Lily. "Go back to the room."

"Where are you going?" She followed my line of vision.

"That way."

"Why? Who is he, Kaleb?"

I downed the rest of my hot chocolate. "His name is Poe."

Terror. Em had told her about Poe. A truck lumbered down the street, blocking my view. Once it passed, he reappeared.

"I know exactly who he is, and I'm coming with you," Lily insisted.

"No way." I couldn't justify dragging her into an unknown situation, and I never wanted anyone else I knew to end up with a knife at her throat. "I've seen what he does to innocent bystanders."

"And I've heard." She nailed me with a look, standing her ground. "Good thing I'm not innocent."

I shook my head. "Go back. Tell Em and Mike what's going on. I'll call as soon as I know something."

"I'm coming with you." She dropped Em's coffee and her tea into the trash, and then pointed down the street. "You don't have time to argue about it, either. You need me because Poe's already gone, and I know exactly how to find his boots."

"Damn." I looked both ways, and then we did some jaywalking of our own across the street. "Once I see him, you're going straight back. If I were just a little bit closer, I could track him by his emotions."

We stepped up onto the curb simultaneously. "You can do that? Track by emotions?"

"I can if I'm close enough to a person, physically or emotionally."

She ducked into an alley, gesturing for me to follow her. "How does that work?"

"No one ever feels one emotion—everything is layered. For example, pure hatred is impossible. It's either tinged with vengeance or sorrow, or something. Pure anything is impossible. Every person has a different . . . flavor."

"You feel people's emotions by tasting them." She didn't sound convinced.

"Kind of."

"What does Poe taste like?"

"The one time I met him? Despair."

She thought for a moment and then shrugged. "Better than gym shorts."

I laughed, in spite of the situation.

"Why can't you track Jack, then?" she asked.

"There are a few reasons. I'm not close to him physically right now, but I was never close to him emotionally. And my dad and I both think Jack could've found a way to block me."

"Why?"

"I thought I couldn't feel what he and Cat were up to because I wasn't paying attention. Dad says he's sure Jack had found a way to keep me from reading him. It would've been very difficult for Jack to operate otherwise. I'd have known something was up." I tried to make myself believe it on a daily basis. If I'd known, things would be different now. We reached the end of the alley. "Which way?"

"Do I get to come with you?"

"Lily."

She lifted her chin in defiance. "Either agree or you can sniff around for Poe's *despair*."

"Okay, okay. Which way do we go?"

She turned left. We were facing the Mississippi River.

And Poe was climbing onto the Riverfront trolley.

Chapter 22

We ran, working our way through the crowd, and managed to get onto the same trolley car as Poe. He headed toward the front and slid into a red leather seat. I followed Lily to the back.

"What's he doing?" I asked softly.

She held on to one of the silver standing poles and swung to the left a little. "Not enjoying the ride like everyone else. He's looking at his phone, texting."

"Now that we're on here," I asked her, "what's your plan for when we stop?"

"Just act like you know what you're doing." She said the words through her fake smile while pretending to point out the window at something in the water.

I grinned back, sure it looked more like a painful grimace. "How about you act like you know what you're doing, and I'll stand behind you?"

Her body tensed, and her eyes darted to the side. "Crap."

I'd turned my back to hide from Poe, and I didn't like what I could feel coming from the other end of the trolley car. "Is he looking at you?"

She gave me an imperceptible nod.

I put my hand on her waist and tried to look possessive. "Laugh, not too loud, but like I just told you a secret or said something inappropriate."

She did, and for a quick second, I wished the situation were different. That I'd made her laugh like that for real.

Poe might not have noticed Lily before, but his spike of interest told me he definitely had now. "Damn."

"What are you getting from him?" She shivered slightly. "Something about his eyes . . . he's scaring me."

"Good." I pulled her closer and spoke just above her ear, into her hair. It was as soft as it looked, and smelled like grapefruit. "You should be scared. He's not a nice guy."

We rode through six stops, people climbing on and off the trolley, the muscles in my shoulders growing more knotted by the second. Poe didn't look in Lily's direction again.

When the driver reached the seventh stop, Lily grabbed my hand.

"Showtime."

We followed thirty feet behind him.

"The Pyramid Arena," I said, when I realized where he was going. "But it's closed. Totally empty since the Grizzlies moved to the FedExForum."

"The Pyramid might be closed, but the parking lot is hopping. Looks like some kind of festival. And can you smell that?" She took a deep breath and exhaled. "Barbecue. We never had lunch."

There were at least twenty red-and-white-striped tents set up in a semicircle. Just over a football field's length away, workers were setting up a stage, complete with speakers and lighting.

"What do we do now?" Lily asked, staring at the closest barbecue stand.

"Watch, wait, and follow." We still held hands. I pulled her away from the food, even though my stomach was grumbling, too. "We'll eat later."

Taking a slow stroll around the perimeter of the activity, we kept at least twenty-five feet between Poe and us. When he broke away and headed toward the Pyramid itself, we hung back and watched.

He completely ignored the huge statue of Ramses the Great at the entrance and took the stairs to the building two at a time. Lily and I rushed to the base of the statue, watching as he pushed through a main door and disappeared inside.

"How are we supposed to follow him?" I asked. "That's not the kind of place you can sneak into. Every single sound will be amplified."

Lily ignored me and walked up the stairs to the entrance, pushing open the main entry door as if she owned the place.

"All righty." I followed.

She let the door shut softly behind me before turning to the left. "He went this way."

"You're following his boots again, aren't you?"

She grinned.

"You take risky to a whole new level." My whispered words echoed off the concrete walls. "And you've got some serious cojones."

"Yes, I do." When she pulled up short, I almost barreled over the top of her. She held a finger up to her lips and pointed. A sign on the wall said EXECUTIVE OFFICES.

No one in sight. My heart beat so loudly I was certain anyone in the building could hear it. Lily remained cool and composed.

Impressive.

She took my arm and dragged me down the hall, looking into each open door, finally ducking into one. It turned out to be a well-appointed office, empty of people, with a perfect view of the Mississippi River. And Mud Island.

"What are you doing?" I asked. "Why did you stop here?"

She pointed. "Because of those."

The far wall was full of backlit shelves, every single one featuring hourglasses.

A few were made of glass and sand, simple, exactly like the kind you could buy in a department store. Others were more detailed. Etched glass, bases carved out of wood or formed from metal. The sand inside several had a different reflective quality from anything I'd ever seen. It shone like crushed diamonds.

One hourglass, carved from ivory, completely drew me in. I had a strong desire to touch it, but some instinct made me recoil from it at the same time. I stepped as close as I dared.

Discovered the spindles that connected the top and bottom of the base weren't ivory but bones. What looked like human bones.

The base was formed from carvings of tiny skulls, each one with black, gaping eye sockets and a wide-open mouth. The mouths seemed to be moving. Seductive whispers in my head grew louder and louder. I raised my hand to touch. So close.

"He's coming." When Lily took my arm, real voices overtook the imaginary ones. She opened a narrow slatted door, pulled me inside, and shut it behind us.

Five seconds later, Poe and a dark-haired woman walked into the office.

Lily leaned against the wall in a half-sitting position. A stack of boxes ended at the back of her knees. She couldn't stand up straight. I didn't know how long we'd be stuck in the closet, but she couldn't hold that position forever, especially if we needed to run once we got out.

The woman's voice was unnaturally soft, yet there was no mistaking her disdainful tone. "I thought this was your specialty."

Through the slats in the door, I saw Poe pull his mouth to the side, making his nose curve more prominently than it had the night he'd paid his visit to the Phone Company. "It's been in my possession a week. Stop making me your errand boy and I'll work on it."

Her laugh was as soft as her voice. "Your skills and those errands are the only reason you're still alive."

"I suppose I'm to be grateful to you, then?" Poe looked much younger in the light of day than he had the night of the masquerade. "Since it's thanks to you I still draw breath?"

"Yes."

Poe set his jaw. His anger spilled across the thick carpet and seeped between the slats of the closet door.

"Have you made any progress?" the woman asked. "At all?"

"It shorts out everything I use. So, no." He held up a slim silver device that looked like a laptop computer but was half the size. "Did you call him?"

"Only because you said 'please.'"

Lily tried to stand up straight, and the boxes behind her shifted when her weight was no longer on them. She wobbled and almost fell when they hit her calves. I put one arm around her to keep her upright, and the other against the wall to brace us. It made a slight thudding sound.

The woman frowned and looked in the direction of the closet.

She tossed her dark hair over her shoulders and started walking toward us. Lily squeezed her eyes shut. I tensed in preparation, planning to get us out alive, no matter who I had to hurt. I didn't know if I could get us both past Poe, but Lily would go free.

Teague walked past the closet and went to the office door. I heard a new voice.

"Hello, Teague."

The woman was Teague. And the man addressing her was Dr. Turner.

Chapter 23

"Hello, Gerald." Teague arranged her expression into a smile. "So glad you could come on such short notice."

When Lily exhaled, I realized how tightly I must have been holding her. The fact that I hadn't noticed spoke volumes about my anxiety level.

"I cancelled my afternoon classes. I hope the matter is as urgent as you made it sound in your message." He'd taken one of the fedoras from the moose antlers in his office and clamped it down over his head of white hair. He removed the hat now, holding it in one hand and tapping it against his other palm. I noticed his suspenders for the first time. They perfectly matched his orange bow tie.

"You'll have to ask Edgar how urgent the matter is," Teague answered, nodding her head toward Poe, who'd taken a seat in the corner.

Edgar? I'd have gone with the nickname, too. I wondered briefly if his middle name was Allen.

"Hello, Poe," Dr. Turner said kindly. "Teague didn't tell me I was visiting for your benefit. I would've made it here much more quickly."

Poe stood and held out his hand. "Sir."

Dr. Turner shook it, and then his eyes caught the device Poe held. He looked from it to Teague, and back to Poe again. "Is this . . . ?"

"We don't know," Poe said, and handed it over to Dr. Turner. Teague hissed between her teeth. Neither of them acknowledged her. "Unfortunately, I can't get it open."

Turning it over and over in his hands, Dr. Turner squinted before lifting his glasses and taking an even closer look. "Like a technological vault."

"Precisely." Poe continued to ignore Teague as she tapped one high-heeled foot. Both men stared at the device. "Whoever stored the information knew how valuable it was."

Dr. Turner whistled. "Those won't even come on the market for at least a couple of years."

Teague's thin patience ripped. "Gerald, can you help us or not?"

"I'm afraid I can't." *A lie.* One he was happy to tell. "I've only read about these, how much information can be stored on them. Not how to access it. There's a USB port here, but if that's what Poe's been using—?" Dr. Turner dropped his glasses back down on his nose to look at Poe, and Poe nodded. "Then I have nothing more advanced to test it."

Lily's arms snaked around my waist. I looked down in surprise, and then realized she was about to lose her balance again. I pulled her close enough to feel the rise and fall of her chest.

"What about the university?" Teague asked. "Wouldn't they have more advanced equipment?"

"You've been out of academia for too long." Dr. Turner shook his head. "We have to fight to get funding for our most basic needs. Skrolls aren't even in our orbit. Probably won't be for ten or fifteen more years."

"I can't accept being this close to information and not being able to access it." She walked to the window to stare out at the water. "We'll just have to keep trying."

Dr. Turner and Poe exchanged a look I didn't understand. The emotion that went with it was mixed—both trust and fear.

"You know, Teague," Dr. Turner said, "doing something rash to this piece of equipment could destroy anything stored on it. Why don't you let me take it—"

"Oh no." Teague spun around and held out her hand. "It doesn't leave my sight."

Dr. Turner didn't let the Skroll go. "Where did you find it? That might give me a clue about how to manipulate it, the right kind of software and such."

"Or give you a clue who to contact for leverage against me." A history of betrayal hung between them, the kind that spoke to the fact that they'd once been allies. Teague wanted to tell him what she knew, and he wanted to hear it, but neither with the intention of helping the other.

Slimier than a snake pit, and even more twisted.

"We should find a way to work together." Dr. Turner said.

"Why would we do that, Gerald? We don't want the same thing." The warmth in her cheeks didn't match the coldness of her smile.

"That's not always been the case. It was different when Liam was here."

All my muscles tensed as a quick flood of adrenaline pulsed through me. Lily rubbed her hand across my back, intending to soothe. It did.

"Liam left because he's entirely too honorable," Teague said, lifting her delicate shoulders. "Always has been."

"I don't think that's the only reason Liam left." Before Teague could ask what he meant, Dr. Turner continued. "Maybe he left because he had information he didn't want to share. With anyone."

Teague frowned.

"Oh, and . . . his son is here, in Memphis. He doesn't know anything about the Infinityglass, either."

I tensed again under Lily's hands. I could feel her heart beating.

"When did you see him?" Teague asked, her expression full of reproach.

"He was at my office." Dr. Turner didn't get into specifics about exactly when.

"And he knew nothing about the Infinityglass?" She assessed his reaction. "You're a human lie detector. If you say he didn't know, he didn't."

"He didn't." Did Dr. Turner have a special ability, too?

Teague conceded with a slight nod of her head. "Did he know about me? What about Chronos? . . . Gerald?"

"He didn't . . . there wasn't . . ." The way he fumbled around for an answer suggested Dr. Turner hadn't anticipated that line of questioning, or prepared an adequate story. And that he was afraid of Teague. "They didn't know much."

"They?"

"There was a girl with him. Emerson."

"What did you tell them?" Teague's voice had gone deadly cool. She knew who Emerson was.

"Very little," he said, pulling at his bow tie, loosening it. "Gave them some generalities about Chronos so they'd go away satisfied."

"What about Jack? Did they ask about him?" Dr. Turner didn't respond. "They did."

"Just if I'd heard of him, or if I knew where he was."

"They're looking." Teague smiled. "Good."

"What are you after?" The fear was in his voice now.

"Finding the Infinityglass has always been the ultimate goal of Chronos, our main purpose for years. We're closer now than we've ever been." Teague had an unnatural light in her eyes as she looked at the Skroll. "Jack Landers picked up the search where Liam left off."

"You think that all you have to do is find Jack, and he'll be able to open the Skroll up and answer all your questions?" Dr. Turner asked.

"If we can't find the answers on our own, I believe he can be persuaded. Especially once he discovers the Skroll is in our possession."

"What about the Hourglass?" Dr. Turner asked.

"If they find Jack for us, they'll be fine." She shrugged. "This isn't a game. Sometimes myth translates into reality."

"What if you find the Infinityglass and it doesn't do everything you hope it will?"

"It will." Teague held out her hand. Dr. Turner gave her the Skroll. She placed it in the top drawer of her desk and then locked it with a small silver key. "That and so much more."

Poe and Dr. Turner exchanged a look.

"Shall Poe and I see you safely out of the building?" Teague asked Dr. Turner.

"You have that little trust in me?" Instead of sounding offended, he seemed relieved.

"I don't trust anyone. That's why I'm still here." She opened the door, and she and Poe followed Dr. Turner out.

We were perfectly still for thirty seconds after they left.

"They're gone," Lily said. "Far enough for us to get out safely."

We stepped out of the closet, and the hourglass made of bones started whispering to me again. I turned away. "We need to get out of here before they come back."

"I'm not leaving empty-handed." She was staring at the desk drawer that held the Skroll.

"How do you plan on making that happen?"

Without another word, she dug around on top of the desk until she found a paper clip. Shoving it in the lock, she wiggled it, opened the drawer, picked up the silver case, and slid it into the waistband of her pants. She took off my flannel shirt and tied the arms around her waist.

Then she looked at me, smiled, and took off toward the hall at a full run.

Chapter 24

"Forget being quiet," Lily huffed over her shoulder, as we flew down the hall and out the front entrance of the Pyramid and into the crowd.

I spotted what looked like a tour group close to the food stands. All wearing the same shirts, broken English touched by a French accent, and a woman holding a tiny red flag above her head.

"Slow down." I took Lily's elbow and pulled her to my side. I'd noticed she got a lot of stares from both men and women in general, but with the appealing addition of flushed cheeks and accentuated curves, it was attention we didn't need. "Try to blend. We're too conspicuous if we run."

"Let's get good and mixed in with this crowd first." She pulled the sleeves tight around her waist again and tied them in two knots this time. "Do you see anyone?"

I scanned the crowd. "No sign."

"I can't sense them." Lily exhaled, but her body didn't relax. Tension pulled her shoulders together, and I reached for the base of her neck to help ease it. I stopped before I touched her and shoved my hand into my pocket.

I was losing my mind.

"I won't feel safe until we get back to the hotel." Her hands went to the small of her back, and then she moved them to her waist, stretching and twisting from side to side.

"You okay?" I asked, mesmerized by the movements.

"Yes. I wanted to make sure everything was secure."

Everything looked secure to me.

"I want to be able to run again if we have to. I'm so scared I'm going to drop this thing."

I shrugged. "Maybe if you do, it'll pop open."

"Not the time for sarcasm."

We stepped back into the flow of the crowd like migratory birds, wayward ducks falling into alignment.

The bird fetish was rubbing off on me.

"Kaleb." Lily's eyes were wide. "Look."

I took a step back, trying to figure out what was off. The crowd was twice as big as it had been two seconds ago.

There were rips.

Everywhere.

"None of the scenery has changed," Lily said in a shaky voice. "It's just extra people. There were fifty people setting up, I blinked, and then there were a hundred."

"The French tourists are here." They were chattering away, checking out the Memphis skyline and the reflective surface of the Pyramid. "And they don't seem to see the rips."

The bodies occupying the crowded space were sharing features, like multi-limbed demigods. They were in the same air space, possibly even in the same cell space.

"So instead of a whole scene, we have a whole crowd. That's freaky," I said under my breath. Facial features blurred like out-of-focus photographs as the living blended with the dead. "That's way too freaky."

Lily's hand tightened on my arm. I didn't know what it would feel like for a rip to walk through me, and I sure as hell didn't want to find out.

A mother, father, and two young boys stopped beside us, posing for a family photo. An elderly woman held up a camera and counted to three. It was all very vacationlike and innocent, unless you saw the man standing with them.

Although the more accurate term was *in* them. One leg rested solidly in the dad, the other, in the mom. His hand was visible on one side of the youngest boy's neck, his elbow on the other side.

"That's too much. I'm going to be sick." Lily closed her eyes and turned toward the breeze blowing off the river, inhaling deeply.

"Stay there and keep your eyes closed. I'll take care of this." When the family finished posing, they turned and headed toward the parking area. I rushed to tap the man on the shoulder, expecting him to disappear.

He jumped, startled. "Can I help you?"

The family had been part of the rip instead of the man. Their Memphis Grizzlies jerseys should have clued me in. "I'm so sorry, sir. No."

"Kaleb?" Lily waited for an explanation.

"My mistake. It's okay." I stayed beside her and scanned the crowd, trying to find someone who was obviously out of place. "The rips don't see us. It should be easy to find one."

"Just like it was a second ago, right?"

Doubt. Fear. More like terror.

"I bet she's a rip." I pointed to a woman wearing white Reebok high tops with fluorescent pink laces. I called out to her. "Ma'am?"

"Yes?" she answered.

I wasn't expecting a response. "I like your . . . shoes."

She hurried away, eyeing me strangely.

"I didn't even know they made those anymore," Lily said, now obviously holding the Skroll in place with her hands, ready to run.

I pushed down a creeping sense of dread. I didn't want to tell Lily, but I was starting to worry that we were becoming planted more firmly in the crowd of rips than in reality. I wanted to run, too. Problem was, I didn't know where to go.

"Trying again." A teenage girl wearing a sweatshirt with the neck cut out was my next target. I could see a shiny spandex leotard underneath. I didn't bother speaking to her; I just stepped in front of her and held out my hand. She walked into it and dissolved before she reached my body.

"Thank God," Lily breathed out.

"Don't relax yet."

Poe and Teague stood on the steps by the Ramses statue, scanning the crowd.

"Run."

Chapter 25

"We're totally not conspicuous," Lily said as we raced through the crowd.

"Stop running, but walk fast."

"That I can do."

We hurried toward the Mud Island monorail and the riverfront, weaving through parked cars. Some of the cobblestones were crumbling. "Be careful."

"I should probably give this a little extra protection." She slid her arms out of my shirt and wrapped the Skroll in it. "Oh no. Duck!"

Call it a stress reaction, but I had the strangest thought she'd gone back to the bird fetish thing. "What—"

"Duck! Poe's boots."

She dropped to the ground behind a Honda Accord and shoved the wrapped Skroll underneath it. Then she yanked my arm, pulling me down with her. On top of her.

When things like that happen in movies, they always result in a longing look, or an almost kiss. In real life, it translated to Lily's eyes squeezed shut in pain. She was the only thing between the cobblestones and me.

"*Holy crap.* You're like . . . a . . . giant." She smacked at my biceps as she choked the words out. I rolled onto my back with my hands on her hips, pulling her with me. She took a huge gulp of air, but instead of moving, she lifted her upper body and straddled me, craning her neck to get a glimpse of Poe. "I don't see anyone. Maybe he wasn't as close as I thought."

I clenched my jaw and stared at the thin white clouds in the otherwise blue sky.

This was about to get really uncomfortable.

"Lily."

"Oh hell. He *is* close. Teague's with him." Dropping back down, she pressed her chest against mine. Her hair tickled my neck.

"*Lily.*" I exhaled through my teeth. A blush of surprise colored her face, but not before a brief second of recognition passed over it. The second when she realized exactly what she was doing to me.

"Sorry." She grinned.

"I bet."

Scrambling to her feet, she squatted down behind the car and looked toward the river.

I took a few seconds to recover, and then crept over to the rear bumper of the Honda and peeked around the side. Teague turned back around and headed toward the Pyramid, while Poe moved to the end of the line forming to board the monorail.

We waited, crouched down. The water lapped against the dock, and hungry seagulls cried out for lunch.

"Too bad I don't have my camera to hide behind," Lily said, pulling the Skroll out from under the Honda and into her lap. "We could have pretended to be tourists."

"How long have you been taking pictures?"

"Abi bought me my first camera when I was twelve. It was secondhand, but it had all the bells and whistles. I had a blast learning how to make it work." *A blip of sorrow.*

"Why does thinking about it make you sad?"

"I'd started to forget things about my family. The house I lived in when I was little. Abi thought being able to keep a record of my life here would help me. So I'd never have to worry about forgetting anything again, and so I'd have a tangible memory." She slid a little on a loose stone and I lightly touched my hand to her back to help her keep her balance. "Been taking pics ever since. I have a digital camera now, but I kept the original."

"Your stuff is really impressive. You could have a gallery showing. Em pointed them out, on the walls at Murphy's Law. Do you want to pursue photography professionally? When you're older?"

"I'm pursing it professionally now." *Drive and determination.*

"It looks like we're in the clear," I said, standing. I reached for Lily's hand to help her up. "You sense anything?"

"No." She held the Skroll close to her chest. "But maybe you should sniff around for some despair."

We made it to the hotel without any further incidents. Neither of us paid attention to the duck parade that was taking place as we hurried through the lobby. We didn't talk in the elevator.

Lily remembered our room number. We'd left without a key, so I had to knock. Waiting for someone to answer was torture. Finally, Michael opened the door and we stepped inside, barely dodging a flying Emerson.

"You scared us to death," she said. "What the hell's going on? Where have you been?"

"Calm down, Em," I said.

"Don't tell me to calm down. You take off in a strange town with my best friend and—"

"We've been with Teague." My words made the impact I'd hoped for. Em sat down hard on the edge of the couch.

"Teague?" Michael joined Em.

"On the way back from getting your coffee, we saw Poe and followed him. He led us straight to Teague's office in the Pyramid, which I'm assuming is also Chronos headquarters." I pulled two different bottles of soda out of the minibar and held them out to Lily. She picked the non-caffeinated one.

"You randomly saw Poe on the street in downtown Memphis. He led you to an abandoned commercial building, and then you followed him inside?" Michael asked. "It could've been a trick."

"It wasn't." I didn't like the implication that I would've put

Lily in a situation like that. "I'd have known if he was trying to trick us, and I'd have insisted that Lily come back to the room."

"He tried to make me come back to the room, anyway, but I didn't listen." She untied the sleeves of my shirt and removed the silver rectangle. I took it. It was still warm from her skin. "If I had, we might not have made it out with this."

"What is that?" Em popped up off the couch and plucked the Skroll from my hands.

"Dr. Turner called it a Skroll."

"Wait. Dr. Turner was there, too?" Michael looked from me to Lily and back again. "Maybe you should start from the beginning."

We explained everything, including the crowd of freaky rips.

"So now we have a device that we don't know what to do with, and we still don't have any leads on how to find Jack," I said.

"Obviously, we have to go back to talk to Dr. Turner." Em felt the edges of the Skroll, looking for a way to open it. "We're taking this with us. First thing in the morning. And we aren't leaving until we get answers."

Chapter 26

*E*arly the next morning, Em and I hurried across Bennett's campus toward the science department.

"Are you just going to plop it down on his desk and say, 'Hey, my best friend stole this from the same office where you were seen with the head of Chronos. What's that all about? And also, do you know how to open it?'"

Em had the silver case in her bag. "No. Maybe. I don't know right now. But when I see him, I'm sure I will."

We didn't even have to go all the way to Dr. Turner's office.

He was in front of the science building, holding his briefcase. A pink carnation was in the buttonhole of his vest.

"Dr. Turner," Emerson called out.

When he heard his name, he turned to face us and smiled politely. "Good morning. How can I help you?"

He seemed a little formal after our encounter yesterday. I

stepped close to him, hoping no one around would hear us. It was around nine, and people were rushing to classes all around us. "I took your advice and checked out the sights. The Pyramid? I saw some things I wanted to talk to you about."

I expected shock, at the very least, surprise. But not confusion.

"I'm sorry, did I give you advice?" Dr. Turner pulled at the edge of his bow tie.

"Yes," I answered, "in your office, yesterday . . ."

He had no idea what I was talking about.

"Dr. Turner, it's me. Emerson." She smiled and nodded, encouraging him to remember. "We were here yesterday morning."

He leaned over to get a better look at her face. "Yesterday morning?"

"During your office hours." She looked around before saying in a low voice, "We talked to you about Chronos."

Distress coated his words. "I don't . . . I wouldn't . . . oh, hold on, my phone . . ." He fumbled around, touching each of his pockets before finally finding his cell. "Hello?"

He glanced at Em and me as he listened to the caller on the other end, his fear more pronounced by the second.

Em's anxiety crashed into mine. "I don't feel good about this."

"You shouldn't."

"Could he be senile, have Alzheimer's or something? Or does this mean what I think it does?"

"His memory is gone." I nodded. "It has to be Jack."

"But he disappeared off the map." She fought her fear, denying the obvious truth. "Lily's been checking every hour."

"More like every half hour."

"Then how could Jack have gotten here?"

"He could be hiding in veils. If he stays inside them, it could block Lily from being able to track the pocket watch. He would exist outside space and time."

"Or he could be stuck. That could explain why the rips just keep getting worse. More screwing around with the continuum equals more consequences." Em made a sound of frustration. "As if things weren't bad enough already."

"Actually, I don't think Jack's stuck. He paid the professor a visit, which would be impossible if he were stuck."

"Why would he take Dr. Turner's memory?" Em asked. "Specifically his memory of us?"

"I don't know." I just knew we were surrounded by enemies and uncertainties, and everything in me wanted to get the hell out of this town and back to Ivy Springs. "Maybe because Dr. Turner told us too much about Chronos."

"He barely told us anything."

I looked at Dr. Turner, paid attention to his appearance, and panic settled in my chest. "We have to go, Em."

"We need to call someone. We can't leave him like this." She didn't move. "Who knows how much of his memory Jack took?"

"Em, don't." I needed to get her back to the hotel. "There's nothing we can do."

Dr. Turner had hung up his phone, and he stood staring at the Gothic arches in front of the science building, frowning at them.

"Please, we have to at least take him to his office. He has grandkids, a family." She pushed away from me. "We want to take you to your office, okay, Dr. Turner? We'll explain once we get up there."

"I'm afraid you can't. I have to get to a meeting shortly." He tucked his phone into the pocket beside the buttonhole that held the carnation. The bright pink, perfectly fresh carnation.

"Don't worry," Emerson said. "We'll be speedy. Just come with us."

She reached out to take his hand.

He dissolved.

✸

Denial came first. A white-hot burst of adrenaline in our chests that flooded out to our arms and legs, making us weak and dizzy.

Reality kicked in, the image outside reconciling with our brain. Panic sped up our breathing, broke us out in a sweat, made us shake.

I'd never felt another person's emotion so strongly in my life.

"Dr. Turner?" Em turned to me. "Kaleb? Was he . . ."

"No," I said, reaching out for her before she turned around. I knew where she was going.

"Rip." Her breath heaved in her chest. "Dr. Turner was a rip. He was a rip, and he didn't recognize us."

"It could have been a future rip," I said, trying to stall her, calm her down. Work out a way to stop what I knew was about to happen.

She shook her head in protest. "No. Michael and your dad said they haven't seen any future rips since all this started."

"That doesn't mean—"

"Kaleb, he was wearing the exact same thing he had on yesterday. He had the pink carnation in his buttonhole. It was fresh. He should have recognized us. Oh no."

"Emerson, don't."

"Oh please, God, no."

She didn't wait for me, just took off running at top speed. My legs were longer, but she ran distance and had fear as a chaser.

"Stop! You don't know what happened up there—stop—Em!"

She skidded through the entrance to the science building. I was two seconds behind because of the time it took to open the door she let slam behind her.

Her footsteps echoed up the stairwell. I heard her wrench open the door to the second floor. I caught it right before it closed.

The receptionist from yesterday sat at her desk, her mouth opening to ask us where we were going. We were too fast for her.

Em opened the door to Dr. Turner's office and stood, frozen, just outside. I stopped in time to keep from running into her.

The fedora he'd worn to meet Teague was on the floor.

The pink carnation was wilted in the pencil holder.

The pipe was cold.

Dr. Turner lay facedown on his desk in a pool of blood, his throat slit from ear to ear.

Chapter 27

After we'd found Dr. Turner, I'd called campus security, and then Michael and Lily. We split the day between the college and the police station, watching the coroner's office employees enter and leave the building as they did their investigation, and then as the police brought in possible witnesses for questioning.

The wound had been inflicted fourteen hours earlier, with a six-inch blade, from behind. The killer had slashed from left to right. The same way Poe cut Emerson.

There was no doubt in my mind he was the culprit.

I kept seeing the knife slice across her throat at the Phone Company, her lifeblood leaving her body. The next second, it was Dr. Turner, a man with grandchildren and a pink flower in his jacket, slumped over his desk, blood dripping to the floor.

Since the moment we'd found him, I hadn't been able to get a grip on my own emotions. Guilt, fear—other things I couldn't name. It all added up to something so out of control my heart kept skipping beats.

Em wasn't any better. We'd returned to the Peabody, where she'd taken a forty-five-minute shower. Now she sat on the couch, wrapped in Michael's arms, a complete wreck. Lily was in the shower, and I sat in a chair in the corner, trying to block everything out. Finally, I couldn't take any more.

"Em." I reached for her hand. She looked at me blankly. "Let me take it."

"Take what?"

Her voice was loud, as if she'd forgotten how to modulate. I pointed at her heart.

"The pain. You want to take the pain." Her words weren't a question. More like an accusation. I didn't expect the laughter that came next, or her short answer. "No."

She was in no shape to handle her emotions on her own, especially when she didn't have to.

"I feel it either way, whether I take them or not," I said, attempting to persuade her.

"I'm sorry my pain is inconveniencing you."

"You know that isn't what I meant." The words came out harsher than I intended. Michael sat forward in his seat. I needed to temper my response. "Don't shut me out when I can make it better."

The bathroom door opened, and Lily emerged with wet hair and pink cheeks. I didn't want her to hear any of this.

"Taking my emotions won't make it better, Kaleb." Em

acknowledged Lily but didn't lower her voice. "If you don't like them, get out. Go in the bedroom."

"The bedroom isn't far enough." I'd be able to feel her on the opposite side of the equator. At least if I took her emotions, I'd be able to control them.

"Then go somewhere else. Leave. Go ahead!" Her shouting caught me completely off guard. The Em I knew was violent with her fists, not her words. I'd never seen her be irrational. Michael's worry and his expression of concern told me he hadn't, either. "Make me worry about you, as long as it makes *you* feel better."

"How far away do you want me to go?" I asked. She was spinning like a top on the edge of a table.

"Oh, that's right. You can leave the situation behind without even leaving the room, can't you?" She cut her eyes in the direction of the minibar. "Just crack a few open. All kinds of teensy little bottles in there that should numb everything right up."

Her refusal to let me help made me angry for reasons I couldn't name. "I offered because I care."

Michael tried to pacify me, "She's just mad. You don't need to take care of her. I will."

"Like you take care of everything, right?" I asked. Something broke loose in my chest, and my rationality flew out the window, right behind Emerson's. "You always swoop in and save the day. You saved my dad. I could have *prevented* his death if I'd been more in tune with Cat and Jack. If I had, my mom would be awake and healthy. And if I'd taken the files out of Dad's safe when I was supposed to, Jack would have never known about Emerson. So it's all my fault."

From the other side of the room, I felt Lily weighing whether or not to intervene.

Michael stood up. "Don't do this. Don't make today about you."

"Oh okay," I scoffed. "Because that's totally what I'm doing, Mike. No, wait. I wasn't making it about me. *You* did that."

"You did that all by yourself," Michael said.

Our emotions reminded me of a hurricane that stayed in one place, churning up destruction and then churning it up again. But there was no eye in this storm.

"I know how Dr. Turner's family feels," I said. "He will *never* go home to them. He doesn't have a second chance like my dad did. There's no rewind or easy out for a slit throat. There was a body. A slit, bloody throat. Someone had to identify him. Someone had to claim him. And now someone has to bury him." I laughed, but there wasn't an ounce of mirth in it. "So, yeah, go ahead and say today is all about me."

"Stop." Em covered her ears. "*Stop it.* Listen to yourselves. You're making it about both of you, and Kaleb's right. A man is dead." She burst into tears, sobbing like she'd never be whole again, and started to slide to the ground.

Michael caught her before she could hit.

Without another word, he scooped her up and carried her into the bedroom, kicking the door closed behind them with his foot.

I grabbed a key card from the table and ran.

Chapter 28

*B*eale Street at night. A person could get away with murder in this kind of dark.

The wind blew colder than it had that afternoon. Music rolled out of every open bar, neon lights in every color of the rainbow made everything seem celebratory, and the crowd ranged through every emotion. *Lust to anger to tipsy joy.*

My fake ID was solid. I needed it to work tonight. I was definitely in the market for some tipsy joy, and maybe a couple of college girls.

I wanted to forget Em's rejection. The confusion I'd seen on Lily's face.

I couldn't even think of Michael's disappointment without boiling the blood in my veins. I'd offered to lay myself open for the girl he loved, and he'd shoved it back in my face. For the first time in a while, I hadn't had one selfish motive, and he'd blown the whole thing completely out of proportion.

I wondered what Dr. Turner's family was doing tonight. What had his granddaughter thought when she heard that she wouldn't be able to take her grandfather flowers anymore, except for the ones she left on his grave?

Turning in the direction of South Main, I walked toward the Orpheum Theatre. After the rip experience at Ivy Springs Cinema, I was glad to see the marquis advertising an upcoming concert by a modern band. It was nice to be firmly planted in my own reality.

Now I was ready to plow myself out of it.

I followed a crowd of frat boys into a bar called the Love Shack. Holding my ID up in front of the bouncer's face as the line went through, I engaged the guy in front of me in conversation. Casual. Cool. Easy enough.

I plopped myself on a bar stool and ordered a gin and tonic. "Extra gin."

The bartender, a ridiculously hot redhead with a name tag that read "Jen," offered me a crooked smile. "Right, baby boy."

"What do you mean, 'right'?"

She scooped ice into a glass. "You aren't old enough to drink."

"I most certainly am." *Indignant* was the perfect word to describe how I felt. Not one I'd use in everyday conversation, but still perfect. "I got in, didn't I?"

"Where's your stamp?" Opening a new bottle of grenadine, she poured some in the bottom of the glass, added two cherries, and topped it off with Coke.

"Stamp?"

She grinned wider. "Stay out of trouble, sugar. Come look me up when you're legal." She slid the cherry Coke across the counter and winked. "On the house."

The guy beside me showed her a stamp on his hand and ordered a beer. I cussed. I'd missed that part. At least I hadn't paid a cover.

I turned around to scan the crowd, cherry Coke in hand, and immediately spilled it all over my right shin and shoe.

Jack. Standing by the front door.

I shoved the glass into an empty hand and pushed my way through the crowded dance floor to the entrance.

Gone.

Stepping outside, I cringed when the cold wind hit the Coke on my pants. Maybe it hadn't been Jack. Maybe my anger was playing tricks. Maybe I needed to find a bar that would serve me.

I blew into my hands to keep my fingers warm, and saw a green trolley speeding up instead of stopping as it approached Beale Street Landing.

The crowd was too thick for the trolley to be going so fast. One drunk stumble in the wrong direction and a person could meet a bloody end.

Then everything flipped to slow motion, too heavy and too thick.

The rip blended, just like the one Lily and I had experienced the day before. The dark made it harder to see specific features, but when a newsboy passed by, hawking the *Memphis Daily*, and then passed *through* a group of Elvis impersonators, I knew time was shifting again.

I rubbed my eyes with my fists and looked around for someone to touch.

A little girl wearing a white dress. She had two long pigtails, and she was skipping. Completely out of place. I reached out to touch her at the same time she dropped a penny. She chased it into the street.

The brakes of the trolley squealed, and the smell of smoke filled the air, along with a mother's anguished cry. "No! Mary!"

What if I was wrong, and the little girl was real, not a rip? I was close enough to catch her. Without another second of thought, I ran, desperate to stop her before the unthinkable happened and the trolley mowed her down. If I was fast enough, I could knock her out of the way and roll us both to safety.

I ran.

I leapt.

I grabbed.

She dissolved.

So did the trolley.

Chapter 29

"Can you tell us again what happened?"

"I don't know what I saw. There was a little girl—she was there and then she was gone. Her mother called her Mary."

She was a rip. No good way to explain that.

"The Orpheum has a few ghosts, but Mary is the most famous. Maybe you have the Sight." The policeman had a round edge to his voice. Definitely a local. "You were here earlier, with the Turner case? After what you've been through today, I'm surprised that's all you saw."

I focused on the scratched vinyl floor, unwilling to make eye contact. The cop walked away.

All the activity in the station faded into the background when I heard his voice.

"The subconscious is a tricky thing."

He sat two feet away from me. Weapons were everywhere, along with enough cops around to take down an elephant if it picked up the wrong peanut. I couldn't touch him. Too many witnesses.

"Jack," I said under my breath.

He smiled.

My fingers gripped the edge of the bench seat. I wanted them wrapped around his neck. "Why are you in Memphis?"

"I'd tell you, but then I'd have to . . . no, wait, I wouldn't. I could erase your memory."

"Convenient."

"I won't, though, because I want you to think about what you saw tonight." Jack leaned over as if we were sharing a secret. "Mary meeting her death in front of a trolley car. Because that's what really happened way back when. No one sacrificed himself to save her, and she ended up as a bloody puddle in the middle of Beale."

Rage burned like flames behind my eyes.

"You tried to change Mary's path," Jack said. "You saw a tragedy about to occur, and you stepped in front of it to spare the life of an innocent."

My arms began to shake.

"We're more alike than you think, Kaleb."

"No, we aren't." I bit off the ends of the words. "I didn't set up an elaborate plan to change that little girl's life. I didn't stalk her, or let her parents die."

"Emerson's parents were going to die either way. I had to let them. Stepping in and changing a time line causes problems just like the ones we're having now—problems Emerson caused by saving Michael. Rips everywhere, trying to break through the fabric of time."

"Don't blame Em for all of this." I paused and made a conscious effort to lower my voice. A young girl with dark brown hair and a black eye seemed to be listening to every word I said. "You traveled when you weren't supposed to. You and Cat did just as much or more to damage the continuum."

"Try to tell me you'd choose otherwise." His voice was oily. "Tell me you don't want Emerson in your life. That you want your father to be dead."

I clenched my teeth.

"You can't. That's what I need you to understand, to embrace. Let me tell you a story."

"I'm not interested."

"I think you want to hear this." Jack looked down at his fingernails. "I understand you. Liam always choosing Michael over you. How you always fall short in meeting your father's expectations. I can empathize."

My jaw grew tighter. I didn't want a sociopath to tap into my feelings, and I hated the fact that no matter how hard I tried, I couldn't tap into his. All I got was a steady hum of self-satisfaction, and that's because Jack wanted me to feel that emotion. Too pure to be real.

"I had a brother who got the same kind of attention Michael does. A blood brother. In our father's eyes, he could do no wrong. Beyond that, he was a hero. I tried to be like him, tried to emulate him, but Father didn't see me. He was blind."

The information Dune found about Jack hadn't included any mention of a father or a brother. Was Jack making this up to try to elicit sympathy from me, or was this really part of his past?

Jack continued, "I did things to make my father look at me. At first, it was good grades, excelling in sports. When that didn't work, I tried other, less pleasant things. A bottle can be an attention getter and a friend. As you know."

I was going to choke him right in the middle of the police station.

"But my father seemed perfectly willing to let me go my own way. I gave it one final wholehearted attempt, sure I'd discovered the solution to making him care." Jack scoffed. "But all that resulted in was one dead brother and one discarded son."

"You were disowned. That's the thing in the past you want to change." I finally understood. "When you figured out how to travel, why didn't you just change it yourself? Why did you have to involve Em?"

"There wasn't enough of the exotic matter in pill form for me to accomplish all the things I needed to do without Emerson. It simply wasn't strong or stable enough." He shrugged. "The further I went back, the faster it burned up, the faster I aged, the longer it took for me to recover."

"So Em was your alternative."

"I thought once I found Emerson, and once she was mentally healthy, I'd just need to help her understand what I'd done for her. I was sure once we connected, she'd be willing to make any number of trips for me. But she chose the Hourglass instead. And then she tricked me by keeping the exotic matter formula disk."

"Why are you telling me this? You always have a motive. What is it this time?"

He smiled slightly. "Because we're the same, Kaleb. The things we want from life. We're always the last to be considered. The second choice. And we both want that to change."

Fury. So much I shook the bench. "We. Are not. The same."

"Keep telling yourself that." He shrugged. "I have answers for you when you want them. Wake up. I can see you. Now you need to try to see me."

A throat cleared. I looked up sharply at the police officer from earlier.

"You're free to go."

"Thanks." I gave him a nod. "I'll be on my way shortly. I just want to finish this conversation."

The officer frowned. "Are you sure you're all right? No headache or . . . lingering . . . anything?"

"I'm fine," I said, smiling. I even threw in a thumbs-up. "And dandy."

He nodded doubtfully and walked away, and I turned back around to face Jack.

He was gone.

But he'd left the pocket watch in his place.

Chapter 30

The minibar stood open.

I could see Em and Michael in the dim light through a crack in their door, curled up in bed. I assumed the door wasn't closed because Michael planned to stay with Em all night. Either he didn't want her honor to fall into question, or he didn't want to break Thomas's rules. Boy Scout.

Lily was nowhere in sight.

Picking up a tiny bottle of Crown Royal, I ran my finger over the ridges of the glass, a perfect replica of the bigger bottle. I was a perfect replica of no one. I wanted out of my head—out of my body. Out of my life.

"Put it down."

Lily.

"Go away, little girl. I don't want to play right now."

I didn't want to hurt her, either, but I didn't need any witnesses.

Still, I was surprised when I didn't *feel* any hurt. I turned around.

The sight of her made my chest ache with an unexpected want.

"I'm not playing." She crossed the room and took the bottle out of my hand, her determined fingers unwrapping each of my tense ones. "You aren't going to do this."

Holding on to my wrist with one hand, she took away the liquor with the other.

"You aren't my keeper, Lily."

"No one is. You're responsible for you. I'm simply reminding you that you're worth more than what you'll find at the bottom of a bottle." She leaned over to put the liquor away and shut the mini-bar. Her hair fell in waves over her bare shoulder, hiding the black strap of her tank top. "Days like today could make you forget."

"How about years like today?"

"I was worried when you took off. So were Em and Michael. I made them go to bed—promised I'd wake them up if you weren't back by midnight."

Gesturing toward their open door, I said, "I don't think they really cared whether I came back at all."

"That's not true, Kaleb. Em insisted on staying up to apologize. That was before she cried so hard she wore herself out. She knows she was wrong and that you were trying to help her because you love her."

I searched Lily's face.

"You do love her?"

"Not like that." I paused, surprised. It was true. "More like a sister. A best friend."

"That role is already taken, but you can audition for understudy. Michael cares, too, you know." When I shook my head, she sighed. "You need a Lily intervention. Come with me."

When she gestured to the other empty bedroom, I almost swallowed my tongue.

"Down, boy. I meant so we could talk at a normal volume. But only if you want to talk. If you don't, I'll flip you for the foldout."

"I'm not flipping you for . . . ugh." I sighed. "My mama raised a gentleman, remember?"

She took my hand. "I also believe you tacked 'in most circumstances' onto the end of that explanation."

In the bedroom, a book lay open facedown on a side table. Its well-worn spine was cracked, and Lily's tiny glasses rested on top. She sat down on the double bed, and since the only chair was serving as a luggage rack, I sat down on the floor. Her back was against the headboard, and her legs were crossed at the ankles. Tiny embroidered cupcakes seemed to dance on her pajama pants. They even had sprinkles.

Due to previous experience, I should've been comfortable in a bedroom with a girl, but Lily looked at me as if she expected me to *say* something instead of *do* something.

"I'm sorry." I blew out a breath. "About earlier. That you had to hear all that. I acted like a jerk."

"All three of you acted like jerks," she confirmed in a dry voice. "But there's an extenuating circumstance to take into consideration. That kind of trauma can bring buried things to the surface."

"Is that your way of telling me I'm off the hook for my behavior?" Lily didn't deserve my sarcasm, but I dished it out, anyway.

She shrugged. "I didn't have you on a hook. But I do have a question. Do you really feel like everything that's happened is your fault?"

"You always get right to the point," I said, half annoyed, half in awe. "There's no messing around."

"Why waste time?" She leveled her eyes at me. "And don't turn the conversation back to me. This is about you."

I tried to calm my own emotions enough to feel hers. *Curiosity. Real, true empathy.* She was trying to see things through my eyes. Nobody outside my immediate family ever did that. "I know it's not rational, but yes. I do feel like most of what's happened is my fault."

Lily nodded, and then she was quiet for a few seconds, processing. "That's the reason you offered to take the pain away for Emerson. You felt responsible. Taking emotion is part of your ability, too?"

She already knew the answer. "Em told you."

"Technically, *you* did. But she clued me in, only because of what I overheard and because I asked specifically."

"It isn't something I do that often," I said tightly.

"Em said that the only emotions you take from people are the painful ones." She looked at the book on her bedside table. Grimm's fairy tales. "I'm guessing there are consequences when you do. Magic always has a price."

"Taking emotions isn't magic."

"What is it, then?" She scooted forward to sit on the edge of the bed.

"Well"—I scrambled for the right explanation—"without permission, it's a violation."

"But you get permission. You take pain with the intent to help, to heal. That's the best kind of magic there is."

"Don't make me out to be a saint, Lily. I'm not."

"But," she challenged, "you aren't like Jack."

The comment set my teeth on edge. "I never said I was like Jack."

"But you think you are. It's the next logical step, especially if you compare your abilities," she said. "Memories and emotions are all tied up. The more strongly you feel about a situation influences how you remember it. There've been studies."

"That you just happened to read?"

"No. I looked it up online." Lily pointed toward the desk, where her computer was open. There was a picture on the screen, one she'd taken today when I hadn't been paying attention. It showed the back of Em's head, which Lily had been in the process of cropping out, and me, with a half smile on my face.

"Nice picture."

"Ah, yeah." She blushed a little and rocketed over to the desk to close the lid of her laptop. "It was a good shot. You, um, have a nice smile. When you pull it out and dust it off."

"Em and I were talking about you. How talented you are."

"Let's get back to talking about you." Very single-minded, this girl. "You've never said it out loud, but I know you compare yourself to him."

I debated telling her that Jack had just made all kinds of comparisons for me, and that the similarities were worse than I'd thought, but I was too worried I'd cave and tell her about the pocket watch. I didn't want to go there tonight, so I shrugged. "Maybe."

"It's only your abilities that are the same." She walked back to the bed, but she didn't sit down. "Jack takes memories and replaces them, and it fractures people in a million ways. And your mom, what he did by taking her memories and *not* replacing them. It made her empty."

I stared up at her.

"You aren't like him," she insisted. "Your intentions aren't the same. What you offered to do for Emerson tonight was a step toward helping her heal. That's what's in your heart, and that's the difference between you and Jack."

"Maybe." The word caught in my throat. How did she see the man that I wanted to be so clearly, instead of the ugliness that was really there?

"Why don't you believe me?"

"Lily, I've made so many mistakes. I've not helped people who needed it. The people who needed it most."

"Like who?" She sat down beside me. "Did you try to take your mom's emotions after your dad died?"

"No," I whispered. "Not until it was too late."

"Listen to me." She took a deep breath before reaching for my hand. "You have to forgive yourself for that, and then you need to take the next step. Instead of beating yourself up because Jack took your mom's memories, you need to focus on how to get them back."

I met her eyes.

On summer evenings when I was little, I'd hold my mom's hand while she snapped the blooms off the bright orange flowers that grew in her garden. Every morning, they would bloom again, beautiful and resilient, ready to take on whatever the day brought.

Tiger lilies.

I had an irrational urge to hold Lily, or ask her to hold me. What would it feel like to lean instead of carrying all the time? I ran the tip of my finger over each of her knuckles before flipping her hand over to trace the lines on her palm. "I don't know how to navigate you."

"That's my life line, not a map." She smiled, but she pulled away. "Did you hear what I said about forgiving yourself?"

"I did. I think . . . I need . . . distance from this conversation." I stood.

"I'm sorry, I had no intentions of crossing any boundaries—"

"Lily. Relax. All I meant is that I need some time to think about everything you've said. Not that I was mad you said it."

"Okay." She stood, too. "Kaleb?"

"Yeah?"

"If you . . . slept . . . in here, in that bed"—she blushed furiously as she pointed at it—"I'd feel a lot . . . better. About you staying out of the liquor cabinet."

"That's it?"

"And I'd feel a lot safer. In general."

"Done. Let me get some clothes." I didn't feel right about leaving her alone, anyway, not with Jack popping in and out of every godforsaken place I went.

"Okay. Oh, and hey."

"Yeah?" I paused at the door.

"I still don't like you."

"I know," I said, smiling. "I still don't like you, either."

She was already asleep when I returned.

I left the door cracked.

Chapter 31

I'd achieved a miraculous feat.

Eight strictly platonic hours in a bedroom with a girl.

Em and Michael didn't ask any questions the next morning. Some dismay came from Em's direction, and I caught her giving Lily a look. Lily shook her head, and the dismay turned to curiosity.

We checked out and carried our bags to Em's SUV. I stepped in front of the trunk before she could pop it open.

"Two things," I said. "First of all, I saw Jack last night."

"What?" Em fumbled her suitcase.

"Where?" Michael demanded.

"At the police station." I recounted the events of the evening, and everything I'd learned. I left out the comparisons Jack made between us. And that he left the pocket watch behind.

"And secondly, I want to give Dune a chance with the Skroll

before we tell Dad about it. If Dune can't get anything after a few days, then we can get Dad involved. I don't want to get his hopes up, and I don't want to be cut out of any information it could provide. Agreed?"

"Agreed," Em waved me to the side and popped open the trunk.

Michael swung the bags into the back.

"Are you in?" I asked.

He nodded, but he remained as quiet as the grave.

So was the rest of the ride home.

Em dropped Lily off first. No one said a word until Em pulled into my driveway. I was already reaching for the door handle.

"Kaleb, wait," Em blurted out.

I sat back in the seat and met her eyes in the rearview mirror.

"I know what you were trying to do for me last night, and I know how much taking emotion costs you. It was a gift that I didn't accept. I'm sorry, and thank you so much." Completely genuine.

Michael ached beside her.

"I'm sorry I yelled. At both of you," I said.

"Don't apologize." Michael turned around. *Regret.* "I called you selfish, when what you were offering to do for Em was completely selfless."

"There were extenuating circumstances," I said, repeating Lily's words. Meeting his eyes. "We were all jerks. But it's okay."

"I hope so." Michael's ache disappeared. The sadness had been for me, not for Em.

"It's really okay."

I'd expected Dad to take a piece out of my hide. Instead, he'd stared at me as if he were memorizing me.

"I'm fine. Everything is fine."

"What about Michael and the girls?"

"They're okay, too." I was surprised he asked about Mike. I figured he'd already know. "Can we go in your office?"

"Sure."

I followed him in, but instead of sitting down, I walked to the hourglass collection on his bookshelf. I traced my fingertips along the edges of the shelves, again noting the absence of dust. "Are you going to tell me about these?"

"What do you mean?" A weak attempt at evasion.

"What's with the collections?" He wasn't going to dodge me this time, and from the defeat on his face, he knew it.

"You're going to find it simple and silly."

"Try me."

"There's a legend. About an object called the Infinityglass."

I tensed, working to control my reaction. "The Infinityglass?"

"The Infinityglass is mythical, or most people think so." He leaned back in his chair, folding his hands across his chest. "There was no evidence to suggest otherwise. Your mother used to tease me about it, her logical husband caught up in a race to find something that didn't exist."

"You think it's real."

"I became obsessed with it. It caused some issues between your mother and me. Part of the reason I never told you about the Infinityglass was because she forbade it."

My mom wasn't the type to forbid anything. "Teague seemed to be pretty obsessed with it herself."

"How did you . . . you found her." He stood so quickly his black leather chair rolled away from him and bounced violently against the back wall. "I gave you permission to go to Memphis to look for paperwork. Not to go on a scavenger hunt through my past."

"We weren't looking for your past, we were looking for Jack's. Teague just happened to be the center point."

"Did you talk to her? Tell her who you were?"

"No. Lily and I eavesdropped on her from inside a closet. Chronos has set up shop in Memphis. Inside the Pyramid. Gerald Turner came to see her while we were there." I thought of his silly brown fedora, the turtle ashtray on his desk. All the people who were mourning him.

"Gerald Turner?" Dad asked. *Terror and relief.*

I nodded.

"He was found dead in his office yesterday," Dad said slowly, as if his lips were out of commission.

"Guess who found him."

His anger didn't shape itself the way mine did. It came fast and hot. "Do you realize what kind of situation you put yourself in? What could have happened to you, to any of you? None of this is a joke. Not to Teague, not to Jack, not to me. Not to whoever killed Dr. Turner."

"I didn't know what I was walking into because you don't trust me enough to tell me the truth. Don't you think it's time? I want to know exactly what the Infinityglass is, what it does, and why Teague is looking for it."

He turned his back to me, rubbing his temples. I waited him out. "The short version is that its intended purpose was to channel time-related abilities from person to person, but it didn't work out that way. Instead, it was a one-way conductor. Whoever possesses the Infinityglass can use it to steal the ability of anyone he or she touches."

Magic, like something from Lily's book of fairy tales.

"Most of the rumors and stories about it are ancient, unchanging. But lately, there are plenty of new rumors."

I narrowed my eyes. "What type of rumors?"

"Reports of its having surfaced again. People suggesting that they know where it is and telling someone. Then those people end up dead." His expression was grim but resigned.

"Then why do people keep looking for it?"

"Power. Control. Endless resources. That's why Teague wants it. And I believe she knows that Jack is looking for it, too. The Infinityglass could give him everything he's ever wanted. It's the perfect alternative to Emerson. That's why he walked away when Emerson wouldn't agree to help him. The promise of the Infinityglass is why he left her alive. Why he left your mother alive."

"Because if Jack finds it before we find him, he can use it to drain us all dry," I said.

"Not just dry. Dead."

Chapter 32

Questions rode a merry-go-round in my mind. "All the time-related abilities, travel, speed . . . they exist because of a gene, one that's backed up by research. The Infinityglass sounds like science fiction or fantasy."

"But it's backed up by research, too. I wouldn't believe the Infinityglass was real, either, if I hadn't seen evidence, years' worth. If I hadn't searched for the truth myself." Dad faced me. "It's real."

"Real enough to kill for."

"You've always thought we left Memphis so I could take the department head position at Cameron. But there were other reasons, too. I'd begun to question the motives of Chronos." Dad was quiet for a moment, lingering in the shadows of a secret. "Even then, Teague was obsessed with the Infinityglass. She was so consumed by her need for power. She knew about the time gene, but she believed all my research was internal. She didn't know I'd been gathering information on people who may or may not have the gene. I never told her about your mother's ability, or yours. She definitely doesn't know Cat and I were trying to develop a formula for exotic matter."

"What would she do with the knowledge if she had it?" I asked.

"Use it. In the worst possible ways."

"What about people with abilities? Everyone else at the Hourglass?" My chest grew tight with unease. "Does she know about them?"

"If she does, it will only give her a bigger incentive to find the Infinityglass."

I stared at him for a long time, sorting through his emotions, putting pieces together. "What Teague and Chronos don't know is what's keeping you—all of us here—safe. If we find Jack and turn him in, Jack could use his knowledge of us, of the exotic matter formula, as a bargaining chip."

"Didn't take very long for you to put that together." He grimaced and then reached up to stroke his beard. "Keep going."

"But if we don't find Jack and turn him in, time will be rewound, and you'll most likely be dead."

"The Infinityglass will only make it easier for Poe to follow through with his threat." Dad focused on a spot just behind my head. "That's why we absolutely must find Jack first, so we can let him lead us to the Infinityglass before Chronos or anyone else. Our lives depend on it."

Chapter 33

I went to Lily's the next morning, after calling to check the location of her grandmother. We met outside the door to her apartment above Murphy's Law.

"How long have you and Abi been in Ivy Springs?"

"Hello. I'm fine. Thanks for asking. And you?"

"Sorry." I put on a cheesy smile. "Hi, how are you, I'm fine, too, and how long have you and your grandmother been in Ivy Springs?"

Lily sighed and opened the door wider to let me in. "Almost since we came to America. I was eight."

I followed her into the living space. "How did you end up here?"

"We were with family in Miami for a little while, but my grandmother wanted to come north." She took my jacket and hung it neatly on a peg by the door. "Ivy Springs was small and still run-down back then. Thomas was just starting his renovations, and a realtor introduced my grandmother to him. The guy who owned the building wanted out, so Abi got it for a steal. It was still a stretch, financially, but we made it work."

"What's it like, living above the shop?" Some walls were exposed brick, others a soft white. She sat down on a couch with bright blue cushions and lime green throw pillows. Everything was tidy, and the room smelled like vanilla and citrus. Like Lily.

"Hard to get away from business. Abi can be a slave driver."

I sat down beside her. "I'd like to meet your grandmother."

"I don't know. If you think I'm tough? She's been known to make grown men piss their pants with one look." She put a pillow behind her back and adjusted her position, flipping her legs over my lap. She rested her head against the padded arm of the couch. "Do you mind? My back is killing me."

"I don't mind." It felt intimate. I didn't know what to do with my hands, so I left them sort of hanging midair. "Do you get to talk to your parents very often?"

"Not really." I felt a flash of the pain I'd seen on her face when she told me she and her grandmother had escaped. "Communication there isn't like it is here. Everything is monitored. Mail, phone calls. Cuban citizens don't have any access to Internet, so even e-mail is out."

"I had no idea it was that bad. I feel really stupid. And Americanized."

"Sometime I'll help you understand. If you want."

"I want."

She noticed my arms were still up in the air and pushed them down on her legs. I went in the shin direction. As opposed to the thigh direction.

"Okay, Kaleb. Spill it. Because I know you didn't come here to talk to me about Cuba, or my grandmother. What's going on?"

"You always say what you think. Your emotions match your words. It's amazing how infrequently that happens."

"Why?" She laughed. "Is everyone else acting?"

"Maybe. I might know what emotions people are feeling, but I rarely know why." I made a show of knocking on my forehead. "It's crowded in here. The filter gets full. After Mom and Dad . . . everything hurt, all around me. Everyone was grieving. That's when the tattoo and piercing thing started." I pointed to my bicep and the end of the dragon tail peeking out from under the cuff of my sleeve. "Pain, meet source. It could be identified."

"That's understandable."

"Dad wants Mom back. So do I. I just don't know how to do it." I stopped short. "I sound like I'm five."

"No. You sound like you love her," she said softly.

"That's only one of the reasons we have to find Jack before he finds the Infinityglass." I gave her a quick rundown of everything Dad had told me. "Dad thinks Jack will lead us straight to it. It's like the Holy Grail of time or something. It could restore everything. Or destroy it."

"Magic," Lily said, sitting up.

"Magic. People have been searching for it for years, possibly centuries. Longer. Teague and Chronos don't want Jack because they want *him*. They just want the Infinityglass, and they think Jack knows where it is."

"Have faith. While Dune works on the Skroll, and Emerson and Michael help your dad with the exotic matter formula, we can work on my abilities. Maybe I was doing something wrong when Jack fell off the map. Maybe I just need to keep trying." She scooted to the end of the couch, preparing to stand. "I'm going to get a map. I'll look at maps of the whole damn world if I have to, until I find the pocket watch. We can get to Jack before it's too late."

"Lily. Wait." I sounded defeated, even to my own ears.

"What is it?"

"This."

I stuck my hand in my pocket and pulled out the pocket watch.

"When?" she asked, barely keeping the disappointment out of her voice.

"In Memphis, at the police station. Not when everyone was there, later. He left this behind."

"He knew. He knew he was being tracked. How?"

"I don't know. But Jack knows how to manipulate a lot of things." I gauged her expression carefully. "I believe you have a theory that would confirm this."

"Ivy Springs as Freak Magnet. Abi and I really did end up here on purpose." Lily made all the connections, and a line formed between her eyebrows. "If he . . . what if he messed with our time lines the way he messed with Em's? How would I know?"

I stared at the ground. "I don't think you would."

She bit her bottom lip and closed her eyes. Her lashes were free of tears, but from the way she was spinning around inside, I didn't think that would last very long. I instinctively reached out to comfort her, but instead, I froze.

Somewhere in the middle of hell and high water, Lily had started to matter.

I stared at the face, the curves, trying to will her back to being an object I needed to use, rather than a living, breathing girl who was beautiful inside and out.

It did not work.

She blew out a deep breath, and I jumped about three feet in the air. "This is a game changer."

"What is?" I asked, a little too loudly.

"I don't have a choice now. I have to ask Abi if I can look for him. The pocket watch isn't an option anymore, and Jack has to be found."

"What are the chances she'll agree?"

"Low." She stood up.

"You're going to do it *now*?" The thought made me a little frantic.

"Why would I wait? The deadline isn't getting further away, and who knows where we'll have to go to get to Jack. Not to mention that I don't know how to actually find a person, because I've never been allowed to do it."

"Wait, Lily, you need to think about what you're going to say," I protested. "You're about to drop time travel and screwed-up time lines and crazy rips and . . . possible death on an old lady."

She snorted. "Don't ever let Abi catch you calling her an old lady. You could seriously end up losing boy parts."

I raised my eyebrows.

"Abi can handle it, but I'm not sure I can. Not alone. Will you stay?"

As long as you'll let me.

I swallowed, hard. "I'll stay."

Chapter 34

A tall woman with spiky silver hair and brown eyes walked into the apartment, and then paused. I stood. The way she was looking at me, I was shocked I hadn't yet burst into flames.

"*Who* are *you?*"

Lily had warned me that her grandmother could make grown men piss their pants with one look.

Pretty much.

Lily spoke up. "This is Kaleb Ballard."

"Kaleb is a friend?" Abi's emotions were a mixed bag. *Distrust and anxiety.* At least she wasn't angry. Yet.

Lily darted a glance at me. "Yes. A friend. Kaleb, this is my grandmother. Everyone calls her Abi."

"I'm pleased to meet you." I held out my hand.

She eyed my hand before she shook it, as if she were checking me for fleas. "I'll put on some coffee. And then we'll talk. Sit."

I sat down at the kitchen table and waited.

An hour later, I didn't know what they were saying, because they were doing it in Spanish, but their combined emotions rolling in my gut made me glad I hadn't gotten around to lunch.

"*Es demasiado peligroso.*" Abi stood and slammed her hands down on the table. "*¡Dije que no . . . y eso es final!*"

"Obviously, it's a no," Lily said to me, tears of frustration welling up in her eyes.

"She's scared," I replied without thinking.

That earned a heated response in Spanish from Abi that I'm pretty sure disparaged my manhood and my intelligence.

I let Abi finish before I spoke directly to her. "What I mean is, if your fear is rooted as deeply as it seems to be, I don't want Lily to be involved, either."

She dropped back into her chair, crossed her arms, and said some more words in Spanish. Then she said, "I didn't peg you for honorable. Unless you're playing some kind of game."

"I'm not playing a game."

"Why doesn't any of this surprise you?" Lily asked. "I just told you about time travel, and people with special abilities, and rewinding time. You should be shocked, or at the very least doubtful."

Abi picked up her coffee mug and sat back in her chair. "There are many things in this world I don't understand. It doesn't mean they aren't true."

Fear. Guilt. The guilt confused me. I leaned forward in my chair, concentrating on trying to read Abi.

"What?" Lily asked, looking back and forth between the two of us.

Sharing Abi's emotions with her granddaughter wasn't my place.

"I just told her you can sense emotion. So she knows she can't hide anything." Lily had covered a lot of information in an hour. She turned from me to Abi. "If you knew something about all this, you'd tell me. Wouldn't you?"

More guilt.

"There's no reason to discuss it." Abi's voice was full of grim determination. "It's the past, and we left it behind when we left Cuba."

"We never discuss Cuba at all. There are things I want to remember. Our home. Our family."

"I do remember. And you are better off not knowing."

"I don't accept that." I saw Abi's fierceness in Lily's eyes and anticipated she'd make grown men piss their pants one day, too. "If you know something, you have to tell me. *¿Por favor?* Please."

Abi put her coffee cup down and walked to the wide, arched double windows that overlooked the town square of Ivy Springs. "People lose things, they look for them. Ask for help. 'Help me find my house key. Where is the grocery list?' It was always funny that your grandfather seemed to know where things were. He just . . . knew. Then your father was born, and he could find things, too. Your father was five when I discovered *el truco de magia*—that's what we called it—wasn't a magic trick."

"*¿Como?*" Lily asked, her face softening with understanding..

"I asked questions. Women didn't ask questions back then. I was silenced, and I never got any answers while your grandfather was alive. I didn't get them until about ten years ago. They came directly from your father, when he started doing survey work."

"I didn't know he did survey work," Lily said. I couldn't imagine not even knowing what my father did for a living.

"Cuba was a trade hub for over four centuries. Ships sank. Many riches were lost. Imagine what someone with a supernatural ability could find with the aid of satellite imagery. Your father saw things he should not have seen, but it was part of who he was. Who he is."

"What kind of things?" Lily frowned.

"The gift seemed to increase in strength with every generation." Abi returned to the table. She traced the rim of her cup. "One of the first things the realtor gave us when we moved in here was a town map with tiny little cartoon drawings of all the planned renovations. He tried to hand it to you, I guess because it was colorful and he thought you'd like it. I jerked it away, telling him I wanted to make it a keepsake, that you were too little and you'd tear it up. I always taught you to touch the maps in your schoolbooks with the eraser end of your pencil. Remember?"

"Yes," Lily answered, remembering. "And when I had to make a topographical map of Tennessee, you wouldn't let me."

"The only time I've ever done your homework." Abi stared into her coffee cup as if it held all the answers. "Your grandfather couldn't find things on maps, but your father could. I didn't know what you'd be able to find."

"I can find things on maps," Lily confessed. "And . . . people, too, I think."

"I suspected as much," Abi said, resigning herself to the truth. "Please understand, my love, I thought by keeping your ability dormant, I was keeping you safe."

"Safe from who?"

Dread settled in the bottom of my stomach.

"From the people your father worked for. They knew about your grandfather, too. It would only make sense that they'd look to you one day. We considered lying, saying that the gift had skipped a generation, but it was so strong in you. You couldn't control it, not at that age. So we left Cuba, and I swore I'd do everything I could to make you forget."

Lily leaned forward. "Papi looked for things on survey maps. On the ocean floor?"

"Knowing the history of a piece of treasure, its origin, and the path it's traveled can increase the worth by hundreds of thousands of dollars. Priceless to museums, collectors, historians, or anyone with money and interest."

"Lily's father can trace provenance?" I asked. "Can Lily?"

"I don't know." She was lying.

If Lily could trace ownership of artifacts, it would make the artifacts more valuable. It would make Lily more valuable.

"Did Lily's father"—I hesitated, meeting Abi's eyes—"did he have to know what the things he was searching for looked like?"

"How could he? They'd been on the bottom of the ocean floor for decades. . . ." She trailed off. "You didn't know that."

Lily's shock coursed through my body as if it were my own. "I thought I had to have seen a thing before I could find it."

"No, my love. No," Abi explained wearily. Defeated. "Not if you're searching on a map. Touching it."

"Abi, I have to help Kaleb find someone. So many bad things could happen if we don't."

"So many bad things could happen if you do. They think we died on a raft in the ocean. But what if they found out the truth? We've been safe for a long time in America, Lilliana, but that doesn't mean we haven't been found out." Abi held her fist up to her mouth and paused for a few seconds. "Any suggestion that you are alive and have a hint of your father's ability, and the people he works for will be here on our doorstep."

"Maybe things have changed." Lily didn't want to believe her.

"Do you think your father works for them because he wants to? The government forces him to work for them, or the highest bidder, and then he watches money go into the pockets of others." Abi's voice got louder and louder. "What do you think these men would do if they could double their intake? What makes you think you'd be treated well, alone on a boat with so many men?"

The thought made my skin crawl. I leaned closer to Lily, resting my arm on the back of her chair.

Abi stared at me for a moment before turning her attention back to her granddaughter. "It's not like it is here. It's not the same."

"I understand that, and I'm so grateful for all you've given up for me." Lily paused, trying to gain control of her emotions. She wasn't having a lot of luck. "But I need you to understand that what I'm asking to do could make the difference between life and death—"

"No." The force behind Abi's answer wasn't just strong, it was harsh. I could tell Lily wasn't used to being spoken to that way, the same way I could tell Abi wasn't used to Lily challenging her.

"Fine." Lily stood, crossed the kitchen, and took her bag and jacket from the peg by the front door. "I'll be home for dinner."

"You no longer ask permission?"

I hated the hurt I felt between them, wished I could erase it and make everything right.

"May I leave?" She didn't meet her grandmother's eyes. "With Kaleb?"

Abi looked at me. "You care for my granddaughter?"

"Yes, ma'am." *More than care.*

"Then you will not let her do anything that would put her at risk?"

"No, ma'am, I won't." I stood up. "I promise."

"Fine, then." Her eyes were dull. "I love you, Lily."

Lily didn't say a word as we walked out the front door.

Chapter 35

*W*e strolled.

I'd never really taken a leisurely trip around downtown Ivy Springs, and definitely not with a girl. Lily's spikes of emotion told me that she was processing all the things her grandmother had told her. I knew that when she was ready to talk, I'd be the one to listen. She trusted me.

That pleased me in ways I couldn't explain.

A pumpkin carving contest took up most of the town square. People were everywhere, spilling out from cafés and sitting on benches. I didn't want to be in a crowd and neither did Lily, so we ended up at Sugar High, a candy shop decorated like a high school hallway. Pep rally and prom ticket posters decorated the wall, there was even the occasional announcement over the loudspeaker. The locker doors were clear and showcased row after row of any candy imaginable. I was currently making my way through a half pound of Atomic Fireballs. Lily watched, drinking mint hot chocolate.

"She loves you," I finally said.

"Of course she does. She sacrificed her life, her family, her homeland, just to bring me here. To keep me safe."

I gathered up the empty wrappers on the table and leaned my chair back to drop them into the closest trash can. "There's not an ounce of regret in her, Tiger. She'd do it a hundred times over."

"I know that, too." She stared off into space, twisting the Styrofoam cup of hot chocolate around in her hands. I jumped when she slammed it down so hard on the table the contents sloshed over the sides. "But she's still forbidding me to use my ability. This whole thing *blows*."

A mom shot Lily a mean look and covered her son's ears before scuttling him to the other side of the store.

"Abi's not being reasonable," she said a few seconds later, wiping the spilled hot chocolate up and shoving the dirty napkin in her cup. "She knows how important it is to me, or I wouldn't have asked. She knows how much I care about Em, and I told her how I feel about you—"

"Me?"

"I . . . I mean, about how I felt . . . like finding Jack was the right thing to—"

"No." I grinned. I couldn't help it. "You told your grandmother how you feel about me. How do you feel about me?"

"We've already established that I don't like you." Her voice was haughty, but her heart wasn't in it. She sighed. "You're exactly the kind of boy my grandmother has always warned me to avoid."

"'Boy?'" I sat up straighter, sticking out my chest. "What kind of *man* would I be, exactly?"

"A temptation." She threw her cup at the trash can, sinking an impressive three pointer.

"Like the snake in the Garden of Eden?"

"No. More like the apple."

"The apple?" I asked.

"Yeah. I'm pretty sure Eve never considered taking a bite out of the snake."

When I realized my mouth was hanging wide open, I shut it. "Okay."

"Back on task." She banged her fist on the table, like a judge calling a courtroom to attention. "Why haven't you asked me to break Abi's rule?"

I tried to refocus. "Your level of respect for her, and how much she adores you. I think because of the life she gave up, you feel you owe her. You only owe her your well-being."

Lily stood up, dissecting the statement as we walked outside to continue our stroll. "How do I owe her for my well-being?"

"Parents, grandparents, whoever—they do what they can to keep us safe. Sometimes that involves secrets." My dad kept the Infinityglass from me because my mom had forbidden it. He'd left Memphis to protect us, as well as his interests. He served as a guardian to every person he'd researched. By letting Jack Landers get away with Dad's personal files, I'd failed to protect the very same people. "Abi thought she was doing the right thing by keeping the truth from you, she honestly did, and you know I know."

"You sound very mature."

I shrugged. "What she said about your dad and the people he works for made me realize how bad things could be if you went back to Cuba. She's not just scared that could happen, she's bone-deep terrified."

So was I.

"And you don't feel the same way about what could happen to you? To your dad?"

"We still have some time. We'll find another way." I didn't even want to think about putting Lily in danger. It twisted my stomach into knots. "So. I'm an apple, huh? The apple of your eye?"

"Kaleb." She stopped walking and her cheeks turned bright pink. "I'm uncomfortably aware that you know how I feel right now."

"I do?"

Hope. Anticipation. Uncertainty.

"Yeah, I do," I admitted. My heart sped up in my chest. "But I try not to rely on my . . . ability in situations where a misread could be fatal."

"Fatal?"

I was losing cool points so fast I was running into negative numbers. "What if I read you wrong?"

"Pretty sure that won't happen." Her expression was as direct as her words. "I was thinking about something last night right before I fell asleep. When people feel emotions, you feel them, too. So it's a . . . mutual experience kind of thing?"

Her perceptiveness was unnerving. Almost as unnerving as the fact that she thought about me while falling asleep. In her bed.

"Mutual. Yes. I mean . . . it . . . it's complicated."

Intrigue. "So how would you feel right now . . . if . . . we touched?"

"I guess it would depend on how you felt about me. There are a lot of triggers with touching. Intensity, circumstances." I lost track of what I was saying when she smoothed her hand across my chest and halfway down my stomach. Her touch made my toes want to curl all the way through the soles of my shoes, and not for purely physical reasons. "I don't . . . I'm not sure."

Smiling, she pulled her hand away and started walking again. No one had ever caught on to this part of my ability before. Except my mom. And that was a whole different thing. We shared happiness when we made cookies together.

Lily was *not* referencing cookies.

I realized she was ten feet away and I caught up.

"It would depend on how I felt," she said. "If I felt good, you would, too?"

"Yup."

"If I felt good physically, or emotionally?"

"Yup. Either. Both."

"Am I making you uncomfortable?"

"Yup." I didn't know why, exactly. It's not like I was shy. Or innocent.

"Knowing that things rebound back to you has to be addictive." When we reached Murphy's Law, she stopped at the stairs leading up to her apartment. "I'd be spending a lot of time making people feel good."

"The appeal of making a lot of people feel good isn't what it used to be. I think maybe I'd just like to focus on one."

"You sure about that?"

"Yup."

And it shocked the hell out of me.

A faint hint of a smile touched her lips.

"Are you going to be all right?" I asked. "Do you need me to go in with you?"

"No. Abi and I have a lot to talk about."

She stood up on her tiptoes to kiss my cheek.

I watched her until she stepped inside, and I knew she was safe.

Chapter 36

The next morning when I woke up I went straight to the pool house. I had to tell Michael that we'd lost our direct connection to Jack, and that using Lily was no longer an option.

I had Jack's watch in my jacket pocket. The morning air was crisp, and steam rose from the pool in a fog. Leaving the heater on and paying the service was such a waste. I didn't know if I'd ever swim in it again. I knocked lightly, but no one answered. Probably still in bed.

After debating whether or not I should wake Mike up, I decided it was too urgent to wait. I turned the knob, and then froze when I heard his voice.

". . . last time I saw you, you were pointing a gun at me. I have no reason at all to trust you." *So much rage.* Not a common feeling from Michael.

"He used me." *Nothing.*

"He's still using you, Cat, and you're letting him. He's traveling, and the continuum is getting worse."

Cat.

She'd been like a sister to me before she turned on my family and actively participated in my dad's death.

My rage blew Michael's out of the stratosphere. I slammed the door open so hard it bounced off the wall. "Why haven't you broken her neck yet? She's a waste. There's no way you're going to get the truth from her."

Cat's arrival must have surprised Michael. His hair was still wet from the shower and he didn't have on a shirt. He stood on one side of the couch and she stood on the other, next to the open sliding glass doors and the snack bar. Her mahogany skin looked ashen, her brown eyes dull. Her short hair had started to grow out, sticking up in awkward angles from her head. She hadn't been taking care of herself. Jack hadn't been taking care of her, either.

"I'm here to ask forgiveness," Cat said, her eyes widening as she looked up at me. An act, just like our entire relationship.

"Don't." I held up my hand. "Don't even open your mouth. If I didn't know Mike would stop me, I'd choke you to death with my bare hands right now."

"Go ahead," Michael said. "My superhero cape is at the cleaners."

"Just listen," she pleaded, holding up her hand, edging closer. "I have information. I can help you."

"Does he know you're here?" I asked. "Does he know you're about to sell him out?"

Sudden movement behind Cat caught my attention.

"I know everything."

Jack, looking pampered and perfectly healthy.

We locked eyes for two seconds before he lunged and grabbed Cat. I rushed him, with Michael right behind me. Propelling myself forward, I reached for Jack's shirtsleeve, my fingers just missing it as he kicked the stools from the snack bar into our path. I smashed into them, Michael ran into me, and we both went down.

By the time we were up, they were gone.

I growled in frustration and slammed my fist into the wall. "Damn it!"

Michael jerked the bar stools to an upright position. "He's not gone forever. Lily can track him through the pocket watch."

I pulled the pocket watch out and swung it by the chain in front of Michael's face. "No. She can't."

"If you have the pocket watch, how did Jack get in and out of here so fast? He needs duronium to travel." Michael sat down on the edge of the couch, his elbows on his knees and his head in his hands.

"I don't know."

"I'm sick of not knowing. What he's doing, what the future holds." He paused, on the verge of telling me something he was afraid to share.

I waited him out.

"She was with you." .

"What?"

"When I didn't make it back. When I died saving your dad. I traveled to the future to make sure she'd be okay. On that time line, before she broke the rules to come back and get me, Em was with you." The honesty cost him. "*With you* with you."

"She loves you." I sat down. "That would never happen."

"Even if I'm dead?" Michael's laugh didn't match the morbidity of the statement. "There's no way to know. Travel used to have rules, and now everything is completely out of control."

I listened. Which was exactly what he needed.

He started to pace. "The fact is that, even if time is rewound, you'll still exist, and Em will still exist. Maybe in a different state of being. She could be . . . sick. She could be the broken Em that was the sole survivor of a terrible bus accident. She could be medicated out of her mind."

"I wouldn't know her if that was the case," I argued. I didn't want to think of Em like that.

"She's in your father's files. Maybe you'll go find her." He lifted his hands. "Or maybe you'll take over for Liam, and you'll see someone like your mom, and you'll want to help her."

"What exactly did you see?"

He stopped and turned toward the window. He could hide his face, but not his emotions. Not from me.

"Michael?"

"You were holding her. On your lap, in your arms. You were on the front porch of your house, sitting in one of your mother's rocking chairs, and you were holding her." He sounded so resigned, like he was willing to surrender without a fight. "You keep showing up, loving her when she needs it most."

"I do love Em. But it hasn't progressed the way I thought it would at first." I searched my soul for the truth. "I don't want to take your place. I couldn't."

He faced me. "I hope we never have to find out if that's true."

"We both know the future is subjective. Just because you saw us together . . . doesn't mean it's going to happen," I said. "And so many things would change. Like Lily."

"She's different for you, isn't she? You look at her when she talks," Michael said, watching me. "Weigh what she has to say."

"Because what she has to say matters," I said. "She matters."

"Have you told her?"

"No." But I'd thought about it all night.

He smiled. It, along with his emotions, was bittersweet. "What are you waiting for?"

"I don't know. That's a lie. I'm scared. That she won't feel the same way. That she will." I stood up and took over Michael's pacing. "I mean, I've never done this."

"One question." He paused until I stopped and looked at him. "Is she worth it?"

I didn't hesistate. "Yes."

"Then tell her."

Chapter 37

I'd been standing downtown for an hour, trying to work up my nerve, watching mothers picking up or dropping off their daughters at the Ivy Springs School of Dance. There was an overabundance of pink, glitter, and hair twisted up in buns. The buns made me think of Lily.

But, then, everything did.

A white van pulled up in front of Murphy's Law across the street, and I watched as a guy in khaki pants took a dolly out of the back and huffed into his hands to warm them before he rolled it inside. A cold front was moving in, the first taste of winter. Storms always followed.

A minute later, the man came out with a full load of bakery boxes. They had the Murphy's Law logo on them, bright blue and white.

When he left, I'd go over there.

I would.

"Kaleb?" I looked away when a girl with really blue eyes and red hair stepped into my line of vision. She had a bun and tights, too. I tried to place her, but all I could remember was that her name started with an *A*. "I'm Ainsley. We met at Wild Bill's last summer."

I smiled, but inwardly I was cussing like a freak. I remembered her now. The night Michael had to come downtown to get me from the bar, right before I met Em. I'd had a little too much fun. How much, exactly, I didn't know. "How are you?"

"Wondering why you never called me." The blue eyes held a hint of disappointment.

Apparently, not calling was a trend with me.

"I thought we had a good time," she continued, and then gave me pouty lips that I think she meant to be sexy. They weren't.

"There's been a lot of . . . stuff happening." *My dad came back from the dead, an attempt was made on my life, I didn't remember you existed.* "Sorry about that."

"Well, it's lucky we ran into each other now." After digging around in her duffel bag, she fished out a permanent marker and grabbed my hand, pulling it toward her. She wrote her number on my palm, and then curled each of my fingers around it. "Don't lose it this time."

And then, right there in the middle of the sidewalk, she kissed me.

Just as Lily came out of Murphy's Law.

"Oh no." I pulled away from Ainsley.

Really? *Really?*

Ava stepped out of the dance studio, raising the lapels of her peacoat together to block out the wind. She had on tights and a scuffed-up pair of pink ballet shoes, and her auburn hair was pulled into a tight bun. I hadn't really talked to her since helping her move in.

"Hi, Ainsley. I didn't know you knew Kaleb." Ava's voice was sweeter than I'd ever heard it.

"I didn't know *you* knew Kaleb." Ainsley's voice was ice-cold.

Ava sensed something was up, either because I'd broken out in a sweat, or because Ainsley was looking at me like I was her lunch money and Ava was about to steal me.

"I do know Kaleb." Ava wrapped her arm around mine and winked up at me. "We go way back."

I looked from Ainsley to Ava, trying to figure out what the hell was going on.

Lily stood fifteen feet away, a bakery box in each hand, her head tilted to the side. And she was *pissed*.

"So is there something between you two?" Ainsley asked. "Do you date?"

I tried to make eye contact with Lily, give her some kind of sign that I wasn't an active participant in what was going on.

"I think 'something between us' accurately describes it," Ava answered.

Lily smiled briefly at the man as he took the bakery boxes and put them in his trunk.

"I guess that was a waste of Sharpie," Ainsley said, gesturing toward my hand before wrinkling up her nose. "I can't believe you're with Ava. She's like a walking skeleton."

"Aw, thanks," Ava answered. "We all have our strengths. At least I don't misplace my panties on a regular basis like some people do. Keeping them on helps with that, by the way."

Ainsley stalked into the studio on straight legs. I craned my neck, trying to catch another glimpse of Lily. She was gone.

"Kaleb Ballard. Please tell me you did not hook up with Ainsely." Ava's voice was full of disgust.

I had to explain things to Lily. A line extended all the way out the door of Murphy's Law, and her emotions had been pretty clear, even from across the street. I could wait until the crowd thinned out.

"Did you?" Ava demanded.

I realized that she was talking to me, and I looked away from Murphy's Law. "I don't think so. I might have been in the process at one point."

"That girl is crazy pants."

I laughed. "Crazy pants?"

"Yes." Ava waved the question away. "It's a thing. Anyway, I'd take a swim in some turpentine before that number soaks into your skin. It might turn into a brand."

"Thanks for coming to my rescue." I fought against sneaking

another glimpse at Murphy's Law, hoping Lily would reappear. "Wait. Why did you? You don't like me."

"You had a panicked look on your face."

"That should make you happy."

"It's true, not too long ago, I would've thrown you to the wolves. Maybe told her you couldn't stop talking about her, that you drew her name inside hearts on all your notebooks, had her picture in your locker."

"That's pretty harsh," I said. "And I don't have a locker."

"Wouldn't have mattered. My hate knew no limits. But," she said, removing her arm from around mine, "I've been thinking about what we talked about in the gatehouse. All the things that happened—that I did—last year."

"What did you come up with?" I asked.

"Jack." She stared at her feet. "I guess he figured out I'd be easier to use and abuse if I felt alienated from the rest of you."

"Separate you from the pack."

She nodded.

"Yeah. Predators always go for the weakest animal."

Ava was so broken on the inside. I wished I could dissect it all, help her figure out the truths and the lies.

"You know, I don't even really know what my ability is. I mean, it's telekinesis, but not the garden variety. I think Jack knows, and I think he took away anything I knew. He'll use it against me again. If he gets another chance."

A couple of raindrops splattered against the sidewalk. "We'll make sure he doesn't."

"It won't be easy. I was valuable to him. Valuable enough to seduce. I just don't know why, or when he'll come back for me."

"Ava, I'm so sorry."

"The worst part is . . . I don't even know if I . . . did anything. With him." She shuddered and closed her eyes. "But the fact that I thought about it is bad enough. He made sure to leave those memories intact."

I understood her blackness a little bit better now.

Ava opened her eyes. "Sorry. That's too much information, I know. I just don't really have anyone to talk to about that kind of stuff."

"If you don't feel too awkward, you can talk to me whenever you want." I frowned down at Ava in dismay, shocked I'd made the offer.

Her expression must have mirrored my own. "Let's take twenty-four hours to think about that. Then we'll reassess."

"Okay."

"Okay," she said. "But thank you. I need an ally. I feel like he's three steps ahead of us in some crazy game, and he already knows who's going to win."

"We will," I promised her. "We will."

"I hope you're right." She shook her head. "Because if you aren't, Hell's going to come down on us like rain."

Chapter 38

I went home.

A month ago, I would have taken off for downtown Nashville, found a bar, and drunk myself into oblivion. Now, instead of holding a beer, I had a measuring cup. And all the ingredients for peanut butter cookies. And chocolate chip.

I fumbled and lost them all when I saw what was on the kitchen island.

A box with the Crown Royal label sat in the exact, dead center. The beam from the pendant light above it shone on it like a spotlight. I dropped the cookie ingredients and picked up the box. Brand spanking new. When I ripped it open, I saw that the seal on the bottle was unbroken.

We had a stare-down, me and that bottle. It won, of course. Whisky doesn't blink.

I twisted off the top with a snap.

Smelled it.

Got down a glass from the cabinet.

There were so many things to run from.

Things Jack *wanted* me to run from.

I realized then who had left the bottle.

I thought of my dad, and all the things he'd finally trusted me with. Michael, and the understanding we'd come to.

And then I heard Lily's voice. *"You're worth more than what you'll find at the bottom of a bottle."*

I put the glass back in the cabinet and upended the liquor into the sink.

"I question your sanity sometimes, Ballard, but I know you aren't an idiot."

"Thank you for the compliment, Shorty."

I was on the couch in my living room, balancing a full plate of cookies on my chest. Emerson stood over me like some kind of military general, wearing her Murphy's Law work clothes.

"You kissed a random girl on a street corner? In the middle of the afternoon?"

"It wasn't what it looked like."

"I've heard that before, maybe I've even said that before, and only because in that case, it actually *wasn't* what it looked like. I'll listen." She picked up my legs by the bottom of my basketball pants, dropped onto the couch, and then lowered my feet to her lap. "What did you do?"

I didn't even bother trying to argue that it wasn't my fault.

"This girl comes up to me out of nowhere, writes her number on my hand, and then lays one on me. Yes, on a street corner, and yes, in the middle of the afternoon."

"And now we're going to discuss why this is a problem."

"Because it happened at the exact same time Lily walked out of Murphy's Law."

"And you care about this because?"

"You're leading the witness."

She crossed her arms.

I sighed. "I care because I like her."

"In *that* way?" She sounded like we were in third grade, hiding under the slide on the playground at recess.

"Good grief, Em, yes, in *that* way."

Her smile almost extended past her ears as she reached out to snag a chocolate chip cookie. "So who was the girl?"

"The one I was with the night before I met you. The night Michael came to rescue me. I didn't even remember her name."

"Not knowing her name does *not* make it better. Why didn't you go talk to Lily right that second? It's afternoon already. Why haven't you tried to talk to her today?" she demanded. "Why are you ignoring her?"

"I'm not ignoring her. Ow!" She grabbed a few leg hairs and pulled, and I was quickly reminded that tiny and irritable didn't make the best combination.

Especially when you poked it with a stick.

"I didn't. I avoided her because I didn't know what to say. Did she tell you anything?"

Leaning over conspiratorially, she whispered, "You want to know what she said about you?"

"*Emerson.*"

She sat up. "Fine. She said that the two of you had a weird conversation about feelings, and she told you she wanted to bite you?" At this, she raised her eyebrows. I nodded. "Oof. No wonder seeing you with that girl on the street hurt her."

"It hurt her?"

"Why do you think she was so mad?" She asked the question like I was an idiot. Which, apparently, I was.

"I don't really understand how this stuff works."

"I love you both. You know that," Em said.

I nodded, and a little bit of the fire in her voice died down.

"If I've learned something from all this crap with Jack," she continued, "it's that living anywhere other than in the moment is a mistake. Like Michael always says, the future is subjective. The past could be a lie—not just my past—but all of our pasts. Even Lily's."

"You still don't think Lily's being here is a coincidence."

"No. Because every time I think I've dealt with Jack and all the ways he's screwed with me, I prove myself wrong." She shook her head. "Do you have any idea how much it kills me that so many of the good things in my life are there because of him?"

"I'm so sorry I didn't stop him when I had the chance," I said. "I'm sorry I didn't take my dad's files before he stole them, before he could find you."

"Where would I be now if you had?"

I sat up and put the plate of cookies on the table, frowning at her.

"If you'd taken the files before he could get to them, Jack wouldn't have known about me and my ability to travel to the past. I'd still be a crazy lump in a bed. Lily could be living somewhere else. Your dad would be dead." She gave me a grim smile. "You could chase the circles of consequence for days. If this had happened, then this wouldn't have. Vice versa. It's mind-boggling."

"There are a hundred different scenarios."

"Exactly, and it proves my point. The present. Right now." Her eyes were more serious than I'd ever seen them. "The exact spot where the hourglass filters the sand from the future to the past. That's where we have to live, Kaleb. Before all the sand runs out, or before somebody shakes it all up again."

"I am so glad I have you in my life, for whatever reason." My vision was suddenly blurry, so I paused and blinked a few times. "So, Lily. I have your blessing?"

"Treat her right, or I'll kill you." She held up a tiny, yet mighty, fist. "I can see how you feel about her. I know how she feels about you. And I guess I wonder . . . how many times have we had this conversation? What if last time you didn't listen to me and you regretted it, or I told you not to go after her at all? Wouldn't you want to do things differently now?"

I ruffled her hair. "Is this what goes on up there in that head of yours?"

"All the time." *The answer was solemn. Melancholy.*

"So I should go clear all of this up and tell her how I really feel."

Her answering smile was genuine. "Absolutely. But maybe clean up first. You have cookie crumbs on your chin."

Chapter 39

The wind slammed the door to Murphy's Law open so hard the glass in the windows rattled.

The shop was almost empty except for two girls behind the counter. One almost dropped a tray of mugs when she saw me. The other, who I recognized as Sophie, spoke as if her lips were numb. "Can I help you?"

"I need Lily." It had taken me well past dinner to get the nerve up to talk to her. Now that I was here, I didn't want to waste time.

"She's roasting beans. In the back. Do you want me to—"

Instead of answering, I blew past her and pushed my way through the swinging door. The air smelled like heaven. Em would get a contact high.

"Lily?"

She stuck her head out from behind the edge of a huge metal roaster. One hand was wrapped around a steaming mug of mint tea, and the other held an open book clutched to her chest. As she stepped around the side of the roaster, her index finger slipped into the book to mark her place.

I wanted to *tackle* her.

"Kaleb." A buzzer went off. She put the tea and book down before flipping a switch on the machine. "Why are you here?"

"I need to talk to you. Please."

She sighed.

"I'm not going to go away until you talk to me." I put my hands flat on the counter and met her eyes. "And I'll follow you if you leave."

Walking to the swinging door and opening it, she leaned out into the coffee shop proper. "Hey, Katie—you and Sophie shut down and then head home early. No sane person is going to come out for coffee once this rain moves in, anyway. Just put the sign in the window. I'll lock up."

The girls on the other side of the door said something I couldn't hear, and Lily laughed. "He's fine. Thanks for the concern."

She came back in the kitchen with a strange expression on her face.

"What?" I asked.

"They were worried. I guess you made quite an impression on the way in."

"I was kind of in a hurry. I really wanted to talk to you."

"You're also as big as a house, tattooed, and pierced. And wearing a black leather jacket."

"Oh yeah." I'm a bad ass. A bad ass who bakes when he's depressed.

"How can I help you, Kaleb?" she asked, the venom finally leaking through the smile.

Two pairs of eyes peered through the circular window that led into the kitchen. "Can we go somewhere more private?"

She hesitated, and then pulled off her glasses, rubbing her face in frustration. "Fine. But make it fast. I don't want my tea to get cold."

I followed her out of the impeccable kitchen through a heavy-duty steel door into an alley. Even the trash was organized, the recycling sorted and stored in neat bins.

"What?" She slumped back against the brick wall of the building, putting one foot against the wall and twisting her apron strings around her fingers.

"I think you misunderstood what you saw yesterday." The wind picked up, and leaves from the red maples that lined Main skittered down the alley.

"What, you mean you and Ainsley Paran?"

"I didn't even know her last name."

"That does not make it better." Em had said the same thing. Lily dropped the apron strings and gestured with her hands. "And, anyway, she acted like she knew yours. And possibly the length of your inseam."

"We met one night, last summer. Downtown. We danced. I might have kissed her once or twice. That's it. And that was not . . . a good time in my life. And as far as the other girl, her name is Ava, and we mostly really dislike each other, but for some reason she rescued me—"

"I know Ava."

I saw a flash of lightning and heard thunder in the distance. "You do?"

"Yeah. I met her when I met Dune."

I wanted to ask exactly when she'd met Dune, and why they were so flirty with each other, but all of that fell strictly into the category of None of Kaleb's Business, especially under the current circumstances. So instead, I just said, "Oh."

"I still don't know why you're here." She looked up at the sky, pushed off the wall with her foot, and headed toward the steel door. "You don't owe me an explanation."

I stepped in front of her. "But I want to give you one."

"Why?"

I put my hands on her shoulders to stop her from going inside. "Because you matter."

"Kaleb . . ."

"That's what I was coming to tell you yesterday when that girl hijacked me on the street corner. You matter. No one's ever mattered before, but you do, and I wanted you to know. So now you know."

She opened her mouth to speak, but before she could get

anything out, the skies opened up. "I let the back door lock behind me and I forgot my keys." Lily had to yell over the pounding rain. "We need to go around to the front."

Lightning flashed again, followed by a huge clap of thunder. This time it was much closer.

"No, come here. The storm's on top of us." I led her to my dad's truck, parallel parked at the front of the alley, and helped her in before hurrying around to the driver's side.

Rain hammered against the roof, but at least we were under cover. Her teeth were chattering.

"Are you cold?" I asked.

"F-f-f-freezing."

"Maybe you should get closer to me. Body heat. It's important in a crisis situation such as this." She cut her eyes at me and I cranked the engine. Flipping on the heater, I pointed all the vents at her. "But manufactured heat will work, too, I guess."

She sat cross-legged in the middle of the bench seat with her back to the dash. The air stirred the tendrils of hair that had escaped from her bun.

"I think my dad has a blanket in here somewhere." When I felt her eyes on me, I stopped shuffling and sat up. "Why are you staring at me like that?"

"You're always taking care of people. You . . . I don't know . . . observe, and then you give others what they need, by instinct." Her right knee barely touched my right hip, but it made my skin tingle. "It's not just an empathy thing. Physical actions go with it."

I shrugged. "If someone needs something and I can give it to them, why wouldn't I help?"

"You . . . are so confusing." She laughed. "And I'm so tired."

"Of what?"

"Of being interrupted, waiting for the right time, trying to figure all this out." She leaned forward and slid her hands into my hair, resting her cheek against mine. "Not getting what I really want."

Inhale, exhale. Inhale, exhale.

"What do you really want?"

She placed a gentle kiss on the corner of my eyelid. If I'd closed my eyes, my lashes would have brushed against her lips. Then she leaned over to kiss my left cheek, pressing her body close to mine.

The breathing thing was getting more difficult.

"Lily. You're messing with me."

"No. Not yet." She moved her mouth to my right jaw, then the left side of my neck, then back up to my chin.

As much as I was enjoying the buildup, I was certain that if there was going to be a payoff, it would outweigh it. But whatever happened next needed to be her decision.

"What do you want?" I repeated.

She hesitated for two seconds before I saw the power in her eyes, felt it coming off her in waves. "You."

Exactly what I was waiting for.

We met halfway. Lips and teeth and the taste of her tongue, the heat of her skin against mine, unexpected through our rain-soaked clothes. Touching her was way more addictive than any substance I'd ever tried.

I wanted to unzip my skin and pull her inside.

Lily twisted her hands in the sleeves of my jacket and pushed back. Her eyes were wide, her voice unsteady. "This is more intense than I thought it would be. And I was banking on intense."

I unpinned her hair and trailed my fingers over her collarbones, into the hollow of her throat. "How is intense working for you?"

She shuddered and grabbed my wrists. "More, please."

I kissed her slowly, taking my time. My hands were on her neck, and I could feel her pulse beating in her throat. I moved my mouth across her jawline and felt it speed up.

"Wait," she gasped.

I stopped, my mouth just below her ear. "I thought you wanted more."

"I do. There's just a steering wheel digging into my back."

"Not enough real estate in here to kiss you." I scooted over and wrapped my arms around her, cradling her, holding her as tightly as I could. "That's a damn shame."

"We could just go up." She leaned back and pointed to her apartment.

I tried not to get too caught up in what arching her back did to her front.

"Although it might be too much real estate. Especially since Abi isn't home."

Lily. Me. Alone. Arching. I groaned.

"What was that for?" she asked.

"The way you feel, and taste, and empty real estate . . . sounds really tempting."

"Yes. I'd like to take you upstairs and kiss you cross-eyed."

"I'd like to be taken upstairs." And do a whole lot more than kiss.

She read between the lines like a champ. "Then any real estate that involves an empty bedroom and a serious lack of supervision probably isn't the wisest choice right now."

"You don't make me feel like being wise." I touched my lips to hers again, pulled her body even closer to mine. "I want to be with you."

"Kaleb."

"Not because of this." I gestured to her in my arms. "Because of you."

A smile teased across her lips. "I have to go close up shop."

"How long will it take you?" I asked. "I'll wait."

She raised one eyebrow.

"Just to make sure you get home okay." I raised my hands innocently. "Swear."

"It's okay. I could be a while." She bent down to the floorboard to retrieve her apron and slipped it over her head. "I should really do a round of baking prep before I leave."

"I'm staying. I don't want you here alone." I didn't want to give Jack any openings to do more damage.

"I do this all the time."

"Now you don't have to. Please. You know I'm excellent in the kitchen."

"You're probably excellent everywhere."

"I look forward to testing that theory." I grinned and leaned over to kiss her again.

"Stop," she protested, but she was teasing. "I will resist your charms. For now. But if you want to help me bake, come on."

"Wait." When my phone rang, I grabbed her apron strings, not ready to let her go yet. It was Dune.

"Yeah?" I held up one finger when she giggled.

"Get over here. I managed to access the Skroll."

The call disconnected. "I'll help you close up shop, but no baking today. We have somewhere to be."

Chapter 40

I went inside Murphy's Law with Lily to do the basics, like double checking that all the machines were off and the doors were locked.

"Okay. We can go. We're all good." She hung up her apron. Before she could say another word, I slid my hand behind her head, pulling her in close for a kiss.

"Yes, we are," I said, not letting her go.

"Do it again," she murmured against my lips.

I did.

I helped her into the truck, backed out, and drove down Main Street, holding her hand. Pumpkins lined the sidewalk, fresh from the carving contest. They'd be illuminated through Halloween. After trick-or-treating, they'd be thrown into a fire for the Pumpkin Smash, a combination dance/bonfire/pumpkin demolition party that happened downtown.

Maybe everything would be resolved by then. It had to be.

I pulled into my driveway and parked close to the pool house. When I walked around to help Lily down from the truck, I took her hand again. "Is it okay if I hang on to this?"

"I'd prefer it."

I held her hand all the way inside, and didn't let go when everyone looked up from the table. Em and Michael smiled at us. Dune seemed disappointed.

"How did you manage it?" I asked, determined to concentrate on the task at hand, and not think about how smooth Lily's skin was. "Did you just keep trying?"

"Do or do not, there is no try," Dune said, looking wise.

Nate entered the living room, so quickly I couldn't tell from which direction. "Seriously, you're like . . . the antithesis of Yoda."

"Oh, look at you, using the big words." Dune clapped his hands like a proud parent.

"Okay, y'all," Em said. "Sheathe your light sabers and let's get down to business."

Nate's eyes grew as big as saucers. "I'm not going to make a 'that's what she said' joke. I'm just telling you. I am not."

I bit my tongue so I wouldn't laugh. I didn't want to give Lily any reason to let go of my hand.

Dune gave a saintly sigh and motioned for all of us to gather around the coffee table. "Okay. There's a USB, so I knew it most likely needed a charge, but I went through six cords before I figured out the right sequence to use to keep it from blowing a fuse."

He grinned at Michael. "You and Em aren't the only ones who are electric around here."

"It's not electricity," Em argued. "Or chemistry. It's physics."

"Anyway," Dune continued, "I knew there was more data on it than I could see. I used the biggest external drive I could buy in town, 3TB, and I still couldn't get it to transfer or open. So I ordered this handy-dandy one from the Internet." He tapped the top of a shiny black box. "I still only got enough to break the encryption."

"The what?" Em had to stand on her tiptoes to try to see over everyone else's shoulders. Finally, she just punched Nate in the arm until he moved.

"The encryption. It makes data unreadable to anyone who doesn't have a key or password. Skrolls are super futuristic and still in development for the masses." He touched a button, and the screen lit up. He flipped it around so we could see it and pulled a stylus out of his pocket. "Everyone sit so you can all see, and so Em will stop punching."

Once we did, he pushed a release button on the side of the Skroll and a flat, flexible screen slid out. It looked like it was made of silicon. Images popped up all over it, and then, with the touch of another button, the backlit screen became a holographic projector. Images, documents, diaries, maps—from the most simplistic to the most advanced—spun around in the air with one touch.

"Sweet," Nate said under his breath.

"How does it work exactly?" Em asked.

"I shall demonstrate. But I need to come clean about something first." Dune put down the stylus. "I've known about the Infinityglass for a long time. It's sort of an obsession. So is Chronos."

"What?" Dune was firmly locked in logic and facts. His ability to control the tides meant he couldn't use it without serious consequences. Like tsunamis. Something as impossible as a mythical, all-controlling hourglass didn't seem like his thing. "How did you find out about them?"

"My dad told me stories when I was younger. And then, as I got older, I did lots of research. The Infinityglass is part of the reason I'm so good at it." He grinned. "What I've learned recently is that Chronos claims that they're widely varied in their pursuits, but the Hourglass isn't the only group focusing on time-related abilities. Chronos has been connected to every important horological discovery in the last one hundred years, at least. Have you ever heard of horology?"

Nate giggled.

"I'm sorry. It sounds dirty. I'm not going to say anything else today. Swear." Nate locked his lips with an imaginary key and then threw it over his shoulder.

Dune shook his head and moved on. "Horology is the science of time and the study of timekeeping devices, from the water clock to the hourglass to the pendulum and beyond. You could call the Infinityglass the ultimate timepiece in the field of horology. Some think it's mythical, others believe it's real. And that's what's on the Skroll. Information about the Infinityglass."

"What is it?" Em asked. "What's it supposed to do?"

"The Infinityglass was initially created for a pure purpose," Dune said. "It was supposed to channel time-related abilities from person to person, but instead, whoever had possession of the Infinityglass could use it to steal the time-related ability of anyone he or she touched."

Helpless. Hopeless. Em's emotions slammed into my chest.

"The Infinityglass is the other alternative." Emerson's defeat had worked its way into her voice. "Jack trying to travel on his own didn't work out, I didn't work out, so now he's looking for the Infinityglass. It puts all of us in danger."

"Not if he can't find it," Dune said, an unmistakable look of determination on his face. "Reports of the Infinityglass dropped off around the early 1900s. It resurfaced briefly in the 1940s, and then again in the 1980s. Both times, it was rumored to be somewhere in Egypt, but then it was lost again."

"*Egypt?*" Lily and I said at the same time.

"There were rumors of it associated with a pyrami . . . oh hell." Dune dropped his head.

"Well, at least half of it makes sense now," Em said. "The headquarters of a mythical time mafia would totally be located in an abandoned pyramid in downtown Memphis."

"That only explains the 1980s, though. Not the 1940s," Dune said. I could almost hear him computing the information inside his head.

"Why would Teague lay down the ultimatum for us to find Jack if she didn't think she was close to finding him or the

Infinityglass?" I asked. "And if Jack was close to finding it, why would he risk so much just to show up to taunt us?"

"Who knows what Jack's thinking," Em said.

"There's so much information about the Infinityglass on the Skroll that you can't access it all." Nate stood up and disappeared into the kitchen, grabbing a drink from the fridge. "Who put it there?"

"I'm not sure." Dune picked up the stylus and clicked a tiny button to turn it into a laser pointer. He used it to highlight documents as he explained. "It holds years' worth of information, and it's all about the history—the very ancient history—of not only the Infinityglass but also Chronos. I've skimmed it, and I haven't processed a quarter of it."

"The history of Chronos?" Em questioned.

"Wait," Michael said. "The Skroll has information about the Infinityglass and Chronos. It doesn't belong to Chronos, or Teague should've been able to open it. So who does it belong to?"

"There's another answer," Dune said. "But I don't like it."

Em looked at Michael, and then me. "Jack."

I stood. "It's time to tell my dad about the Skroll."

Chapter 41

I'd been keeping so much from Dad. Jack's appearances, Lily's ability, the Skroll. I was going to be in a world of hurt when I spilled my secrets.

Since I was pretty sure Dad was going to kill me, Em offered to take Lily home. I left her at the pool house.

After a few good-bye kisses, of course.

He wasn't upstairs or in his office. I finally spotted him in the sunroom, his back to the glass doors. When I opened them, he jumped and clamped his fingers down on the edge of the blanket he'd wrapped around himself.

Something was way off.

Not just the stoop of his shoulders, or the way he sat still, especially without a book in his hands. Since my dad had come back home, one thing had been constant. His ache for my mother.

It was gone.

I wanted to run. Instead, I stepped around the front of the couch.

"Dad?" I asked cautiously. "What are you doing out here?"

He remained still, his expression blank. I focused on his face. Saw that he wasn't in there. What was left sat on the couch in front of me, fingertips picking at the threads of the blanket. I could barely breathe, barely move. I dropped to my heels and put my hands on top of his.

A seeping black hole of nothing. It was what Em must have been like after Jack Landers took her memories and left her to recover in a mental hospital—what my mom would be if I could break through the wall that separated us. So empty and so, so dark.

Jack had robbed my father, and he hadn't put anything in place of what he'd taken.

I fought to keep my voice steady. "Dad?"

He blinked a few times. "Kaleb?"

He knew me. A tiny spark of hope flashed under the surface. "Yeah, Dad, it's me. What happened?"

"You're so . . . big. I don't know how you got to be . . . you're a man, not a child." His voice was frail, more like an eighty-year-old man's than my father's. How would I take care of him? How could I fix this?

"It's okay, Dad," I lied. "It'll all be okay."

"Nothing looks like it's supposed to. I know this house, but not why I'm in it. It's like my world stopped, but the rest of you went on . . . your mother. She's upstairs in a room . . . there are machines. She won't wake up."

I swallowed the tears that burned in my throat. "What's the last thing you remember, Dad? About me?"

"Middle school, your first day. It didn't go well. I talked to Cat about starting an Hourglass school—even if there were just a few students and private tutors at first. For you. For kids who'd struggled the way we did."

The first day of middle school had ripped me wide open. It had started the second I stepped on the school bus in the morning until I got off it again in the afternoon. It had been so important to me to attend school with my friends. The earlier grades had been easy— my mom was kind to my teachers and they gave me a little extra room when I got too emotional. They were always so impressed with how much sympathy I had when someone's feelings were hurt, but less so when I latched on to someone's anger or fear.

The middle school had twice as many students as the elementary school, and way more hormones. I'd done all I could on that first day, determined to make it work, but the second I'd seen my house come into view, my mom waiting anxiously at the end of the driveway, I'd lost it.

I'd managed to hold off the worst of the crying until the bus had pulled away. She held me there until I stopped.

She applied for homeschool status the next morning.

A month later, we'd all moved to Ivy Springs, and the Hourglass had been born.

"Five years, Michael. He's lost five years." I stared out the window into the cold, gray morning.

Usually by this point in the fall, my mom had cut back the monkey grass lining her flower beds, pruned her rosebushes just so, and mulched every plant in sight to help them survive the winter. All I saw this year were frostbitten petals and wilted leaves.

I'd called Michael for help, and he'd dispersed the crowd and come up to the main house by himself. We'd spent all night trying to help Dad remember anything, but we'd only upset him. Finally, he'd yelled, told us both to go away. Locked himself in the bedroom with Mom.

I'd sat outside their closed door, listening to him cry himself to sleep, my knees pulled up to my chest like I was a little kid. I'd wanted to call Lily, just to hear her voice. But I couldn't. What would I tell her? What would I tell everyone else?

"We'll make it better," Michael said, breaking into my thoughts. "We'll fix—"

"Don't tell me we'll fix this. I don't know how we can. I can't make Jack give them their memories back." If Jack had wanted to break me, he'd succeeded. I had no family left. I was alone. I fought against the desolation that threatened to overwhelm me. "Even if we do manage to find Jack before Chronos does, we'll have to turn him over. Mom's and Dad's memories go with him."

"We'll find the Infinityglass before Jack does, use them both as leverage," Michael argued. "We'll hold him, make Chronos leave him with us if we hand the Infinityglass over, and we'll find a way to force him to restore your parents' memories."

"We might as well accept the truth." I spun around to face him. "Jack's beaten us. He's won."

"You still have options."

My lips stretched over my teeth in a grim smile. "I can't ask Lily. There are reasons."

It would put her in the direct path of danger. Abi had said people were watching. I believed her.

I didn't want to lose anyone else.

"I don't think you have a choice." Michael started to lower himself into my dad's empty office chair, but he stopped and stared at it. Not willing to take Dad's place. "Lily's going to have to be involved, whether it means she looks for Jack or for something else."

"What else?"

"Lily could look for the Infinityglass." Michael walked around the desk and sat down in the armchair. "You need to talk to her, Kaleb. Tell her what's going on with your dad. That things have changed. If she finds the Infinityglass . . . Poe said it could help set the continuum right without any consequences. Maybe it can fix all of this."

I was so sick of false hope and almosts. So tired of Jack screwing with my life.

"I'm supposed to pin my hope on something that could be

fictional?" I grabbed one of the hourglasses from Dad's shelf and slammed it to the floor. "Something made of sand and glass?"

"Kaleb."

"No. I want my parents back. I can't make it happen. An object can't make it happen." I swept my arm across the shelf, knocking every hourglass over, breaking two more. "All of these represent a failed attempt. All the hourglasses in Teague's office represent a failed attempt. What makes you think we'll find the Infinityglass when all these people haven't?"

"Faith. Stupidity. I don't know." Michael folded his hands over his chest and considered me. I felt his concern and love, and for the first time in a long time, it was welcome. "But there's so much to lose. I'm on your side, brother. I'm here for you. It's just the two of us now."

"Not just the two of you," Em said, from the door of the office. "We can do this, Kaleb. We can do it together, I know it. But I agree with Michael. You're going to have to talk to Lily. She's on your side, too."

Chapter 42

Lily's grandmother was in North Carolina, meeting with an organic coffee supplier. Unhappy about leaving Lily alone, she'd insisted that Lily lock the doors and stay inside.

"I don't think she understands that locks don't keep someone like Jack out." Still, she secured all three and leaned back against the door. Then she reached out to hook a finger into the collar of my shirt. "Why are you all the way over there?"

I let myself sink into her warmth and the taste of her lips. Her kiss told me I didn't have to explain anything. That she already knew the question, and she had the answer.

"Let me help," she whispered, with her mouth still on mine.

I pulled back slightly. "I can't."

"I told you once that you aren't like Jack." *Frustration.* "I was right, but I was also wrong."

Now I stepped back a full foot. "How were you wrong?"

"Let me explain why I was right first." Taking my hand, she led me to the couch. "You don't take advantage of people and use what they have to benefit yourself."

"You say that knowing I need your help to find Jack. Putting you in danger, going against your grandmother's rules. That's taking advantage."

"Not to benefit you," she said, disagreeing. "To benefit people that you love. I know that's your desire, and that's the thing that comes first. You don't have to ask me, Kaleb. I'll do whatever it takes to help you."

"But your grandmother, and the men and the fact that they could be watching—"

"Focus," she said. "I have a point to make."

I kissed her on the forehead, breathing in the citrus scent of her hair. "I'm focusing."

"On what I'm saying." She pushed back and took my hands in hers. "As for how you were wrong . . . I think, in trying so hard to be different from him, you missed some really important similarities. In doing that, you've missed some answers."

"Explain."

"I've been thinking about this since the night we talked in Memphis. Jack takes memories hostage. You take terrible emotions and keep them away from the people they hurt. How tied are emotions and memories?"

I stared at her.

"You can't separate the two. Jack keeps telling you killing him would be a mistake, that the two of you are alike. He's telling you the truth. If you kill Jack, you kill your mother's memories with him, and now your father's. If he goes, so do they."

"Are you saying he's the key to restoring my parents?"

"No. I'm saying you are."

"How?"

"The memories Jack took were the ones that were most important to your mother." Lily spoke slowly. "Her love for your father and you, all the personal moments that tied you together. If those memories aren't tied in emotion, I don't know what is."

"Finding their memories, their emotions, inside him? Taking them back, and then transferring them over?" I shook my head. "It's impossible. I wouldn't even know where to begin."

"That's why you're going to practice on me."

I followed her to her bedroom. It was on the small side, with clean white walls and photographs everywhere. Built-in bookshelves lined one wall, crammed full of every kind of book and organized by color. It looked like a perfect rainbow. She sat down on the edge of her double bed, leaned back on the red duvet cover, and held out her foot. I stared at it, and then looked at her.

"Knee boots?" She grinned. "Can you help me out?"

"Oh yeah." I pulled the right boot off while I was facing her, but for the left, I turned around to give her a view of my backside.

"Are you kidding me?" she asked, laughing.

"I enjoy yours all the time. I just figured I'd give you a chance to enjoy mine." I gave a little wiggle before I faced her again. "What's with the socks?"

They were lime green with pink stripes.

"I think what a girl wears under her clothes is just as important as the clothes themselves. And I like a little spice underneath." She looked directly at me as she peeled off the socks in a striptease fashion, swung them around in a circle, and threw them over her shoulder. One landed on the bookcase, the other in a corner.

"You're trying to kill me. No, correction, you are *going* to kill me. And how can you make me laugh like this in the middle of all hell breaking loose?"

"It's a gift." Lily scooted to the middle of the bed and sat cross-legged. "I'm ready when you are."

"I told Abi I wouldn't let you put yourself at risk, and I meant it. Don't act like what your grandmother wants doesn't matter when it does." Still, I sat down across from her.

"Looking for memories isn't a risk. It's my memory," Lily argued. "If we can do this, you can figure out exactly what to look for with your parents. It should be even easier with them, because the three of you shared most of those emotions and memories."

I sighed, and then put my hands on her hips and slid her toward me. The movement threw her off balance. She gasped and grabbed my forearms to keep from toppling over. I stared down at her fingers on my skin for a second before meeting her eyes, and then leaned forward to touch my lips to hers.

Our combined heat gathered in my chest and radiated out through my skin. She put her arms around my neck and pulled me closer.

"This isn't why we came in here," I whispered.

"I know," she whispered back. "But it's a nice side benefit."

"Are you procrastinating? Changing your mind about letting me inside your soul?"

"No."

"It's intense for me when I take emotion. I know it's not going to be easy on you to give it." I frowned. "And it's going to be even more intense this time, because I'll be concentrating on the memories that go with the emotion, too. What if I do something wrong? What if I hurt you?"

"You won't." She touched my cheek. "I'm not afraid of anything when I'm with you."

This time, I put my hands on her knees instead of her hips.

"Before you do anything, I think the memory you look for needs to be significant."

"You've thought about this."

She nodded.

"What do you want me to take?"

"The day I left Cuba."

"Lily. No. What if I can't give that back to you? And do you really want to relive it, twice more? Because if I take it and give it back, I'm pretty sure you will."

"I *want* to relive it." She bit her lip. "I've pushed the memory away for so long. But I think I could do with some remembering. What do I need to do?"

"I guess . . . focus on that day, the way you felt, anything you can remember about it. I know you were young, but even one specific detail would be good, what you were wearing, the weather, something like that."

She took a deep breath. "It was sunny, after about a solid week of rain. My mom was always super protective of me, but this day . . . I was so happy to be outside, free. She was hanging clothes on the line. I stretched out on the grass for a minute, just to feel it against the backs of my legs. Everything after that gets kind of . . ."

"That's enough." I could see the day on her emotional time line. It was a big one. "Promise me you're sure."

"Yes."

I leaned forward, took her face in my hands, and looked into her eyes.

Emotion flooded through my system almost the second I touched her. Visuals I didn't understand made her feel trapped, and then there was pain. Happiness and a swing set. White clouds and flapping sheets. *Worry, anxiety.* Shiny black car, feet, the ground. *So much fear.*

Hope. Hope and a red crayon, a lined piece of paper. Crude drawings and . . . *pain.*

A doll with black yarn for hair.

Then everything clicked into sharp focus, but it all moved in slow motion.

Brake lights.

A woman who looked like Lily, but rounder, with brown eyes instead of hazel. Whispers. *Love, forgiveness.*

Words. I knew they were said in Spanish.

The pain of the memory was jagged around the edges, grief like broken glass, and I was dragging Lily through it, slicing open fresh wounds. I heard her sobbing, felt her cries in my chest, in my bones.

The sharp focus faded and everything began to move quickly again.

Then there was only emptiness.

I knew I was falling backward, but I couldn't stop myself.

Blackness.

Silence.

Chapter 43

"*P*lease, please wake up." Lily was shaking me. I wanted to open my eyes. I tried, but all I got was a flutter. Her fear was fresh, and it was already too much for me to manage.

"I'll be right back," she said, scooting to the edge of the bed. "I'm going to get help."

"No. Stay." I tried to wrap my arms around her, but I couldn't lift them any higher than half an inch.

"Kaleb?" She threw her body across mine and curled around me like a cat. "One second, you were fine, the next, you went pale and fell back on the headboard. You have a huge knot on the back of your head. I should call someone."

"No." The pain in my body was way worse than my head, and different from any I'd ever experienced. My joints ached, and I thought I could feel my blood moving through my body. Too slow. "Just . . . stay."

"What's wrong?"

"Intense. It'll pass." My voice was ragged, like it had been run through a thresher.

I hoped it would pass.

"What do you want me to do?"

"Calm down. You're freaking me out." Her emotions were everywhere, and they were making the pain worse. "I think I got a triple whammy. Your emotions, my reaction to them. Your fear now. You don't need to be afraid; I'm fine."

I opened my eyes. The afternoon daylight was gone, and her room was almost dark. "You're not calming down."

Panic. Loss. Emptiness.

She took my hands in hers. They were freezing. "I can't remember. I know what you took, but I remember even less now. I just know it came out of my mind going backward. It was hard to make sense of it all."

I cursed. I hadn't prepared her for the blackness. I struggled to sit but could only manage to prop myself up on my elbows. "I'll fix it."

"You don't need to fix anything right now. You can't even sit."

"No." I gave up and stayed on my back. "Part of you is missing. I didn't even think about the way it would make you feel."

"I don't want you to hurt yourself."

"I hurt you. When Jack takes things, he leaves empty space. Pain. That wasn't my intention, but that's what you feel, right?"

She nodded and rubbed her chest with her hand, as if her heart ached.

"I'm afraid if I don't give it back now, it'll . . . I don't know, dilute or something. I didn't see what I took that clearly, but when I give it back, you should. I think." I hoped. I rolled over to my side, facing her, and put my hand on her waist. "Come here."

She scooted closer. A lot closer. Toe to toe, hip to hip, chest to chest. I had almost half a foot on her heightwise, so I had to lean my head down to touch my forehead to hers, but otherwise we fit together perfectly.

"After I do this, there's a really good chance I'll pass out again."

"I'll stay with you." She lifted her chin and pressed her lips to mine. "Until I know you're okay. Right here."

"Hold on to me." I tightened my grip on her waist. "Focus on what you see, and I'll try to go slowly. Lily, this isn't going to be easy. I think you're going to feel it . . . like it's fresh. Like it just happened."

"I'm ready."

I focused on the emotion and the memories. When I pushed them through my mental space into hers, they went backward for me, like a movie on rewind. Giving them back made me feel as if someone were scraping the inside of my soul away, leaving an open wound.

When I finished, she was crying as if she'd never stop.

I held her as close as I could and concentrated on not passing out. She needed me, and I wanted to be there. "Tell me what to do."

"What you're doing right now." She shuddered. "It didn't go backward that time. It was like I was watching it happen, like I was right there. I haven't seen my parents that clearly in . . . well, in nine years. I look like my mom."

"You're both beautiful." I tucked her head under my chin.

"And my dad . . ." Her voice caught. She turned her face into my chest. Sobs shook her body, but she didn't make a sound. Tears soaked the front of my shirt.

After a few minutes, she stopped. "The emotions are so much clearer . . . the things I saw, I remember so many more details."

"Like what?"

She lifted her head. "Feet. Shiny black shoes. Three men, and their faces. And my mom. She was trying to protect me."

I nodded and waited for her to absorb the next memory in the chain, the one I didn't understand.

"They came for me that day, Kaleb."

I stayed silent.

Confusion, shame, sorrow.

"That's why we left Cuba when we did, and so quickly. Because the men had already come to take me away."

Chapter 44

I held her until nightfall, watching the darkness weave a cocoon around us.

"What are you going to tell your grandmother?" I asked, stroking her hair.

"Nothing." Lily stared at the ceiling. "How do I explain what you showed me?"

"Tell her the truth."

"I don't think I can. I don't know how she'd react, or if she'd be angry." She rolled over to face me and I brushed her hair away from her face. "I'd like to keep you on her good side."

"I thought she'd already made up her mind about boys like me. I'm a bad influence. A temptation," I teased. "The apple, I believe you said?"

"You know . . . I never did get a bite." She put her hands on my cheeks and gently grazed my bottom lip with her teeth.

I kissed her without thought or hesitation, tasting her without caution. Slipping my hand under the hem of her sweater, brushing the skin of her stomach with the back of my hand. Her breath caught.

"Too much?" I asked, watching her.

"Not enough."

I missed her lips, so I went after them, sliding my hands around to her back, the curve of her waist, the flare of her hips.

I wanted to be skin to skin with her, so much more than I'd ever wanted it with anyone else.

I wanted all of her.

Lily touched me greedily, as if she were afraid one of us might disappear. Her palms found their way under my shirt, and she pulled it over my head. Her lips were everywhere—my neck, my chest, the fading bruise on my ribs from the night of the masquerade. The night I'd met her.

"You're beautiful." I brushed her hair over her shoulder, away from her face, watching her kiss her way back to my mouth. "Every single bit of you."

I stopped breathing when she tugged her sweater over her head to reveal an ivory lace camisole. "You haven't seen every single bit of me."

I was a hell of a lot closer than I'd been five seconds ago.

Reaching out, I drew a line with my index finger from her bottom lip to the button on her jeans. "Taking your memories of that day feels so personal. Taking something that important to you away, and then giving it back, it was even more intense than I expected. It reminded me of . . ."

"Kaleb." *A skip of desire.*

"You know, *making love* has always sounded so lame to me. Maybe because I've never done anything like that, either. But I think I understand now."

She tilted her head to the side. "I didn't think . . . you're not a—"

"Um . . . no." I kissed her again to soften the words. I couldn't tell exactly how much that mattered to her. "But everything is different with you. I'm closer to you than I've ever been to anyone."

She leaned over and put her lips right next to my ear.

"Get closer."

I opened my ability as wide as I could, staring into her eyes.

She wanted this as much as I did.

When I didn't respond immediately, she turned away. "I'm sorry. The timing is . . . *so* wrong. I shouldn't have—"

"Don't." I put my hands on her hips, sliding her close, flipping our positions. I eased her back onto the pillows and traced the line of her cheekbones with my thumbs. "I only hesitated because I wanted to feel what you felt. Know you were sure about me. Us."

"I am." She slid her hands into my hair and arched her back, pressing into me. Tightened her legs, pulling me closer.

"I know."

I directed every ounce of focus I had to Lily. I knew exactly how to kiss her, to touch her. Not because of her sighs, or the way her muscles tensed and relaxed in response to me, but because I was wrapped in her emotions. Everything I gave, she returned.

Pleasing her pleased me. I stopped the second she was unsure.

"Tiger," I said, pulling away, "I'm not in a hurry."

Her cheeks were flushed, her hair dark and tangled against the pillowcase. Exhaling shakily, she said, "I know."

"Do you?"

She nodded.

"People underestimate the benefits of taking their time. Slow is just as good as fast." I grinned, running my fingertips across the exposed skin between her jeans and the bottom of the camisole. "Usually, it's better."

I saw the sadness in her eyes as much as I felt it.

"What is it? What's wrong?"

"Taking our time." She traced the outer edge of the tattoo on my bicep. Her touch was warm. "I wonder how much we have."

I didn't want to think about that.

Leaning over, I kissed her forehead. "Thank you."

"For what?"

"Trusting me enough to let me in. With Cuba, your parents. With this." I gently placed my hand just above her heart. "I know how many risks you've taken, how hard it is for you to trust me. Why do you?"

"I've watched you go from stumbling to sure, and you're getting even stronger. You consistently take risks for people you care about." She covered my hand with hers. "Also, maybe I'm in love with you a little. But that doesn't mean I like you."

This girl was a miracle. A miracle in love with me.

"I don't like you, either. But I'm a little in love myself."

"We'll find Jack. You'll take your parents' memories back, and then we'll turn him in to Teague. We just have to—" Light flickered across her face, and she sat up quickly, pointing out the window.

Shock.

Ivy Springs was going up in flames.

Chapter 45

The sound of sirens bounced off the buildings lining the corridor of Main Street.

"We need to get out of here." I scooped Lily's sweater up and handed it to her along with her boots. "There's too much smoke to see well, and I don't like being on the second floor when I don't know where the fire is."

Lily pushed her arms into her sweater sleeves as she took off for the door. "I have to check on the shop."

"Wait for me." I shoved my feet into my shoes and pulled on my shirt as I followed her.

I felt the back of the door. It wasn't hot, but when I opened it the acrid smell of smoke billowed through. It burned the inside of my nose. Lily started coughing immediately, and I slammed the door shut.

"We need towels."

In the kitchen, she pulled open the drawer beside the stove and took a handful of dish towels. I turned on the water, and she held them under the faucet until they were soaked.

This time, we covered our noses and mouths before we went out the door. We hurried down the back steps, and I watched as Lily fumbled to unlock the back door of the coffee shop. "My key won't work."

She handed it to me and I tried.

"Something's wrong," I yelled. "It won't even slide into the lock."

"I don't know. Go to the front. I'll be okay once I know there's no fire inside."

We rounded the corner to the front of Murphy's Law, but then we stopped dead.

The whole north side of town was on fire. Main Street burned with complete abandon.

Even from two blocks away, the heat pushed across the pavement with a physical force. Closer to the blaze, the asphalt became pliable again. The glass in storefront windows popped, cracked, and then exploded.

"How? This couldn't have happened this fast." Lily was shouting, but I could barely hear her. The roar of the flames sounded like a waterfall. "We would have heard something, smelled something."

"Where are the fire trucks?" I took her hand and drew her close, assessing the situation. "I don't even hear them now."

"I don't, either. Where did they go?"

"Lily! Kaleb!"

Tires squealed as Michael pulled over to the curb in front of Murphy's Law. Emerson jumped out of the car and flew toward us at top speed, with Michael right behind her. She launched herself into Lily's arms. "Where have you been? We haven't heard from Kaleb since this morning, and neither one of you was answering your cell."

"We drove down here to look for you," Michael said, pushing down his fear, choosing concern instead. "And now . . . the fire. . . ."

"I can't get in touch with my brother." Flames reflected in Em's tears, and two escaped to roll down her cheeks. "This is everything he's ever worked for, and it's literally going up in flames. He and Dru both worked tonight—there was a party for the community theater troupe. Thomas always keeps his phone on him."

"Thomas and Dru are at the Phone Company?" I asked, looking from Em to Michael. His frown deepened as he looked north.

Shock.

Em's fear had become so familiar to me that I knew the second it came.

The Phone Company was on the north side of town.

"Emerson, no!"

Michael wasn't quick enough. She'd already started racing toward the smoke. We followed.

The closer we got to the fire, the more something about it pulled at my memory. The base of the flames was beyond blue, almost an electric purple. The flames consumed stone and wood, burning both with the same speed and intensity. Only one person could make fire like that, and only one person could spread it so destructively.

"Hurry. Em hasn't reached the Phone Company yet." Lily pulled at my arm and panted for air. "Come on!"

"This isn't normal fire."

"What?" She let her arm go slack, but I held on to her hand tightly.

"This is the kind of fire that burned my dad's lab. Jack and Cat did this." Maybe Ava, although I hoped that wasn't true. "Look around. Why aren't there any people on the street? Where are the cars? This doesn't look like Ivy Springs; it looks like a movie set, or a ghost town."

Doubt. Realization. Fear.

I squinted over my shoulder through the smoke, from the direction we came. "Lily, look."

No pumpkins sat on the street waiting to be lit for Halloween. Gone were the decorative pots of flowers and wrought-iron benches used to adorn the spaces between red maples and pear trees. The replica gas streetlights remained, but only a few were lit, and the rest was broken sidewalks and weeds. A power surge hummed, and everything went dark. The only light came from the fire glowing orange in the night sky.

Now Lily squeezed my hand. "Something is wrong."

Very wrong. "I don't think we're really here."

"What?" Lily breathed.

"I think we're in a rip."

Chapter 46

"How are we in a rip?" Lily asked. "We saw the fire from inside my apartment. We even heard sirens."

"But we didn't hear any more sirens after we came out of your apartment. And your Murphy's Law key didn't work." I didn't want to think too hard about the possible implications. We started running toward the Phone Company again.

"I've never heard anything about Ivy Springs catching fire. That would be a huge part of our town history," Lily said, panting. "Especially with all the post–Civil War building that was done here."

"If Jack and Cat started that fire, and I think they did, this rip is from the future. Only my dad and Michael have ever seen those. The whole situation escalates every time another rip shows up." My feet pounded the sidewalk in time with the thoughts pounding through my brain. "Time has started traveling to us."

Rips were having an impact on people who were alive. If that were the case, and Emerson ran into a blazing fire . . .

The Phone Company came into view just as Em approached the side of the building, the very place I'd first met Lily the night of the masquerade. "Wait!" I shouted. "Don't let her go in."

Michael caught Em by her upper arm. She'd been running so fast she almost lost her footing. "Let me go," she demanded, trying to jerk away from him.

"You can't go in there," I insisted when we caught up. "Look around—this isn't the Ivy Springs we know. It's a rip."

"A rip?" Em stood completely still, staring at the building. The Phone Company sign was gone, as were the usual impeccable landscaping and lighting, signatures of Thomas's work. "What the hell?"

"A future rip." Michael's face paled as he considered the circumstances. "One we can all see."

"Rips are tangible now," I said, thinking out loud. A concentrated wave of intense panic pulsed through me. Coming from Em. "Does that mean we could change the outcome of an event, even though we aren't *really* here?"

"It's a possibility," Michael said grimly. Defeat made his voice and eyes tight. He didn't look at Emerson. "What we do now could flow backward or forward."

Em broke free from Michael, shaking her head in denial. "If my brother and Dru are in there, I'm not leaving them. I've already broken rules. What's the difference now?"

Lily reached out for Em. "Maybe there's another way—"

"No." Em cut her off and backed away. The flames were no more than fifteen feet away from the building on the left side, maybe twenty feet from the back, burning as if possessed, bent on total destruction. I felt a memory clawing at Em's insides, tearing her open, so strong I had to bend over at the waist. "I know what burning feels like. It sears your skin, but it's almost cold. Then there's the smell." Her nostrils flared. "You can't escape it. There's nowhere to go."

In Emerson's original time line, she'd been horribly burned in a fire, caused by the shuttle bus accident that killed her parents. Jack's machinations, as horrible as they were, had saved her from that. He'd taken that time line away.

She shouldn't be remembering it now.

"Em, please." Michael moved slowly, keeping his eyes on her. "Don't. They might not even be in there."

"'Might not be' isn't good enough." She took another step back. *Determined.* "I won't let them go. Them or their baby."

The roof from the building beside the restaurant crashed to the ground. The vines climbing the iron fence on the dining patio burst into flame, and I shook my head in disbelief when the iron immediately glowed red. The glass in the French doors that led in popped, and the fire slid inside.

Too hot. Too fast.

"I can't lose them, too." Emerson took one more step back, and then rushed the heavy oak front doors, pushing them open and throwing herself inside.

"Emerson!" Michael followed.

"No!" Lily grabbed my arm, digging in her heels when I tried to take off after Michael. "You won't help if you go in there now."

Terror bled under the doors of the Phone Company. "I can't . . ."

"If we make the rip go away, we can end this." She yelled over the sound of the fire, which grew more ardent every second. Her desperation was barely under control. It matched mine. "Please. Think."

I stepped back to gauge the path of the flames. Half the roof was already gone. Ending the rip would be the fastest way to get us all out of danger. "We have to find a person, and I haven't seen one since we landed here. Unless . . ."

If Jack and Cat started this inferno, they'd stick around to watch it burn. Just like they had the night they killed my father.

I shouted instructions to Lily. "We have to find the origin of the fire. Let's try the midpoint."

Lily nodded instead of screaming back.

Everything in me fought to run toward Em and Michael instead of away from them, but I knew Lily was right and that we had to make the rip go away. The heat coming off the buildings made my eyes water, and the closer we got to the center of the fire, the thicker the smoke became.

But there was nothing was left to burn.

I wanted a second to shut everything out, to quiet my hectic mind. But I could sense Em and Michael, which meant they were still alive, and I didn't want to lose the connection. My focus on maintaining it almost made me miss seeing him.

Jack. Ashes, falling like snow, covered his shoulders.

Reaching out for Lily, I tagged her shoulder and pointed at Jack. I held my finger up in front of my lips. We both stopped short, and I moved in front of her.

More terrifying than the sight of him was what I could feel.

I could read him.

I now knew for certain that he'd been blocking me for years, maybe as long as I'd known him. Peeling back layers of emotion was part of the necessary process to read someone deeply. Jack's outer layer was black, the same kind of blackness I'd felt from Ava so many times. Peeling away his emotions like an onion, I half expected to find some kind of redeeming quality, but it never came.

He was rotten to the core.

It felt like the read had taken hours, falling through the darkness of Jack's soul, but it had only been a few seconds. I'd never experienced that kind of decay. Utter corruption. Greed and deceit. Desolation and desperation. The teeming need for control and power. The need to destroy.

If I could get out of this rip, I'd kill him. I'd find him, and I'd kill him for all the things he'd done to me and to the people I loved.

My rage flowed out of me through my fingertips, uncontrollable. I wanted revenge, and I wanted it now.

I charged him. He turned around and his mouth formed an O of surprise. Then his fear came.

As I crouched to spring, Lily grabbed my wrist, and I pulled her with me as I tackled Jack.

He dissolved.

Lily and I both landed on our knees on the sidewalk in "our" Ivy Springs. The flames were gone.

So were Emerson and Michael.

Chapter 47

The town stood unscathed.

The air smelled like rain, spicy mums, and the decomposing jack-o'-lanterns that lined the street, their decaying faces sinister and secretive.

"Where are they?" Lily's voice shook as she scanned the sidewalk. "I don't see them."

I got to my feet, dusting off, and pulled her up with me. "Are you okay?"

Her jeans had ripped, and the open flap of denim exposed a bloody knee. She didn't seem to notice. "Did they make it out? Or are they still in the rip?"

"Lily? Are you okay?" I repeated, taking her shoulders and looking into her eyes.

"We have to check the Phone Company. That's where they were, maybe that's where they landed."

We ran down the street to the restaurant, reaching it just as Thomas stepped outside the door and began counting the number of people waiting in line to get in. "Hey, you two," he said when he saw us. "Why are you covered in ashes?"

"Long story," I said, trying to catch my breath. "Can you get Em and Michael for us?"

He looked at me strangely. "They're at your house. I'd asked Em to fill in as hostess tonight because Dru is having a hard time with morning sickness. Em said she couldn't because something was up with your dad."

"Are you sure you haven't seen them?" Lily asked. "Could you just stick your head inside and check again?"

"Okay." Thomas pulled open the door and leaned back, calling to someone inside. "Clint? Have you seen my sister anywhere?"

Lily took my hand. I felt her hope while we waited, and her desolation when Thomas turned back to us. "No, they aren't here. Is everything okay?"

"It's fine. Must be a misunderstanding. Looks busy," I said, gesturing to the crowd. "We'll catch you later."

Lily's tears started to fall the second we turned away.

"Hold on. Let's just get out of here and get back to your apartment." I squeezed her hand. "We'll come up with a plan."

"We have to get back inside the rip. How do we do it?" She bit her bottom lip, staring at me and waiting for an answer. "Kaleb?"

"I don't know." I looked at the ground, avoiding her eyes. "I've never seen the same rip twice. The Jack that I grabbed was a rip.

I . . . wasn't thinking. Thank God you were holding on to my arm, or I would have left you behind, too."

"Don't tell me we can't save them. We have to. We can't just . . . we have to." Her voice shook. "There has to be a way."

"I can think of one." I didn't want to say it, but it was our only alternative. "There's one thing that can repair the continuum without personal consequence."

"The Infinityglass."

I nodded. "We don't have a choice, Lily. We have to find it. You have to find it."

Chapter 48

*E*ven though most of Ava's belongings were still in the gate-house, it had an empty, abandoned feeling. The air was stale and cold. I flipped on a small lamp in the living room and cranked up the heat. It was the most remote place I could think of, a place where no one would look.

I made sure the blinds and curtains were drawn before I clicked on another lamp. I immediately turned it off. The darker the better for now.

"Ready?" I asked her.

Half of Lily's face was cast in shadows. I didn't have to see her to feel her sorrow.

"I am so sorry it's come to this," I said.

"I was willing to help before I was forced into a corner. We'll make this right. Together."

We sat down on the couch and put the Skroll between us.

Stealing it from Dune's room had been easy enough; he slept like a rock.

Trying to remember how he'd opened it was a little harder.

"Dune said that everything he'd seen in the Skroll related to either the Infinityglass or Chronos. We're just going to cross our fingers and hope there's something specific, some clue that points us in the right direction. To the right map."

"I've never looked for anything I haven't seen before." Lily's legs bounced as she waited. "What if I can't find the Infinityglass? What if I find it and it's in Africa? What will we do then?"

"If Jack or Teague thought the Infinityglass was in Africa, they'd be in Africa."

"But—"

"Listen to me." I put my hand on her leg. "It has to be close. All the key players are here. This isn't a coincidence."

"I hope not."

"Here we go." The holographic screen appeared between us, bright in the dim room. Lily reached over to turn off the tiny lamp and then faced me again.

I tapped the map icon on the screen with the stylus. Maps rotated in a circle as they projected from the screen.

"Any you feel good about?" I asked.

Lily watched them spin. "Let's start big and work our way in. There's a modern world map."

I touched the corresponding map on the screen, using the

stylus, and it projected into the air. I did it again, and the map spread out across the screen.

"Okay, close your eyes. We'll practice." I took her hands and put them on the screen. "Now try to find the Lincoln Memorial."

She tapped her fingers across the map; once she hit DC, she stopped. "Here."

"You got it." I changed the dimensions and size, as well as turning the map sideways. "The Space Needle."

She found it immediately.

"Don't open your eyes. The Arc de Triomphe."

Her fingers felt every inch of the map twice. Her mouth turned down at the corners. "I don't feel this one."

"That's because it isn't a map of France."

She growled at me.

"Okay, try the Leaning Tower of Pisa—"

"There." She opened her eyes. "I think I've got it."

Her cheeks were flushed, and the excitement in her voice was contagious. I took her face in my hands and kissed her hard on the lips. "You can do it."

"We can." She pointed at the Skroll. "Let's start with North America."

✺

Two hours and seven continents later, we had nothing.

"I don't know what I'm doing wrong." Lily stretched her neck from side to side and rolled her shoulders. "We haven't even gotten a hint."

"Take a break," I told her, touching her cheek. "Maybe we're pushing too hard."

"What if it doesn't exist, Kaleb?" She leaned against the couch, dropping her head back and closing her eyes. *Hopelessness.*

"My dad thinks it does." I had to hold on to his belief. I might not have seen the evidence, but he'd seen enough to make finding the Infinityglass one of his life goals. I knew how much he loved my mother, how pure it was. He'd never risk their relationship on something that couldn't be real. He wouldn't.

I navigated back to the main page of the Skroll and spun through every icon, hoping we'd overlooked something. One file didn't have a title at all. I tapped twice to open it.

The hologram displayed familiar writing.

I used the stylus to quickly advance the pages. "No way."

Lily sat up and opened her eyes, focusing on the image hovering between us. "What's wrong?"

"These are my dad's files, the ones that Jack and Cat stole. They've been scanned in. They list everyone he's come across in his research who could have a time-related ability." So many names. I sped through faster and faster. "It doesn't make sense. Unless . . ."

"What?"

"Dad expected Jack to use the files as a bargaining chip with Chronos. How did they end up on the Skroll?"

I advanced to the letter *C* and saw Emerson's name. It felt wrong to read it now.

"Will you . . ." Lily sounded strange, as if she was trying to stop herself from asking the question. "Will you go to the *G*s next?"

"Why?"

"I want you to look for me."

I advanced the pages. "Nothing."

She exhaled. "Try *Diaz.*"

"Diaz?" I went backward from the *G*s. "There are three on the list. Jorge, Eduardo, and Pillar."

Lily gasped.

"Do you know these people?" I asked.

"Pilli was what my father called me, a pet name. That's why my *abuela* chose Lily once we got to America, because it sounded similar and was less confusing for me. My real name is Pillar Diaz." She stared down at the Skroll. "Does it say what I can do?"

"Not you. It just says your grandfather and father had seeker abilities. There's a question mark by Pillar's . . . by your name."

"You know what this means."

"I do."

"Jack couldn't get to my father or grandfather, so he brought Abi and me here. He found us, just like he found Emerson. And just like he wanted to use Emerson to change his past, he wants to use me to find things." Her voice was steel, but her heart was broken. "He had to get me to this time, and this place, so I could find the Infinityglass."

The door opening behind me caught me off guard. Lily's scream tipped the balance.

The blow to my skull did the rest.

I opened my eyes, but I still couldn't see.

Blindfolded. I couldn't move my arms or legs, and I was gagged. My left wrist felt like someone had taken a hammer to it.

Worst of all was that I couldn't feel Lily's emotions, no matter how far I stretched.

But the stale air of the gatehouse was familiar.

I rocked side to side. Once I had momentum, I pitched my chair over, pulling outward with my legs. I landed on my right shoulder, and pieces of chair went flying the second I hit the ground.

I pulled off the blindfold and removed the gag. My wrist was blue, and possibly broken.

Lily's jacket was still on the floor, but she and the Skroll were nowhere to be found.

I got loose from the remaining pieces of chair, somehow managing to cut a five-inch slice on the inside of my right arm with an exposed screw.

Then I ran like hell for the main house.

Chapter 49

"*I* can't feel her."

Ava and I sat in a corner of the emergency room, which was blessedly empty. She'd insisted on taking me to the hospital.

"That doesn't have to mean the worst."

"I put her in this situation. Nothing can happen." My voice broke, and I stared at a framed print of Monet's water lilies on the wall until I regained control. Lilies. "It's been three hours. The sun is coming up, her grandmother is home, and she'll know Lily's missing."

"Are you sure you've told us everything?" Ava asked. "It's going to be easier to find her if we know every detail, especially if you have to wait for X-rays and a cast and we have to go looking by ourselves."

Ava looked toward the sliding double doors of the emergency entrance. Dune and Nate walked in, holding four cups of coffee.

"Fracture?" Nate asked, looking at my arm.

"Don't know yet."

I doubted Dune would ever forgive me for breaking into his room and stealing the Skroll. Even so, he asked, "Are you okay?"

"I can't feel Lily. Has anyone heard from Emerson or Michael?"

Nate stared up at the red exit sign, blinking as if he was holding back tears. The fact that he was serious scared me as much as anything could.

"No," Dune said. "Thomas has the cops on it. He freaked when Em didn't come home last night."

Almost everyone I loved was in danger, and I was in a hospital waiting for stitches and an X-ray.

"I don't know who has Lily." The possibility that it was Poe sent ice down my spine. Jack wasn't any better. He'd keep her alive long enough to use her ability to find the one thing he wanted, and then he'd discard her. "I need to get out of here. My arm can wait."

"Ballard?" A young, smiling nurse with pink scrubs, red hair, and white shoes called my name. She had a clipboard in her hands and a pen stuck in her bun.

"No," Ava argued. "Your arm is all bendy. You can't leave without seeing a doctor."

"I'll be fine. Let's just go." I stood up.

"*Dude*," Nate said. "You'll be useless if you don't get that arm fixed. Trust us to look for Lily. We want her found, too."

He waited for me to read him. *Loyalty, fear, conviction.* The same feelings came from Dune and Ava.

"Ballard?" The nurse had removed the pen from her hair and was now tapping it on her clipboard, looking at us pointedly, but still smiling.

"Thank you." I could only whisper.

"Go," Ava said. "You'll know you the second we find anything."

The nurse, Mary Ellen, forced me to put on a hospital gown, and then she started an IV.

"Seriously? At worst, I need an ACE bandage, not an IV. Why do I need a hospital gown?" It wasn't wide enough for my shoulders, so no matter what I did, it wouldn't close in the back. The nurse kept averting her eyes. "Can't you just slap on a Band-Aid and send me on my way?"

"Don't be so grumpy. Let us take care of you. The IV will keep you hydrated." Mary Ellen slid the needle under my skin quickly and almost painlessly. "No eating or drinking. We need to keep your stomach clear, in case that's a break, specifically a compound fracture, and requires surgery."

"Surgery? I can't have surgery. I don't have time. I have to . . ." In that second, everything in the room softened around the edges. I forgot what I was mad about. "What did you just do?"

"I gave you a little something for the pain, and to calm you down. You're rather . . . agitated." She frowned and took a step back before leaving the room completely.

"Agitated? You haven't *seen* agitated." Panic couldn't eclipse the meds rushing through my system. Drugs that strong could have the same numbing effect as alcohol. I wouldn't be able to feel anyone's emotions, not even my own.

Not Lily's.

I struggled to sit up, to keep my eyes open, but the nurse must have given me enough of the painkiller to take down a horse.

I don't know how, but that's when the wall between Lily and me tumbled down.

I'd known we were connected, but the pain I felt now was so sharp I could've been in her skin. Every emotion was amplified. She was pissed off and scared and worried. The pissed-off part made me hopeful for one brief second, and then my muscles spasmed as if I'd been running for days. My stomach twisted in knots.

She wasn't okay.

Fear. Desperation. Fear. Desperation.

I fought against both as I fell into a deep sleep.

Chapter 50

My eyes flew open.

Fear. Desperation.

Lily.

Her pain was coming from a clear direction, and it wasn't just emotional.

The clock said 5:00. An hour before sunset. My left arm was wrapped in a half cast. I pulled the two IVs out of my hand and climbed out of bed. My legs were steady enough, and my headache had settled into a dull throb. My clothes were neatly folded inside a cabinet, and I put them on as quickly as possible, considering my injury. I couldn't find my cell phone anywhere. Lily's emotions were coming more steadily now, ripping me in half with anxiety.

I stuck my head out my door and looked to the right and the left, and then I took off for the stairs.

Once I made it to the street, I started running, holding my

injured arm close to my chest. The hospital was only a few blocks from downtown proper. Barricades blocked all the through streets, and the sounds of music and laughter floated on the evening air.

I'd forgotten it was Halloween.

Deadline. The word took on a whole new meaning.

The crowd was thick with costumed ghosts and witches in pointy hats. Superheroes, villains, mummies, vampires, and werewolves filled the sidewalks and streets. The rush of emotions ranged from giddiness to disappointment, and combined with the remnants of my pain-med buzz, it all blocked out the clarity I'd felt coming from Lily ten minutes ago.

"Focus. Just focus." I stopped to lean back against a tree and close my eyes. I recalled what it felt like when I kissed Lily, when I held her. It only made things worse. I'd be better served by remembering her fear, since that's what she was feeling now. The night she saw her first rip, the one of the hanged man. And then the way she'd felt when we'd landed on the sidewalk after leaving Em and Mike behind.

I opened my eyes.

She was in the center of town.

I pushed my way through the crowd, trying to avoid the little kids. A pissed-off parent could hold me up, and I didn't have any time to waste. I almost tripped over a little boy with white-blond hair. I reached out to put my hand on his head for balance, and hit a tree shoulder-first when he dissolved.

He'd saved me from entering into a full-blown rip.

I ran faster.

The main stage was set up right in front of the chamber of commerce, which meant the throng of people got even thicker as I got closer. I worked my way around to the far right side of the bandstand, finding an open stretch of ground in front of one huge speaker. Volunteers wearing bright orange PUMPKIN DAZE T-shirts walked in and out of the office building, carrying things like glow sticks and coolers of iced-down water bottles.

Lily was here, in the clock tower.

I felt her fear.

I couldn't feel who was causing it.

Jack.

Chapter 51

I sneaked into the building behind a volunteer who was holding a tray of caramel apples, and immediately headed to the meeting area at the top of the clock tower, following Lily's emotions. I flattened myself against the half wall that blocked the stairs and slid closer, listening. I could only see Jack.

"I'll keep looking as long as you want." Lily's voice was raw. Relief still flooded through me at the sound of it. "But I don't know what I'm looking for. Is there a certain size, any specific details? Can you give me anything? There are so many maps. Maybe if you could just give me the place of origin?"

Agony replaced my relief when the screams started. They became pleading sobs that faded into whimpers. Each one sent fury racing through my veins. If I wanted the chance to get her out of here, there was nothing I could do but ride it out.

Through it all, Jack remained statue still. He didn't even have to move to inflict pain.

The most frightening enemy has weapons you can't take away.

"Any other complaints?"

She didn't speak. What memory had he shown her?

"Get it together and keep searching. I thought the first five times we went through this made that clear. Understood?"

"I understand," she answered, her voice faint, broken. I was going to make him sorry he'd ever even looked at her. I scooted to the right just a bit, and Lily came into view.

Blood poured from a split in her lip, and a fresh bruise bloomed on her cheek. He'd put his hands on her, too. I had to breathe through my rage to keep the grip of my fingers from splintering the wood of the top stair.

Sitting with my back to the half wall, trembling, I tried to figure out a plan of attack. Killing Jack with one hand would be difficult. But not impossible.

"This is just sad." Jack. Right beside me.

He was smiling.

"Too afraid to deal with me so you knocked me unconscious?" I sneered.

"Less about fear, more about convenience." The smile got wider.

"Go to hell." I stood and jumped the two steps left on the staircase. In a split second, he was at Lily's side. Holding Poe's duronium knife.

"How did you get that?" I asked. My stomach dropped. It was impossible to keep him from seeing the way her fear affected me. "It was you. You killed Dr. Turner."

He didn't answer directly. "How about we come to an agreement? Let your flavor of the week find what I want, and then I'll decide if I feel like killing anyone *today*."

"You're forcing her to search for the Infinityglass?"

"No. Waldo."

Lily flipped through the maps as quickly as she could, the holograms lighting up her bloody mouth and bruised cheek.

"Why?" I asked. "It doesn't exist."

"Then why were you looking for it? Your father believed it was real."

Lily's fear escalated, and I caught myself before I said anything else. She hadn't told Jack we couldn't find the Infinityglass. That was probably the only thing keeping her alive.

"Dad doesn't know what he believes anymore. You took the last five years of his memory."

Jack's focus kept returning outside, where the sunset flamed hot pink and lavender. "I should've wiped him clean."

"Like my mother?" My rage tried to push its way through again, but Lily's fresh panic kept it in.

He sighed and walked to the window, turning his back on us.

I caught Lily's attention, and mouthed a single word. *Lie.*

It took her a second to grasp my meaning, but when she did,

she regained control. I saw fierce determination in the set of her jaw and the straightness of her spine.

"Hey, I think . . ." She cleared her throat. "I think I've found something."

Jack's expression changed as he looked over at the map. She took it from the floating hologram to the touch screen, forcing him to move closer to her. "What?" he asked.

Partygoers cheered as they threw pumpkins into the fire for Pumpkin Smash. I took one step toward Lily and Jack.

"I think it could be in Memphis, not the Tennessee city. The Egypt one. It's faint, but it was definitely there. It might still be there." Her fingers moved furiously over the map.

I stepped closer, tensing my muscles, ready to spring.

"Egypt?" Jack said. "Why do you continue to lie?"

He raised his hand.

"No," Lily argued, her eyes bright with fear. "Look, right there."

Closer.

"Right where?" Jack asked impatiently.

"Yes. Right where?" A female voice dragged the question out.

All three of us looked toward the stairs.

Teague.

Chapter 52

I'd have given anything to be inside the panic I saw in Jack's expression. Fear like that made your skin too tight.

"Teague." He said her name with a reverence that should have been accompanied by a bow.

What did Teague know, or what could she do that would make Jack act that way?

Teague smiled serenely at me, absolute calm bleeding from her pores. "Liam's son?"

"Yes."

Footsteps echoed on the stairs behind Teague.

Poe.

Lily's fear. Teague's calm. Poe's despair. And still, nothing at all from Jack, except a vein pulsing steadily in his forehead.

Teague didn't acknowledge Poe, just continued to focus on

me. "Where is Emerson? I expected to find her here. She *is* the reason Jack wants the Infinityglass."

"Emerson's gone." It took effort to keep my voice from breaking. "So is Michael."

Jack whipped his head toward me. "Gone?"

"We ran into a rip at the Phone Company. A fire. Em ran in, Michael ran after her." I paused, hearing my weakness. When I'd regained control, I said, "Neither one of them came out."

Jack stared at me, searching for a lie. Hoping for one.

Teague seemed unaffected by the news. She shook her head and made a tsking noise. "If Michael and Emerson are gone, what will you do, Jack? Continue to use Poe to try to get what you want? Make him do things, and then steal his memories?"

"Poe offered," Jack said coldly.

"Is that true?" Teague kept her eyes on Jack but directed the question to Poe. "Did you offer Jack use of your ability?"

"No. I didn't." Poe stared at the wall behind Teague, his hands shoved into the pockets of his leather jacket.

What the hell was going on? Poe claimed not to be a traveler the night we met him. How had Jack used him?

"It's fine, Poe. I wouldn't expect you to remember if you did," Teague said.

Poe turned to Jack and held out his hand. "I want my knife back."

Jack played with the blade for a moment, weighing his options, and then he looked at Teague. He aimed the blade toward himself and passed it over to Poe.

"Are you done with me?" Poe asked Teague.

"That will be all." Teague waved her fingers toward the exit.

Poe slid the knife into his boot and and disappeared down the staircase.

"So many lies, Jack," Teague observed. "Have you told Kaleb the truth yet?"

I flinched when she said my name, and thought I saw pleading in Jack's eyes.

"About what?" I asked.

"Jack's full of secrets. Where he comes from, where he's been. He's taken so many risks to cover it all up. Ruined so many lives. Kaleb, I think it's about time you met your uncle Jack."

"Uncle?" The word was a solid kick in the gut.

"Jack's a bastard," Teague said. "Conceived by his mother in an extramarital affair, one your grandfather Ballard was loath to admit but for which he was honor bound to take responsibility. You spent every other weekend with your 'extended family' growing up, right, Jack?"

Jack growled under his breath and his face became an ugly mask of bitterness and rage.

"You had another uncle, too, Kaleb, but he died when he was just a toddler. Jack's the only one who remembers exactly how." Now Teague looked at me. "You have his name."

"My father never . . . told me." I didn't understand.

"He couldn't. His memories aren't clear because they aren't true. Jack manipulated them to serve himself. That's why Jack wants

Emerson. He wants to change the past and make himself a hero to his—"

She broke off when she noticed Lily. Or rather, what Lily held in her hand. The Skroll.

"Where did that come from?" Teague's voice turned cold, with an edge like a razor blade. "How did you find it?"

"Him." Lily pointed toward Jack without a moment of hesitation, lying so smoothly I almost believed her. She was playing to the most likely ally.

"You little bitch," Jack spat at her. "I stole it from you."

Lily shrugged.

Jack turned to Teague. "The girl knows how to find things. She has the gene. Her real name is Pillar Diaz and her information is in the files I sold you."

"Did you find it?" Teague asked Lily. "The Infinityglass?"

"Say I did," Lily mused, tapping one finger against her lips. "I wouldn't be willing to tell Jack what I know, but I would be willing to tell you."

"Why?"

"I want something in exchange." Lily met Teague's eyes and spoke clearly. "When I'm done giving you the information, Kaleb and I walk away. And while you and I are talking, Kaleb gets five minutes alone with Jack."

Teague looked from Lily to me and back again as a slow smile spread along her face.

"Deal."

Chapter 53

The second Teague and Lily turned away, I rushed Jack.

He wrestled with me, digging his fingernails into my arms, kicking at my shins. I grabbed his face with my good hand, ready to let my ability open up wide. He anticipated my plans.

And opened up a world of pain instead.

Every ocean in the world roared in my ears as he pushed memories on me. Mom, when she heard about Dad, wrapped in grief, curled up on the floor. My face when she told me what happened. Dad, his fear the minute before Jack erased five years of his life.

Showing me Dad's memories was Jack's first mistake.

Those five years were so fresh I could see them perfectly. Taking back the emotion that went with them was like siphoning the foam off a cold beer. Pulling the love away brought memories, all of them. I held them inside me, and then I was riding a wave through Jack's brain space.

Now I knew what to look for, and finding my mom's memories was easy. They flowed like water, slipping away from Jack and into me, making me stronger. My dad, movie sets, shared kisses in her trailer, their wedding on a beach in Bali. My birth, me as a toddler learning to walk. Laughing, with peas smeared all over my face. From a preschooler to a teenager in fast forward, with my dad aging the same way. More images: cooking together, watching me swim. Then ones I didn't understand . . . a white house on a hill . . . swamps . . . an older couple . . . a much younger Teague?

I slowed down the flow to try to examine that image. It gave Jack enough equilibrium to push back.

His defense involved showing me things I didn't want to see. Emerson broken and burned. Michael and my dad confiding in each other, Dad clamping his hand on Michael's shoulder. The word *son*.

The pain was so quick and sharp that I almost faltered. Then somehow, I knew it was a lie.

I could hear Lily from across the room, her voice low and insistent, as she gave Teague the information she wanted.

I dug my thumb into Jack's cheekbone, and pushed back harder. I saw memories he'd taken from Ava, Emerson, Michael, even Lily. Some things I was glad to see. Others not as much. Deciding what to share with Jack's victims was going to be a long and painful process.

Even so, I took it all.

Once I was certain I had everything I needed, I let him go. I had my parent's memories, and now I could have my revenge.

I stared at him, helpless on the floor, for what felt like an eternity. I wondered if taking other people's memories away from him would leave him with the same kind of empty blackness he caused. I could only hope.

I used my cast arm to slam his head into the floor.

"Have we met our end of the bargain?" I asked, cautiously approaching Lily and Teague.

Teague watched Lily begin the process of shutting down the Skroll. "Yes."

Lily's face was carefully composed.

"I'd just started to figure this out earlier," she began, after looking to Teague for permission. When she got it, she continued. "I touched every inch of every map in the Skroll, every corner of the whole world. I'd started to believe that the Infinityglass wasn't real, and then something hit me. I stopped looking at maps and started looking through all the information."

"Lily discovered the one thing that has eluded seekers for a century." Teague took it from Lily and slipped it under her arm. "The Infinityglass isn't a thing."

Now Lily held my gaze. "The Infinityglass is a person. I told Teague how sorry I was that I couldn't help her anymore. Since I can only find things."

"Thank you for the information, Lily. Should I need you again, I know where I can find you. And don't worry. I'll take care of this, for all of us." Teague looked down on an unconscious Jack with a wicked smile.

Lily and I walked out of the clock tower together.

Chapter 54

Lily held my right hand as I approached my mom's room. Dad was on my left side. His simmering hope was encouraging and distracting.

"What if it doesn't work?" My greatest fear.

"It will," Dad said. "You restored me."

"He's right." Lily squeezed my hand. "You gave memories back to both of us. It will work."

The early morning sun shone through the octagonal window at the top of the stairs. I hadn't slept all night. Dune, Nate, and Ava had regrouped, and were out searching for Michael and Emerson. No one was ready to give up hope.

They couldn't be dead.

"Are you coming with me?" I asked Lily. Her grandmother had been caught in a freak snowstorm in North Carolina. Lily's Abi always said that if she was supposed to drive in snow, she wouldn't have been born on a tropical island. I hoped to escape the convo where Lily filled Abi in on the latest happenings.

"This is between you and your parents. I'm going to be right here, though, saying prayers and thinking good thoughts, with everything I have crossed." She squeezed my hand again.

"Are you ready?" Dad asked.

I nodded. Lily leaned against the wall, waiting.

We went in. Mom had lost weight while she'd been in the coma. Her black hair was shot with silver now. I couldn't wait to see her reaction to it when she woke up. If she woke up. She'd never been vain, even though she was beautiful, but I had the feeling the gray hair was going to be a shock, and not the only one.

What was she going to think about her tatted-up and pierced son?

Dad shut the door behind us. "Are you ready?"

"As I'll ever be."

"Even if you revive her, you realize that much of her memory could be fragmented."

"Some of her is better than none at all."

"I agree wholeheartedly. Kaleb?"

"Yeah?"

"You and your mother are the lights of my life. If anything had happened to you yesterday—"

"It didn't."

"Just know that no matter what happens here I love you." He put his hand on my shoulder.

"I love you, too, Dad."

I pulled the chair he'd been sleeping in up to her bedside. It was the same one I'd sat in when I tried to take away her pain—too little, too late. This time, it was going to be different, because this time, I was going to restore her joy.

I took both of her hands in mine and kissed her forehead.

Closing my eyes, I focused my energy on gathering up all her most precious emotions and memories, bundling them up carefully.

And then I pushed.

I pushed with all the love and determination I had. I focused on giving them back chronologically, as close as I could get for the parts I hadn't personally experienced, and one at a time. Clarity was the top priority, after bringing her back.

Her skin began to warm against mine, and her breathing grew labored. I finished with the memories I didn't understand, one in particular, and held on, afraid to open my eyes.

The machine monitoring her heartbeat sped up, and an alarm went off on another machine.

"Dad?" I stood, stepped back, and looked at him instead of her, but I didn't let go of her hands.

Anger. Fear. Despair. Pain.

The rush of emotions sucker-punched me. I might have gone down if they hadn't been followed by *love. Gratitude. Joy. Relief.*

Her blue eyes, the mirror image of mine, opened. She was smiling.

"Mama?" I used the name I'd called her as a child, and my

voice broke. I buried my face in her neck, feeling her pulse, strong and sure. "Are you . . . are you okay?"

"I knew you could do it." Her voice was weak, and then she was crying.

I touched her face, held her hands. Felt the overwhelming love Dad had for both of us rush over me like healing water.

"I could hear. I knew how you tried to save me. How you blamed yourself, and I knew when your father came back. I just kept holding on."

Then she caught a glimpse of Dad behind me.

"Liam?"

He rushed past me, wrapped her in his arms, and kissed her.

Every lightbulb and electrical appliance in the room blew at once.

I turned to sneak out, to give them time to reconnect, but my mother called out to me.

"Kaleb?"

I turned around.

"Where's Lily?"

My mouth dropped open. "What?"

"She's such a lovely girl." Mom smiled again, as if she had a secret.

I guess she did.

Chapter 55

Lily and I escaped to the front porch.

"Are you okay?" Lily asked, putting her hand on my shoulder. I covered it with my own.

"I don't know. Mom and Dad. It's amazing." I stared across the dewy grass and breathed in the smell of a new morning. But it wasn't a fresh start. "Emerson and Michael . . ."

"There's hope." I heard it in her voice, felt it in her soul.

"Lily? What aren't you telling me?"

"I know where the Infinityglass is."

"What? How?"

"I lied to Teague. Once I figured out the Infinityglass was a person, I looked for it on the map. It's in Louisiana, near New Orleans. We can save them, Kaleb." Her smile was full of promise. "We just have to find the Infinityglass, and we can make everything okay."

I touched the bruise on her cheek, ran my thumb under the cut on her mouth.

"I hope you aren't going to let a fat lip stop you," she said.

I barely touched my lips to hers, but rather than seek her emotions, I paid attention to my own.

All I felt was love.

Until other emotions pushed between us.

More relief. More gratitude. So much more love.

Michael. And Emerson.

I turned to see him, along with Emerson, perfectly healthy, standing right in front of us. I stared at them in wonder, and then I jumped off the porch steps, grabbing Mike to make sure he was real, reaching out for Em's hand.

They didn't disappear.

"How?" I asked, once everyone had hugged and been hugged at least fifteen times. "We were sure you were gone, forever."

"So were we," Em said. "Once we got inside, I realized that the Phone Company didn't look like the Phone Company anymore. No one was inside, and there weren't tables or chairs or . . . anything. I turned around to run back out, but the smoke was so thick. . . ."

She'd been terrified. Being trapped, compounded with her fear of fire—I could feel the tightness in her throat, the shaking of her arms and legs.

"But I could see her," Michael said, reaching for Em's hand. "I knew we had one chance."

"We couldn't travel," Em said, her voice stronger now,

"because we didn't have exotic matter. But we had our duronium rings, so we could get inside the veil."

"The rip changed while we watched," Michael said. "The Phone Company went back to normal."

"But we couldn't get out of the veil." Em shuddered. "We were trapped."

"If you were trapped, how the hell are you standing here right now?" I demanded. That's when I felt him.

Poe stood two feet away from us, just outside a veil.

"Edgar," Em said, with pink cheeks. "Jack and Cat used him as a tool. Just like Ava, just like me."

"I'm still not following," I said. At all.

There was extreme fierceness in Em's voice. If Poe was going to have a champion, the girl he'd tried to kill was his best chance. "He's not a traveler to the past or the future, but he can move through space. Kind of like . . . teleporting."

"Explain." I stared at Poe, trying to get any other emotion besides sadness from him. It was all I could find.

"I use duronium to get inside veils." His voice was thin, and it seemed as if he could barely stand. "I use exotic matter to get from place to place. Jack used me to do the same."

"You were using Cat's exotic matter," I realized. "Did Cat help Em and Michael get out of the rip?"

"No."

"How did you get them out?" I asked.

"I have my own source of exotic matter."

I let the possibilities of that statement sink in.

"If we're done with the happy reunion, I'm not just here for kicks and giggles." I noticed a red spot on the front of Poe's shirt growing wider by the second. He swayed to one side, blinking furiously. "I came to warn you. Landers. Chronos. Together . . . mistake. Huge mistake."

And then he collapsed.

Acknowledgments

Thank you to:

Awesome Agent Holly "The Death Kitten" Root. You never cease to amaze me. They say choosing an agent is like choosing a spouse. I totally leveled up.

Fab Film Agent Brandy Rivers. Your advocacy for *Hourglass* has been tireless. Southern girls are the best. Thank you.

Everyone at Waxman Literary, for handling all the details.

Excellent Editor Regina Griffin, and the whole team at Egmont. I can't even begin to list all you've done for *Hourglass* and *Timepiece*!

Lissy Laricchia, cover photographer, whose mind I'd like to crawl inside for an extended vacation, and cover designer Alison Chamberlain.

My foreign publishers, along with every sales rep, bookseller, bookstore, reader, and bookpusher alive. Where would I be without you?

Twentieth Century Fox, for being able to see the potential in *Hourglass* as a feature film. If it happens or not, the possibility is the real gift.

My writer friends. Beth Revis, for the Firefly reference; Victoria Schwab, for the thin blue line; MG Buehrlen, for kite string and shin kicking elves; Jodi Meadows, for an always open chat box and the kindest approach; CJ Redwine, for ledge wrangling and peach tea runs; and Rachel Hawkins, for the endless laughter and the "hurts me in my feminism" line. Half up, half down, Hawkins.

Cuban ladies who came to my rescue! Christina Diaz Gonzalez, and Chantel Acevedo (who made phone calls to Marta and Aris to make sure I got Lily right!). Empanadas for everyone! (But one of y'all are going to have to teach me how to make them.)

Jen Lamoureux, for being a precious friend and a tireless worker on the Murphy's Law fan site.

Katie Bartow and Sophie Riggsby, for being seriously spectacular. (Can't wait for you to find yourselves between the pages.)

Clint Redwine, for taking three rolls of film in Sedona. (You made it in, too!)

Writer/readers who helped more than they know: Bill Cameron, Valerie Kemp, Tessa Gratton, Natalie Parker, Jeri Smith-Ready, and all authors repped by Freddy the Moose (who makes an appearance—because he never stole my cranberry juice).

Friends, readers, and supporters: The WHOLE of #Team-Root. YOU GUYS. SERIOUSLY.

Also, Joanna Boaz Nash, Jessica Katina, Amelia Moore, Carol Schmid, Sally Peterson, Laine and Brian Bennett, Kim Pauley, Karen Gudgen, Tammy Jones, Tracy and Phillip Dishner. Dishner. That's DISHNER.

Bloggers, including but not limited to: Mundie Moms,

Twilight Lexicon, Novel Novice, YA Sisterhood, Twilight Facebook, MTV Hollywood Crush, VH1's Fab Life, Amanda from Book Love 101, Young Adult Books Central, and Sabrina Rojas Weiss (who took the chance that helped change everything).

The first teenage readers to send me e-mails and make me feel like a REAL!LIVE!AUTHOR!: Julie Daly and Harmony Beaufort.

Teachers I missed last time: Mrs. Ruth Ann Street, Dr. Gerald Wood, and Dr. Robert Turner. One or two of you might find a part of yourselves in here. And, um, sorry about that. It's not because I don't love you! Swear.

Sandra Ballard, again, for telling me I could write when all I needed was permission.

To my family, who means everything. Wayne and Martha Simmons, Keith and Deborrah McEntire, Elton and Mandy McEntire, and my new nephew, Carter, who has all the hope in the world in his eyes.

To Ethan, who still feeds me and the boys when I forget to, and to Andrew and Charlie, who will one day (hopefully) understand why their mama walks around with her brains leaking out of her ears.

And finally, to my grandmother, Doris, who was brave enough to take a ten-year-old to Memphis on a plane, and to my godmother, Carol, who didn't hesitate to pull a perfectly good dollhouse out of the garbage so we could have our way with our imaginations that week, and who didn't get mad at all when I dropped my plastic jelly slipper off the paddle boat at Mud Island.